No Surrender

Love United Series #2

No Surrender

Love United Series Book 2

By Melyssa Winchester

Copyright © 2014 Melyssa Winchester

This book is dedicated to my four real life angels. Never give in, never give up and most of all never settle for less than you deserve.

PROLOGUE

Graham

SIX MONTHS PRIOR

I can't believe it. He is giving up. What kind of person calls themselves angel and then walks away without finding another way? Is that how it all worked in Heaven, you just give up when the going gets tough?

I wasn't going to let that happen. Gabriel may have extracted himself from me in an effort to keep me safe from everything going on but he didn't know me. He didn't know that I wouldn't just lie down and accept defeat. That it isn't my style.

I have to save Serenity. I could not let her go through with this sham of a wedding to Ryan and then sacrifice herself to Lucifer. She might think she's doing the right thing but anything that takes her from this world before she's meant to go is not the right thing. I don't care what anyone says. This cannot be the way things end.

Sure, I might feel this way because of the history between the two of us. I might be pushing so hard to save her because I don't want to lose her in yet another lifetime but I don't care. I just got her back in my life; there is no way in hell I'm letting it end this way. If Gabriel won't do anything then I will.

The church that Lucifer is using for his sick plan is one that I know well. Hell some of the spray paints on the outside; I actually put there myself five years ago. It was the place me and Jimmy McNeil used to go and hang out in when we didn't want to go home, which with as sick as my mom ended up getting had been a lot more then I like admitting to.

I knew that place better than anyone. Ryan had no experience with how to get out undetected. I was the master. Fear of getting caught by an adult is an extremely good motivator for a kid. If Gabriel had just given me access to my own body I could have gotten him out with no problem. Too bad the angel decided that I was better being kept in the dark.

As I made my way around the side of the building I noticed the unlatched basement window. Exactly the way it had been years before when Jimmy and I had used it to slip in and out undetected. Yes, this was it. This was my in.

Sitting on the ground I lifted the window with my hands and slowly, making sure I don't call any attention to myself slid through my legs first before allowing the rest of my body entrance and jumping down onto the floor.

Looking around the basement I realize not much has changed since the last time I was here. There are boxes of unknown origin still in the corners, large amounts of cobwebs covering them, beside bookshelves full of hymn books that have seen better days. Thankful that the light is still out with only the street lights outside to illuminate the space I now occupied, I began to plan my next move.

Based on my location, Serenity would be directly above me. Close enough for me to get to her easily enough but still too far away for my liking. I had to make sure before anything else that I got to her and made sure she was okay.

While Gabriel had given up on her the minute he found out that Lucifer had put some form of a brand on her, I wouldn't do the same. I needed to move and get her and I had to do it now.

As I made my way towards the stairs I heard the sound of footsteps. Moving back and crouching, I made sure the height of the boxes hid my location. The last thing I needed was to be caught before doing what I came here to do.

The voices came next and as I struggled to hear them clearly I realized that I recognized one of them. Ryan, the supposed demon but who he was having the conversation with I couldn't tell. Another guy for sure but given what Serenity and Gabriel had told me about Ryan, I couldn't be sure that the other person he spoke with is even a person at all.

"You have lost sight of the larger picture. Why I am doing this at all. If it takes torturing you for you to fully accept the inevitable then so be it."

"I'm never going to understand or accept what you're doing."

"Yes I was afraid of that but after watching the woman you love succumb to her injuries and die in front of your very eyes, I'm sure you'll change your mind."

"You really hate the world that much?"

"Look around you boy. Just as I predicted the world is crumbling down around itself. Murder, rape, and even more horrendous acts of violence have taken over what was originally supposed to be a place of light and love. It has nothing to do with hate. Not anymore."

"So it's just about you proving you're right then?"

"Yes. My father needs to see exactly what his faith and true belief has caused. He needs to see just how right I was."

Wow this guy has some serious daddy issues. I thought as I listened to what I could only assume was Lucifer explain his actions.

Not that there really could be an explanation for the level of insanity going on inside his brain. If he'd been human I'd have figured he was the kid that threw tantrums when he didn't get his way. No wonder he was cast out.

"I know the struggle you face Ryan. You want nothing more than to find a way around my plan and save yourself as well as your bride to be but there is no other way to be found. I can assure you of that. So you must stop this silliness now. It is not becoming of a demon."

"Don't you mean half-demon?"

"Semantics Ryan, that is all that is."

"You know what I've always wondered but could never figure out on my own?"

"No but I am sure as is the human way you are going to tell me regardless of the fact that I do not care to hear it."

"Why did you choose me in the beginning? What did you see in me that a full demon couldn't give you?"

"Your level of power is what drew me to you at first. For a hybrid you are remarkably strong. From there it was your temperament. You always remain in control of any situation you put yourself in. Finally, it was your social standing. That was the in that I needed in order to gain control of your more basic instincts."

6

"What do you mean my more basic instincts?"

"You are human but your more basic instincts lean towards the demonic. You are evil Ryan; surely you must know this by now?"

"That's what you believe. It doesn't mean that it's true."

From the very beginning when I met Ryan standing at Serenity's door I had known what Lucifer is trying to get him to see about himself. I knew there was something off about him and it had been confirmed when Gabriel told me that he wasn't exactly human.

I believed him to be evil and given what Serenity is about to sacrifice for him, knowing what he is, it made my goal even more clear. I needed to get her out of here before he turned back into what he was underneath. There is no doubt in my mind that he would. It was only a matter of time.

Their footsteps began receding as they climbed the stairs back to the upper level and to where Serenity was completely alone. I had to get to her and I had to do it now.

Moving out from my hiding spot I made my way in the direction that Ryan and Lucifer just occupied. Taking each step guarding for any and all possible scenarios, I reached the stairs and bending over the staircase, was happy to see that no one awaited me.

Wherever they had gone, they didn't stop for any more conversations, which worked in my favor. Taking the steps slowly, careful to make sure my feet with each step made little to no noise, I reached the top. As I turned to make my way in Serenity's direction, content that I accomplished my first goal I heard a smooth voice speak from behind me.

"Well, what do we have here?"

Serenity

God these heels are a pain in the ass.

Whoever thought up the bright idea of wearing tight black polyester needed to be shot. Add to that the thin veil on my head made of the same stupid material and these god awful heels that I

7

swear were longer than my actual fingers and I was already sick of this plan.

What is waiting for me beyond those doors was scary but nothing as scary as this clothing choice. If it wasn't bad enough, I'm itchy as hell on top of it. I just want this entire thing over with. I'd face death if it meant I could finally be taken out of these clothes.

The door opened behind me and Ryan entered, making sure as he did that the door closed firmly behind him. The only visitor to the room since he had been here with Graham had been the demon in charge of making sure I was ready and presentable. Oh and that I didn't take off running the first chance I got. I was definitely up for a better distraction.

Unlike me he wasn't dressed yet for our upcoming wedding. Whether that's because he was still trying to find a way around the branding Lucifer had put on me or because he was just not the suit wearing type of guy was not important but there is a part of me that wanted him to feel as uncomfortable as I did. At least then we'd be sharing our pain together.

"Did you get Graham out safely?" I asked.

"Yeah, though it wasn't easy. This place has so many doors it's no surprise it got shut down. I have no idea where I'm going."

"You should have just told Graham to show you the way out."

"What do you mean?"

"Graham spent a lot of time here when he was younger. I mean I moved here after he'd grown out of the break and enter stage but before that you gotta figure he did it a lot seeing as this has always been his home."

"So he knows every part of this place?"

I nodded and his lips turned downward frowning. Just what it is that made him upset about what I said I had no clue but he definitely didn't look happy. Maybe the whole soul mate thing was a turn off to the guy you were about to marry.

"We don't have much longer now. From the sounds of Lucifer, he's got everything ready to go. I just wanted to check on you one more time before we go through with this."

"Well as you can see, I'm as dark as I'll ever be." I said, pointing to the dress and towards my heels, which caused him to laugh, a sound I hadn't heard since I'd gotten us into this mess. You never know how much you miss something until it comes back to you.

"Yeah, that outfit is tradition if you can believe it. If you ask me I think that he went above and beyond with you though. Can you even move?"

"Barely." I muttered as he moved closer, bringing his hand out and touching the fabric gently. "So tell me about the wedding. What exactly is going to happen in there?" I asked, trying to take my mind off the way the small touch of his fingers on the dress made my body overheat.

I'm facing death and here I am getting hot and bothered just from a guy touching me. I have serious issues with priorities.

"Serenity, you look really uncomfortable. Are you sure you wanna talk about the wedding?"

Damn him and his perfect mind reading skill.

"Yeah, of course." I answered, hopefully succeeding in my effort to sound interested. I really wasn't feeling comfortable admitting that I could care less about the wedding as long as he had his fingers anywhere near me.

Taking my hand and locking our fingers together he moved over to the pew where I'd been sitting only minutes before. Once seated he pulled me into his arms and the heat I felt when he'd just been fingering the fabric exploded. I really wanted to focus on what he was about to tell me but much more of this and I was sure I'd be a puddle on the floor.

Other than my one time with Graham I had never felt anything remotely close to this. I was torn between acting on it and possibly making a fool of myself or breaking the contact just so I could think clearly again. Ryan affected my body in ways that right now I couldn't afford. I needed to stay focused on what was coming, not on how badly I wanted the man beside me.

"I feel it too Serenity, you don't have to try so hard to fight it."
"Huh?"

"You have no idea what you do to me do you? You're like a freaking magnet. I mean I can be on the other side of the room and the pull between us is insane."

I had to go back and give more thought to the earlier mind reading statement. I experienced this before with him, especially when talking about the abilities we shared but this was a whole other ballpark. Could he really know what I'm feeling that easily?

"How do you do that?"

He looked up at me, his eyes filled with question. "How do I do what?"

"Just know what I'm feeling and thinking. I mean I could have looked uncomfortable because of the dress yet you knew it wasn't that."

"You think I'm reading you don't you?" he asked.

"The thought crossed my mind. I mean Gabriel was able to read my mind. I gotta figure you're able to do the same thing."

"I can't. I can read you because of how I feel about you and because we're similar with our expressions. That's it. I swear to you I wouldn't keep something like that from you."

Well at least now I had answers.

"So about that wedding…"

"It's a pretty formal affair. Lucifer likes to go all out for them which is why you're dressed this way. Though making you look like a street walker isn't appealing to the guy that you're about to marry. Just wanna put that out there now."

"It's not appealing to the girl that's wearing it either."

"I bet."

"So what else can I expect?"

Ryan went silent as he thought out what to say next. I'd never really given it much focus before but whenever he was deep in thought his eyes squinted just a little. Another thing about him I found absolutely adorable.

"I honestly don't know Serenity. I mean I know the ceremony basics but given what happens afterward I'm not sure there really is a plan going in. It's a dark ceremony that worships the very person that is about to take you from me. Just expect the unexpected."

It wasn't much to go on but I had to be content with it. Given that he is supposed to be taking part in this as a willing participant and was doing anything but I had to accept any morsel I was given. All I really needed to know is that we'd be married by the end of it anyway. Nothing else mattered.

"I wish I could get you out of this. I put you in this position and I can't do a damn thing to stop it." He said his frustration showing as he ran his hands through his hair and rubbed his face.

I understood completely. There is nothing I wanted more than to stop this before it went too far but there was no way that I could. Just like Ryan was bonded, I am too. We were both stuck with the outcome, whether we liked it or not. He just needed to realize that it wasn't his fault. The choice had been mine.

"You didn't put me here Ry, I did."

"That's only because I decided to tell you the truth and didn't fight you when you said you wouldn't let me deal alone. If I just fought you harder maybe none of this would be happening right now."

"Let's say you did fight me…I might not have to face my mortality the way I am now but I might be worse off. What happens if Lucifer decided I wasn't good enough for him and just had me killed? You can't blame yourself. I made the choice and I'm standing by it."

"Yeah, you made the choice because you want to save me."

I couldn't argue with him because that had been the reason I said yes but it had not been his fault. He didn't made me choose it, I did it all on my own.

Nodding in agreement I spoke again, this time my eyes locked on his so he could see the truth in them.

"You are not meant for this and deep down I think you know that. So if it means that I have to save you, I will do whatever it takes. I would make the same choice all over again and that has nothing to do with you. It's all me. That's what you don't get. Lucifer wouldn't have given me a choice and I don't think Heaven would have either. You did and I made it."

His body relaxed and I breathed a sigh of relief. While he might never be okay with it, he now understood where I was coming from and wouldn't fight me for blame anymore.

"I should probably leave. I know at any moment he's going to tell me it's time and I don't want to be around when he finds out I'm not ready."

I didn't want him to go. The fear only set in when I was alone and if he walked away now I knew it would come back. As concerned as I am with everything I'm about to do I was more concerned with making sure he stayed in one piece. All of this wouldn't matter at all if Lucifer did something to take him away from me.

"I don't want you to go."

"I know you don't but I don't have a choice. Just like you can't get out of this, I can't stop what he's already set in motion. The only difference is I'm being physically pushed into doing the things I do and you're just stuck here."

"As long as you're here with me I know you're okay but the moment you leave this room everything is up in the air." I argued.

"While he may want the demon side of me to win Serenity, right now he isn't getting his way. You must trust me. I will be fine."

I knew I had to let him go. That no matter how afraid I was at the prospect of losing him, it would be a lot worse if we didn't go through with things according to the plan. It didn't make it any easier though.

"Trust me pretty girl, I'm going to be just fine."

He turned to me and placing his hands on both sides of my head pulled me into him, his lips pressing roughly against mine, gently prying my lips apart with his tongue as he deepened the kiss. Time seemed to stop around us as we grabbed on for dear life, neither one of us willing to stop, caught up as we were in each other.

He broke away first, the urge to come up for air overpowering. "If I don't go now I'll never go…"

"Please be careful."

"I will be, trust me on that. I'll see you soon pretty girl."

12

CHAPTER ONE

Graham

I can't believe I had been so stupid.

I thought I'd given them enough time to make their way up the stairs, even going so far as to keep checking as I slowly made my way up after them. I hadn't seen a sign of anyone around, so how had he found me so easily?

I had no idea how angels and demons worked. I knew they had powers because I had seen Gabriel use his own before, even if it had been in a limited capacity. I just had no idea how far those powers extended and if Lucifer had powers that the angels didn't. Had he been able to sense me without me realizing it? Is that why I am on the receiving end of his evil grin now?

"I know you." He stated. "You are most familiar to me yet I cannot place you. What is your name human?"

The thought crossed my mind not to give him anything. To play dumb and hope I was able to escape from here with my life but I didn't do that. Instead I cowered and gave in. I had no idea what would happen to me if I did what I wanted and I couldn't help anyone if I was dead.

"Graham."

He lifted his head in acknowledgement, as if just in hearing my name he is able to place where he knew me. While I knew of him and what his long term plans were, I could safely say I'd never come in contact with the man before so how he knew me was leaving me at a loss.

"You're the host."

Shit. He knows me because of Gabriel.

I wanted to tell him there is more to me than just being the host for an old school angel but again, I didn't follow through. I was much safer if I just agreed with him. I could only hope anyway.

"Yeah, that's what they call me these days. I still prefer Graham."

"Of course you do. You would never understand the magnitude of being chosen as a host for an angelic being. That in being chosen you have proven yourself to be worthy."

What the hell is that supposed to mean? Did he really think that because I didn't want to be known as Gabriel's host that it meant I didn't get what an honor it is? I have to admit, living with an angel inside of you isn't the most fun but I knew what it meant. Well I knew what it meant in being chosen anyway.

"You really hate us don't you?" I asked. After what I heard only a few minutes earlier, I knew the question didn't even have to be asked. He hated anything remotely attached to the world, humans like me most of all.

"Of course and your lack of respect in speaking with me is just further proof of that."

Man this guy needed an ego check and badly. "What would you rather me do? Get on my knees and worship you?"

"That would be a start yes."

"Never gonna happen man, sorry to disappoint."

"So tell me human, does my brother still reside within you or has he finally smartened up and cast you aside for a better option?"

I didn't want his statement to affect me but it did. Gabriel had ditched me just the way Lucifer said. Whether or not he was going to call on another host is doubtful but the fact remained that he had split away from me. He hadn't believed me to be strong enough to handle this.

"It's just me."

He seemed to think on that as I surveyed the area around me. If he was going to leave me hanging then I was going to come up with another way to get out of this while he did. I didn't exactly have time to waste.

"Why are you here alone? I would have thought my brother would have sacrificed himself before sending in a human to do his dirty work for him. Has he really changed that much since our time together?"

14

It was funny hearing him talk. He sounded a lot like Gabriel in that every statement could be taken in multiple ways. With the way he spoke of hanging with his brother it made another image entirely come to mind. I just couldn't allow myself to act on it. I could not make a smart ass remark and laugh.

If I did it then I might possibly end up dead or whatever equally damning punishment he saw fit to give me and I couldn't afford that.

"I thought angels, or in your case demons were supposed to be smarter than this? Why are you asking me questions about Gabriel? I told you, my name is Graham. You wanna know what your brother is up to I figure you should ask him."

"Silly human. I am not a demon. I am still an angel. If you knew anything then you would know that I am just one of the fallen."

"So tell me, do you get your kicks calling people 'humans' all the time? I mean it sounds a little childish doesn't it?"

"Silence!" he yelled. "Enough of your mindless chatter."

"Fine. I'm more than happy to shut the hell up. Now if you don't mind I'm going to find my friend." I answered as I took a step to move around him.

I knew it wasn't going to work. I would never get away from him that easily but I'll be damned if I wasn't going to try. He talked about mindless chatter yet here we both were standing around talking about nothing. Seemed like a good idea to get back to what was really important.

"You know at first I was planning on killing you right where you stand. Hell could always use another soul, whether one that is good or not. A few lifetimes of torture would strip you of that rather easily. Now though, I think I have a much better idea for what to do with you."

I didn't like the sound of that. If he wasn't going to kill me then what he had in mind for me had to be much worse.

"I want a vessel. A body that I can strip until it is only a shell of its former self. It was supposed to be Ryan but I think you may be a much better candidate."

Am I really being checked out by the angel of darkness?

15

"Nah man I think you had it right the first time around. Ryan is your guy; you should definitely stick with him."

"What you believe is of no importance to me. Yes, I see it now. Ryan for all of his potential is a weak link. While my original plan must go on without a hitch, I do believe I will change the ending."

I swallowed the lump in my throat, a chill slowly making its way through my body at his words.

"W—what are you g—going to do with me?" I stammered, fear slamming into me like a freight train. If he is planning on using me for something than it meant that Serenity was going to be officially on her own. I couldn't do anything to save her.

"For now, I will take you and keep you hidden. As I said, the plan must go off without a hitch. When the time is right I will come to you and then and only then will the real plan truly take form."

While he wasn't making even the slightest bit of sense talking in circles, I knew that I was trapped. I wouldn't get out of here alive. Lucifer had plans for me and in the grand scheme of things; I knew nothing good would ever come of it.

I was a dead man.

Lucifer

The best laid plans have a way of going awry. Nothing can ever truly be written in stone. In order to truly succeed one must prepare for such things. If you are prepared for such an instance then you can plan around it and come up with an even better end result then the one you previously prepared.

This is the case with the human that stood before me now. While I knew him to be the vessel for my estranged brother Gabriel there wasn't much information attainable to me. That is until the fear set in. His fear of me and what I meant to bring to the world was enough to open the vessel up like a stuffed pig.

I could now feast on his very insides. See the parts of him that he until that moment had been keeping under lock and key. Yes he is most definitely going to be of use to me.

Not only was the human a vessel for the most holy of angelic beings but he is also the very link I needed in order to garner complete control of the human known as Serenity. He is her soul mate. News that came as a surprise to me given I had previously been unaware of any such attachment.

The bond between soul mates has been very well documented over the years, both through Heaven and the humans alike. They all believed themselves to have one yet that is not the case at all. Having a soul mate is a gift given to only a select few beings and it would seem that Serenity was one of them.

The bond between them is strong, passing through many a human lifetime which gave me all the information I needed in order to move forward. I would definitely use Graham but not in a way that was visible. He had to remain a secret until the time is right. I would most definitely not risk this gift I am being given.

Truth be told Ryan had become a disappointment to me. While I always knew it was a risk, him being both human and demon alike, I never thought that his human soul would control the rest of him so strongly.

I had effectively garnered control of him from a very young age and planted just the right seed to make him see this plan through to the very end. I was confident in his ability, his loyalty to me and the cause. With his father being one of my most trusted earlier confidants, I knew that Ryan would fit perfectly.

My only failing is that I did not see the connection that could be made between the agent of heaven and the half demon. If I had known it was possible before going through with the endeavor then I may have thought twice about using him. As it was, I went ahead strictly based on his loyalty and his eagerness to see it through to the end.

Heavenly beings are unable to mingle with the beings born of darkness. It had been written that way before my extraction from Heaven. Up until this point in time there has never been a documented case of the two forming a lasting bond. That is until Ryan came across Serenity. That is where what was written and the art of human emotion collided.

Given their similarities, their combined levels of power of which neither is fully aware and the situation I had presented them with it was inevitable. They collided and it would take a great deal of work to pull them apart. This is where the soul mate connection would come into play. This is the only bond that could shatter the one created between the angel and the demon.

I would use it to my advantage and it would be my information alone. Ryan would go to his death believing that he was the chosen one, when in reality; I had a much better option handed to me.

Graham is one of the stronger humans I have come across in my time on the planet. That strength alone makes him a suitable vessel for me. It means he will be able to handle the magnitude of having a being of my caliber within him. Already having hosted Gabriel in the manner in which he did is just further proof of that fact.

There is only one thing that needs to be done before I can use him to his full potential. He is very strong willed and inherently good which means I am going to have to break him down. He was chosen by Heaven for the level of light within him and I would need to break down that light piece by piece. It is the only way that this can succeed where the other plan has failed.

It's settled. Ryan will continue believing that he is the vessel to which I will join after he takes the very life force of his true love. He will go to his death believing in the lie while I will work on the real successor to the power I hope to gain.

Yes, everything is coming together perfectly. Where one plan goes awry, another rises from ashes, presenting itself so boldly that it would be horrible to ignore its magnificence.

I cannot wait to begin.

CHAPTER TWO

PRESENT DAY

Gabriel

I have been keeping a secret. A secret that when it gets out will surely cause the people it affects unimaginable amounts of pain.

The scene that I witnessed upon my first visit back to the little house in Green Haven still has the power to bring me, a guardian of Heaven, to my knees.

On Earth you hear talk of natural disasters. Events that take place that are not under anyone's control. All of them are expected in Heaven due to the fact that our father, the creator had placed them into his design but to the humans that inhabit the world they are an unforeseen occurrence. They are most unexpected and unwanted.

The level of devastation that I bore witness to as I appeared at Graham's residence could only be described as being that of a natural disaster.

One could not ignore that it had only occurred to the one house on the entire block. He had been singled out for whatever reason and if Graham himself wasn't a casualty of the damage done it would be a miracle.

What had once been a brown and red bricked house with a black roof is now reduced to a colorful almost powdery substance over the very foundation on which it previously stood. The grass surrounding it was burned until no color remained. What had been a wooden fence blocking the house off from the others around it, now a pile of boards blown into the street in front and the greenery behind.

There was nothing left.

Not much had changed in six months. The town had taken care of the bare essentials in removing the remnants of the damage but no further action had been taken to rebuild, which meant that not only is Graham missing but his mother as well.

When I'd chosen Graham to be my vessel I had done so in order to protect Serenity. I let my own selfish desires override everything else and caused the situation I now found myself in. I used every available ounce of power that was afforded me to locate the man and it had been to no avail.

Wherever Graham was, he is shrouded from me, which could only mean one thing.

Lucifer had him.

I had known it from the very moment I laid eyes on the mass destruction of his childhood home and the more time that passed with no word, no trace of any part of him whether good or bad it just solidified what I had known from the start.

I needed to tell Serenity what I knew. It is the right thing to do but given her own recovery and that of the man she loved I didn't want to burden her further. The last thing she needed to focus on at a time like this was Graham and what Lucifer may or may not have done to him.

She would never forgive herself and I couldn't allow that. Not when there wasn't anything that she could have done to prevent it. No, this was all on me this time just as her choice had been six months earlier.

I had let my estranged brother access my mind, giving him the ability to manipulate me for his own selfish gain never believing for a second that I would have had to worry about such a thing. In allowing him access the way I did, he turned me around from my original goal and brought about nothing but death and destruction ever since.

Serenity had chosen the path of saving the half demon because of the decisions I made. Instead of following through with my guardianship of her and by extension the human host I had chosen in Graham, I followed my own path and turned her towards the very darkness that wanted nothing more than to end her.

I had been able to save her but at what cost?

Ryan died in his attempt to redeem himself in the eyes of our father and it all could have been prevented had I just blocked myself from the brother that I still believed could be saved.

She would most definitely not handle this news well. So I would hold onto my secret believing that in doing so I would be following through with what had been my true path from the start.

Protecting Serenity.

Serenity

They say that time passes differently in Heaven. That what you experience on Earth in one month is actually more like a year there. If that's really the case then for the past six years I've been watching the man I love fight for his life.

The life he lost trying to save mine.

No matter how many times I remember it never gets easier. For a while after Uriel brought me here to heal, I had a hard time placing the events that led me to this point. I remembered what seemed important like the people in my life but not the events that surrounded it. I had no idea at first just what Ryan had done for me.

Michael had been the one to tell me. In fact most everything that I've learned in the last six months has been courtesy of him. As irritating as he can be, I'm more than a little thankful he gave everything to me straight. Where I think anyone else would have sugar coated it, he didn't.

I knew that Ryan attempted to kill the very man he had sworn his loyalty to. A decision he made all in an effort to give me time to regenerate my light and live. Even though the very part of him he fought so hard against was being controlled by the demonic angel himself he still fought against what he was being told to do.

Lucifer had killed him by taking the very weapon that had been used to extract my life force and stabbing it through his chest. Michael and Raphael managed to get him out of there but not before his physical body died, leaving only the demon behind.

Which is what is so hard about what's going on now.

He will always be a demon. It will always be a part of him regardless of how he is regarded in Heaven. At least that's what I'm told anyway. Ryan will always have powers the same way that I do though the level may change. He may never be as strong as he was before he died because in order to save him they have to use the very demonic essence within him.

The healing process, where they revive the human part of him looks extremely painful. His body though in a coma still reacts to what the angels surrounding him are doing and with every twitch his body makes my heart breaks that much more. He is going through all of this because of his love for me.

In loving me he put himself on the line and no matter how much time passes I will never have the right words to express what that means to me. There really are no words or actions that can convey it the way it needs to be. Everything I can try and come up with just seems to fall short.

The only good thing to come from all of this is that in doing what he did, his light was magnified to Heaven and the moment the knife plunged into his chest he was redeemed. That's where I'm different from everyone else because I believe it happened before that moment. I saw the light surrounding him for days beforehand. While the rest of Heaven believes that redemption occurred at the moment he died, I just don't.

Apparently that makes me stubborn. Since it's Michael that said it I just like to believe that it's the pot calling the kettle black. There is no being alive more stubborn and set in his ways then Michael. Given that he was the leader in the brigade of angels that saved me though I can't hold it against him. If anything it made it just a little bit easier to tolerate him.

With Gabriel losing the majority of his powers due to what happened to us that day, I've been stuck with Michael. I'm not entire sure what went on with Gabriel other than the time he spent blaming himself for the way everything happened but he's here less and less these days.

According to my new best friend he's being sent to Earth strictly in an information gathering capacity and is unable to use his power for anything other than going back and forth. I've wanted to ask him about going back with him the way the Almighty wants but anytime he is home he seems to go out of his way to avoid me. If I wasn't so focused on Ryan and his recovery, I'd fight it but as it is I just don't have it in me.

No one thinks I realize it but I know why Gabriel has been spending so much time back on Earth alone. It's about Graham. I know they can't find him. I learned of that shortly after I was healed enough to shake the constant angel care. Gabriel feels responsible for whatever happened to Graham but he's not the only one. I let him down too.

Gabriel clued me in to the fact that he separated from him before the wedding but after that he is at a loss which means that I am at a loss too. I know why I didn't focus on Graham the way I normally would have and it's because of the wedding and then the horrible aftermath but Gabe is taking the fact that he didn't pay attention hard.

Given what he is I guess it's almost against the law to abandon someone entirely the way he did. In putting his focus on me and finding a way to save us all he had taken his attention off his human host and that just isn't something heard of here.

I want him to look at things differently and not blame himself for what was probably the most natural response in the world but it just goes to show you that I'm not the little angelic ball of light everyone believes me to be. In wanting Gabriel to relieve himself of the guilt, I'm proving myself more human by the second.

I'm told that it's almost the time. That soon I will have to make my entrance back into the land of the living but I'm not ready for it. I can't imagine going back down there with Ryan still the way he is now. Leaving him would be leaving the best parts of me behind and I just can't do that.

"Serenity…"

"Yes Michael." I state as I turn to face him. If he is here with me now, it meant that I'm being summoned.

"Father would like to speak with you now."

"You know how I feel about leaving him." I say motioning to Ryan. "Can he wait?"

23

The look on Michael's face told me everything I needed to know. There would be no waiting because while the Almighty is the most powerful of beings imaginable, he is also the most impatient. What needed to be said had to happen now.

"Ryan is still adapting to the healing Serenity. I can assure you that he will not wake up in your absence. You must go and speak with father now. You know how he is about such matters."

Michael's right about that. I do know exactly how Father is. Just in the brief time since I had been admitted entrance to Heaven he had already called on me more times than I could count and was upset when I didn't show up right after his call. I'm breaking rules that I'm not even aware of.

Seeing as though only a few months ago I just assumed I was the flaw in God's design and not the gift sent to save the world, I would have thought he would have understood my trepidation in meeting with him. Apparently that's not the way it worked.

"Will you stay with him?"

"Don't I always?"

This I could not deny. Only a few months before Michael had been the very angel to remove me from Ryan's bedside on his father's orders. It's said that they did it to help me but really I just think the idea that a being from the light caring so deeply for one born of darkness scared them more than they wanted to admit.

"You know what to do if anything changes."

"I have a feeling that if anything were to change you'd know about it before I would Serenity but yes, I will inform you of any changes."

With just a mere thought I found myself standing before him, my creator and he looked none too pleased to see me.

"Serenity…it is time."

CHAPTER THREE

Graham

I'm close to giving in to him.

He knows how strong I am, in fact he's making a point of pointing it out every time he floods my mind with memories. I thought that in seeing parts of my life flash before my eyes I'd be able to handle it and remain calm but the more that he shows me the more I feel myself breaking down. There is only so much a person can take.

It started with memories of my time with Serenity. He seems to know that's my trigger so he floods with those more so then any others. He enjoys flooding me with the night she kissed me more than any other. I suppose if you're going to torture someone through their mind, showing them the memories they most want to recreate would be the way to go about it.

I would give anything to be able to go back and do that moment with Serenity over. When she'd taken the chance and kissed me despite the way she had always been beforehand, I loved it but in typical idiot fashion I didn't admit to feeling the same. Instead I treated her like just any other drunk girl making a mistake and taken her home.

When I told her that things had been different from that moment on I wasn't lying. We still hung out together, as Lucifer insisted on showing me but it had never really been the same again. There was a distance between us, one that only seemed to grow even bigger when she moved away to school.

Showing failures is the worst kind of torture. I couldn't handle seeing Serenity as she smiled at me anymore. The smile that right from the first moment I'd seen it forever changed me. I swear if it's possible I fell in love with her because of that smile. There really is nothing in the world better than that, at least for me.

Lucifer seems to agree because every good memory he insists on showing me in an effort to break me down, she's always smiling. He knew what she meant to me and what her death did to me inside. Knowing what I did about the two of us now, that she is dead and I would never see her again killed me. Her death would eventually be my death and that evil son of a bitch was going to use it for all it was worth.

I never understood why Gabriel had given up on her that day but as it turns out the more time that passes without rescue I realize that he might have made the right decision. If I hadn't gone back in to the church determined to save the girl I love then I wouldn't be where I am now. He wouldn't have gotten to me and basically turned me into his bitch.

I would have been able to visit with her mother, talk about her and plan life without her. I would be able to mourn her the right way surrounded by all the people that loved her. Instead here I am locked and chained with no escape and living with the overload of memories as they flooded my brain.

There is one particular memory that I wouldn't dare show reaction to but that got to me more than any of the others. She wanted to step out of her comfort level and asked me to be her date for one of the many dances our school liked to put on. I always just saw them for what they were. A chance for the popular kids to get drunk and make asses of themselves but she had seen it differently. At least she had with this particular one.

I agreed to go with her. Of course this was before the kiss so we didn't think of it as a date, at least not that either of us knew. It was just my way of being her best friend and supporting her in something she felt she needed to do.

Serenity would never admit it but she looked beautiful that night. Showing up at her door and having her be the one to meet me, in full dance attire, was one of the moments where I'm sure my heart stopped beating in my chest. She'd taken my breath away that easily.

*****

"Graham! You're early!" she said backing away from the door and motioning me inside.

"Well I didn't want to risk showing up late."

"I'll just be another minute. My hair doesn't seem to want to cooperate."

"You're beautiful the way you are. You should leave your hair that way."

Her hair is down, something she didn't do often but a way I enjoyed. She had the wavier parts clipped behind her ears with a pink clip, butterflies on the ends. This was a way I'd never seen her before and I couldn't help but enjoy it. I knew after tonight I may never get the chance to see it again so I was going to take all I could get of it now.

Her blush at my words only made me appreciate the view more. Anytime I complimented her she did this. If it took the rest of my life I would make her see her beauty, one compliment and blush at a time.

"Thank you but seriously I really need to fix this."

"Can you please tell my daughter that she looks beautiful just the way she is Graham? I've been listening to her whine about her hair for the last hour." Serenity's mother said as she made her entrance into the doorway.

I had never really spent much time around Serenity's mom but she never seemed happy with anything her daughter did. In seeing the way she interacted with her on the times I was over I knew where a lot of Serenity's issues came from. The woman did not go easy on her.

"Of course, Ms. Richards. I told you Ser, you look perfect. Your hair is fine."

"Says the guy that just rolls out of bed, throws a beanie on his head and calls it a day." She shot back with an eye roll.

"It's not my fault I was blessed with perfect hair."

"Sure it's not." She says grinning. "Fine, I'll leave my hair alone just for you."

There is something in the way she said 'just for you' that made my heart skip in my chest. It had been happening more frequently lately but I didn't want to mention it. The last thing I needed to do was act on the way I'm feeling and end up pushing her away.

"Great, so are we ready to go then?"

With a nod of her head, I held my arm out to her and as she latched her arm around it, my body tensed at the electric shock it received at the connection.

"We'll be back early Mom so don't bother giving me the speech." She called as we made our way back out through the door.

I had no idea why she even bothered calling out to her mother given that the woman had already walked away from the door. It is just another glaringly obvious way that our families were different. My mother had spent thirty minutes bugging me with questions before she let me leave the house.

"Your mom…"

"I know Graham. We've been over this before. She thinks I'm insane so she doesn't want to get too close. I'm okay with it."

I wasn't entirely sure I believed her but was willing to let it drop. The last thing I want to do is ruin her night given the struggle she must be going through in doing it at all.

"You really do look beautiful."

There it was again, the blush. Even in the darkness of the night I could see it clear as day. I couldn't help myself. With the way the light pink dress fell over every curve of her body, playing off the fairness of her skin, it was hard not to notice how beautiful she looked. I almost wanted to pinch myself to make sure this is really happening.

"Stop it Graham Cracker. You know I hate it when you lie."

*****

She might have thought I'd been lying to her that night but she was wrong. I had never been more honest than I had been in that moment. She had always just been Serenity to me but that night it was as if I finally got to see her for the woman she was becoming. The woman she is now.

My soul mate.

For the first little while after he locked me away I noticed he wasn't himself. It might not have been obvious to anyone else but to me I could see it. Where he had been strong and in charge the day he'd taken me hostage and buried me in this basement he is now an emptier shell. He had marks on his body, ones that spoke of agonizing pain.

It is because of him this way that the torture became more extreme. Some days it would go on for hours without so much as a break and then others it wouldn't last long at all. He had been injured so his need to use me had been heightened but at the same time I think he wanted to prolong it for a better result. The more lengthy the torture, the easier it would be when he used me for his purpose.

His current method of torture isn't Serenity but my mother. He hadn't come out and said it but he hinted at her death. It was now that he is showing me just what he'd done to her before she ultimately died. He showed me what he did to the home I grew up in and what her final moments had been. If Serenity hadn't broken me then he was determined this would.

It is having the desired effect. Seeing the way he cut her, torturing her for information about me, my childhood and my way of being is brutal. It had only gotten worse as he blew the house apart with her trapped inside. She met her end in a blaze of fire, fitting for the King of Hell. Even remembering the vision now is enough to tear me apart from the inside out.

My mother had done nothing but love me and she deserved better then what she ended up with. The guilt I felt over her death was unbearable. If I had never agreed to be Gabriel's vessel I would have still been there with her and she'd still be alive. She may have been sick but at least I wouldn't have been alone the way I am now.

I only hoped that in her death she passed on to the other side. If that happened then surely at some point Gabriel would come across her and I might have half a chance to get out of this alive. If spirits could talk to Serenity then they should be able to speak with angels in Heaven just as easily.

So I continued holding on even when all I wanted to do was give in. I could not let him have his way. I am stronger than that. The very reason he wanted me to begin with would be the very thing that would be his undoing.

I would not let him break me.

CHAPTER FOUR

Serenity

Well it's official. I'm going back home.

I would be heading back to Earth alone, going back into the only existence I have ever known until Gabriel began appearing in my head. Ryan is still in no shape to be moved in order to come back with me and there were no more excuses I could use. I had to do this.

While there was a small part of me that is ready to get out of Heaven and back to my life and more importantly, back to Emma I just didn't feel right about leaving Ryan behind. As beautiful a place as Heaven is he is still very much a demon and who knew what they would do to him once I wasn't there anymore to fight for him.

I needed to have faith and trust. That's what I've been told since the moment I arrived here but it isn't something I can easily give. Gabriel kept things from me to a point where my entire life was changed because of it. If an angel can do that so easily then my lack of faith in them isn't surprising.

As worried as I am for Ryan I know that I have no other choice. While I may be going down alone, I would never truly be that way as I had a two way communication system with Heaven in my head at all times. It also helped that I would have an angel on call with me again for the duration once I touched down.

When Father told me that I would not be alone in terms of support during my entry back I assumed he meant Michael would be coming along for the ride. As much as I tolerated him during my time here I really wasn't sure I could handle the way he was going back to my human existence. Where I once believed Gabriel to be a pretty cut and dry guy, Michael was even worse. If he did experience anything remotely human he never showed it.

I was wrong though, it wasn't Michael.

*****

"The time has come Serenity for you to continue with the undertaking. You must make your presence known back on Earth."

"You know how I feel about that. I'm not going anywhere without Ryan."

"I am afraid you have no other option. I have put up with your feelings toward the demon for long enough. You are needed on Earth now. Ryan will stay here until he is fit to travel."

"What if I say no?"

"That is not an option. You must see this through to the end or your lifetime on Earth will be complete and you will reside here forever."

He knew that was something I couldn't handle. I could not allow myself to be stuck here forever. Not when there is so much that I still need to do, finding Graham being at the top of the list. As much as I love Ryan, I owe it to Graham to make sure he is okay. If I didn't go through with it then he would be lost forever.

That was just something I could not accept.

"You will not be doing this alone."

"What's that supposed to mean?"

"You will be accompanied by one of the greatest warriors."

"You're sending Michael with me aren't you? Look, I know I've been a pretty big pain in the ass since I've been here but I don't need a babysitter."

"Michael is needed here. You will have Gabriel with you."

Gabriel. Great, I was going to go back down with the angel that had been ignoring me for months. Somehow I didn't see that working out any better than Michael coming. It might even end up worse.

"Does he know he's stuck with me again?"

"Gabriel has been made aware of everything as it pertains to this mission. He is to resume his position as your guardian but in the original capacity. He is to keep you from harm but that is all."

"You mean there's another way he could be with me?"

"Serenity, you are aware of the connection between the two of you. It is that very connection that opened Gabriel up to manipulation by Lucifer. We cannot in good conscience go down

31

that path again or it will end far worse than was originally intended."

Well he is right about that. I did know about the connection between Gabriel and me even if I didn't fully understand it. I also knew that it is one of the reasons things had gotten to the point they had a few months before. Being the beloved of an angel is a job I obviously suck at.

"You said that he is only to keep me from harm and I get that you don't want his feelings for me interfering with what you believe I'm destined for but why is he unable to use his power in any other way?"

"That is information you need not concern yourself with. Your only task is to fulfill your destiny. That is all. Leave everything else to Michael and the rest of the angels."

*****

So now I'm preparing myself to head back down to Earth with none other than my beloved by my side while the man I love fights for his life here without me. I only hope they know what they are doing because from the way it looks to me this is going to go all sorts of wrong.

"Serenity…"

"Yes Michael?" I asked turning to face him.

"I witnessed the conversation between you and Father and I believe I have the answers you seek."

"You have answers about what exactly?"

"The reason that Gabriel will be without his full powers during his time with you."

Michael knew the real reason that Gabriel was limited and he is waiting until now to tell me? This is exactly why I have my doubts about leaving Ryan in their care. They didn't seem to get that what they deemed unimportant was always the things that actually were the most.

"So why is he powerless?"

"He has been stripped of all but the basic guardian powers due to what happened leading up to the battle with Lucifer."

"Oh come on. It wasn't even his fault. I'm tired of everyone else taking the blame for the decision I made."

"I agree with you in that regard. It is you that made the decision and it was the rest of us who determined what we would do from that point on but there's more that you need to know."

"What else could there possibly be?"

"Gabriel did not succeed in regard to the plan he set forth the day we came for you and Ryan."

"What is that supposed to mean? You got us both out and he killed Lucifer. How could he fail?"

"Lucifer was not slain in the attack and it is Father's belief that Gabriel planned it that way but has been unable to prove it positively."

"You're saying Lucifer is still alive?"

"That is most definitely what I am trying to tell you."

Well now everything was beginning to make sense. No one trusted Gabriel because he hadn't taken care of his brother. While I watched them all mourn his passing he hadn't really passed on at all. Did Gabriel spare him out of loyalty or is there more going on that none of us are aware of?

It made my decision that much easier given the knowledge I had. If they couldn't figure out what Gabriel's master plan was then it is up to me. I would do what they wanted me to and at the same time I would get answers once and for all.

I would find out just what side Gabriel is really on.

Gabriel

When Lucifer had been planting thoughts in my mind I felt I was becoming human. It wasn't an idea totally without merit given that Serenity is indeed my beloved and I would in time adapt to the form she found herself in. Knowing now that he was the mastermind behind the entire production and that I hadn't really been human at all left me feeling empty.

When Father told me that I would be her guardian and that I am to remain strictly in that capacity I felt more human than ever before.

33

I have been spending the last several months distancing myself from her, allowing her the time to be with Ryan in his recovery. It has been easy given that I was given free roam of Heaven and then my search for Graham on Earth. The human action of avoidance is one that I am learning first hand in dealing with Serenity these days.

Knowing that I would be placed with her again in much the same way I had been originally caused me great discomfort on many levels. Facing her again with the basic knowledge I had regarding her soul mate Graham, information she would want to know and that I had been keeping from her was upsetting me. Add into that the fact of our very real connection and I was afraid that it would only be a matter of time before I put her in the same danger I did the first time around.

They were both very human responses. I know that Father is using this as a test. In stripping me of only the most basic powers he is giving me a chance to redeem myself by seeing Serenity through to her real destiny. There is only one thing wrong with his test. I didn't have the faith in my own ability anymore.

I caused her to turn her back on the light the last time we were in a situation like this. What happens if we are placed in the same place again especially given the knowledge that Lucifer is indeed still alive out there? Could I really trust my ability to keep her safe again? Am I worthy of being given this very small chance?

Having overlooked the light inside of Ryan was also part of my undoing. It is something that even the newest of angels should be able to tell and I completely ignored it. While father may be willing to give me this chance I do not believe I deserve it. There are too many variables to consider and I couldn't risk Serenity's life, not again.

My concerns fell on deaf ears though as the decision was made and there would be no talking Father out of it. No matter how hard I tried.

*****

"This is your chance to rectify what you believe to have been your most egregious error. While I am confident in your ability to

see this through. I do believe you need to do so with a limited power supply."

"So you want to punish me?"

"This is not a punishment but there were mistakes made the first time around and we must be sure they don't repeat themselves. You must block the beloved connection and focus solely on the two objectives I have made you aware of."

"You mean Graham and Lucifer."

"Yes. It causes me a great deal of distress not to be able to track the young Hudson boy. Knowing that Lucifer has not perished only adds to that. I believe what you found when visiting his former home is the key to everything. That level of destruction could only have occurred by Heaven or the most powerful of fallen angels. It is my firm belief that in order to find the human we must find Lucifer."

"I don't know how he survived."

"That is a mystery to us all but given what you have told me about his ability to walk through the holy fire, it is safe to assume he has levels of dark power now that even we are not aware of."

"If that is true then wouldn't you be better served sending Michael or even Uriel down with Serenity? They would be in a better position to protect her then I am given my lack of power."

"It is not your lack of power that makes you unable to care for her. It is your lack of faith in your abilities Gabriel. You must embrace the light again and soon in order to do what has been asked of you effectively."

"And if I can't do that?"

"Then Serenity will perish. There is no other alternative. You must do this Gabriel or we all suffer."

*****

So that is it for me. I don't have any other options. I would have to be the one to travel with Serenity back to her life on Earth, to protect her as I have been trying to do from the beginning while still managing to find out everything there is to know about what happened to Graham Hudson and just what my brother has planned for him.

When push comes to shove I will rise above my own fear in my abilities and accept the task set before me but there is still one very large problem I have to deal with before we could begin the transition.

How am I going to keep my search for Graham from his other half? Could I really maintain the lie in order to save one and protect the other? Or would my connection to her manifest itself and ruin it all before it even began?

CHAPTER FIVE

Lucifer

It is in times such as these that I find myself missing the ease of working with a half breed.

The way in which I had been able to manipulate Ryan into following my path had been easy, taking no real effort at all to reach my long term goal. He was a most willing participant in my plans. I had not lied when I spoke of him being my eventual successor. His very DNA spoke of how perfect he was for the position.

That is at least until he met the light known as Serenity. It is then that everything had changed. I had seen the change occurring, keeping my eye on it as the bond between the two of them had become stronger. It was then I realized he was not the person I believed him to be.

Working with the human Graham is much more difficult. He is built of nothing but light and stripping him of it is becoming a tedious task indeed. I wanted nothing more than to destroy him on the spot, finding an easier target and working with it instead but I knew that was not to be.

It had to be Graham. Just based on the immeasurable strength he held inside of him whether born of the light or not kept me going.

I enjoyed his stubbornness, the way in which he handled his time with me each day. The sarcasm I witnessed on our very first meeting carried itself over for months as I flooded his mind with visions he had long since forgotten about. He fought me every step of the way until he couldn't anymore. It was then he began begging me to end it.

To cease the torture and just do whatever it is that I wanted to do with him. I could not accept his words though because despite the fact that he was cracking under the pressure, the light still remained as strong as ever. Until such time as I am able to break the hold that his goodness held over him he would be of no use to me.

I longed for the ease of Ryan McGregor and his acceptance of his gifts. With Ryan I would have no issues with light as he was born of darkness and humanity, both things easy to manipulate and guide in whatever path I chose. I needed that with the human now. I needed the ease of turning him so that I would be able to join with him and finish what I had started months before.

Not only had Ryan betrayed me in not draining the life of Serenity the way I intended him too but he somehow managed to earn the favor of Heaven in the process. The ways in which he let me down were many and I am determined to bring my own version of hell down on him if ever in his presence again.

While it looked as if he died I knew the minute my brothers got him out of the church that he would not be meeting his end. I would bide my time and when everything was right and ready, I would make sure Ryan McGregor paid for his betrayal of the very life he had embraced.

"It seems to me that you are reaching your limit human. It won't be much longer now and we will be able to move forward."

"Why not just…do it now?" He choked out his voice filled with defeat.

"I am sure you would like nothing more than for me to end your suffering but it is that suffering that will make you most viable."

"Viable for what exactly?"

"What is it with you humans? Your need to constantly have things repeated is very unbecoming."

"What are you talking about? You…have…never…told…me…anything." he spat out slowly as if believing that I am like his kind and need such things. It is just further proof of why they needed to be obliterated once and for all.

"You seem to forget our earlier conversation, during the time at which you were attempting to stop what had already put into motion."

"Fine, I don't remember. Why don't you just clue me in again?"

38

He is trying the levels of my patience. I believe I now know why Father wanted to create the world the way he did. Dealing with humans is like dealing with my brothers. Their level of intellect severely lacking. It annoyed me to no end.

"You are to be my vessel Graham Hudson. Do you not recall the conversation in which I made that apparent to you? That you would succeed where Ryan had failed me?"

There are many ways a human can appear when they remember something and watching Graham now I am witnessing one very way first hand. When they recall something they enjoy, there is a dream like peace that envelopes their features and makes them appear free no matter if they are naturally dark or light. Then there is the way they look when they remember things they wish they couldn't which is the look I now saw cross Graham's features.

He was sickened and there could be no denial of it. From his eyes to his lips his entire face sagged as he began to recall the conversation I spoke of. If the torture of previous memories hadn't been enough, the realization of what is to come would surely be the thing to push him over the edge.

There is really no way out for him. Not even my angelic brother could save him now. His path is set in stone.

"You've been doing all of this so that you can ride around in my skin?"

"Precisely. For a human you do catch on alarmingly quick. That will be of great use to me in the future."

"Great. That's just great. Anything I can do to make your life easier."

"Your unique ability with sarcasm will also be of use so please continue."

As difficult as he had been to break I did rather enjoy our sparring when it occurred. It wasn't often that the two of us actually spoke to one another as I spent my time focused on the long term goal but they happened enough to make quite the impression on me.

Yes, I would very much enjoy walking around in this man's skin, especially when the time came for me to come face to face with the pretty little object of his affection. Oh, there would be no greater joy then that moment.

It would literally be the day the Earth stood still. Only this time I would come out the victor.

Graham

When he came into the room I prepared myself for the onslaught of memories that were sure to follow. When he just stood watching me I began to wonder just what was running through his mind. For months he had taken pleasure in watching me break apart and now here he is bathing in the glow of what he accomplished.

I didn't like the way his eyes felt on my body, wanting no more than to get him close enough to me so I could really show him what I thought of him but when he didn't move an inch it was obvious I would never get my chance. I really am at his mercy.

From the moment of capture the days had been running together making it impossible for me to know exactly how long it had been since the fateful moment he caught me in my attempt to save Serenity. The way the time moved seemed to affect me in being able to remember exactly what was going on around me as well. He told me what he planned for me but until the moment he brought the past to light I had been unwilling to remember.

Where Ryan failed him he wanted me. In falling for Serenity he had broken some form of bond that the two of them shared and now I was paying the price. I wanted nothing more than to hate the demon for what he caused but I couldn't. He had only done the very thing I had done more than two years beforehand and fallen in love with the most beautiful girl on the planet. Giving him shit for that would be laying blame at my own feet and I couldn't do that.

Being reminded of exactly what Lucifer's plan is only brought to the surface everything I had learned since. The role I played in killing the first vessel that Ryan's own father inhabited, taking the life of a human whose only mistake was being in the wrong place at the wrong time.

40

I've never been a violent person, at least in this lifetime which is really the only one I remember. I choose to figure things out with words before using fists. That isn't the case with my previous lifetimes. No, I was actually quite the cold blooded killer even if I was defending another woman's honor at the time.

Is that why Lucifer wanted me, because deep down I have the ability to get the job done even if it's buried so deeply I'm unaware of it? Am I about to become his vessel because deep down I'm as evil as he is?

No, you can't think like that. If you do then the very thing he is trying to accomplish will come to pass. You can't let the guilt consume you.

The pep talk my inner voice wanted to give me is accurate but not one I am willing to listen to anymore. I just couldn't be the person that Lucifer wanted me to be. I could never be Ryan.

"What you believe about yourself is accurate."

"What would that be oh wise one?"

"You believe yourself to be dark in nature due to your past lives and you would be accurate in your assumption. It is why you are the perfect vessel, even more so then Ryan before you."

"Do you really expect me to believe anything you have to say?"

"Of course not, I know how you feel about me given everything I have put you through. You will trust in yourself though and deep down you know that what I say is made of the truth."

"No. You're wrong. The only thing I know for sure is that you're a sick son of a bitch."

If I expected my words to affect him I was in for a shock. While calling another man what I just called him would have probably gotten me in a fight, it didn't seem to affect him at all. Probably another thing he had been expecting. If he knew as much about humans as he claimed to then his reaction was obvious.

"It's alright Graham. You may remain on the defensive, it is actually expected. Soon you will be unable and I will own you completely, so please enjoy the last remaining days of free will."

41

Just what the hell did he mean by that? Am I really that close to becoming his vessel? I know I had been feeling drained and defeated lately but I hadn't let my guard down in a long time. I never allowed the weakness I showed the one time to come through again.

"Don't I have to allow you entrance?" I asked, calling on my knowledge of my time with Gabriel and hoping that in some small way they were similar.

"It is no longer about getting your approval. You have already given it to me in your darkest moments. It is now strictly about breaking the light within you."

"That won't ever happen."

"You naïve little boy, it has already begun and you have been powerless to stop it. It is only a matter of time before you crack completely and I will be here at the ready for that moment."

"Over my dead body."

"That can be arranged."

I don't know what freaked me out more. Knowing that if the light didn't break inside of me that he would take me over dead or the fact that he believes I am   almost ready anyway. Either way I didn't like it, not one bit.

"Come on Gabe...realize what's going on here please. I don't think I can hold out much longer."

CHAPTER SIX

Serenity

I really didn't know what to expect seeing Gabriel again. He didn't think I was aware of it but I know he's avoiding me. I just wish I knew the real reason why. While Heaven might believe he had spared Lucifer for some reason that is less than genuine I am having a hard time agreeing with it.

If he wanted Lucifer alive then he wouldn't have come to save Ryan and I at all. He would have let the plan go down the way it was supposed to and he would have let us die. He didn't do that, instead choosing to grab his brothers and come to our aide.

Graham going missing had been hard on him. We'd spoken about that before he separated himself from me. He is carrying the disappearance on his shoulders alone, believing that it is all his fault which is why he's pulling away. At least that's what I'm choosing to believe.

I know that when Michael told me everything I planned on getting answers but seeing the way he looks now I don't think going hard at him is the best option. It wouldn't serve anyone's best interests alienating Gabriel now. I have to get close to him again. That's the only way I am going to get the answers we want.

His light isn't as bright as it had been that day in my dorm room. I hadn't had a whole lot of opportunities in Heaven to be around Gabriel and his light but here now, back in my old hometown, it was noticeable that whatever he is going through is affecting his brightness.

I wondered how he felt about losing his powers. He has always been the more emotional of the angels I have been in contact with. He reminded me more of a human then the celestial being that he really is. Maybe that's why when he backed away from me I felt the loss so powerfully. As focused as I had been on Ryan, it didn't mean that I wasn't also concerned about the fragile state of the only angel I had ever truly known.

43

"I'm sorry you got stuck on babysitting duty. You probably want to be anywhere else right now."

"This is not what you refer to as babysitting duty Serenity."

"Well it's not like you've wanted to be around me much since everything happened. So what would you call it?"

"I would call it what it is. We have a job we must do. You must live your life and I must protect you while focusing on other pursuits."

"Okay fine then, you're on protection duty."

"Even after everything you still refuse to acknowledge how important you are. I would think that after all of this time you would at least be able to come to terms with that."

This is definitely not the same Gabriel I'd known and cared for. With the way he seemed to want to lecture me he is reminding me of his father. I didn't like the way he sounded. I wanted the Gabriel from before back and I wanted him back now.

"I know what I mean to the world Gabriel. I've actually dealt with that and the powers I have. I just don't think it's as great as you all seem to think it is."

"You are the key to true peace. How can you not see that as something truly extraordinary?"

"I don't know," I shrugged. "I guess it's because I've only known about all of this for six months where you've known it my entire life. Maybe I need more time to get used to it."

"I wish I could grant you that time Serenity but I can't. We no longer have time for you to adapt."

His final statement made my blood run cold. He was talking about Lucifer. We didn't have time because of him and the fact that he was still alive and probably planning his next attack as we spoke.

"So what exactly am I supposed to do now? " I asked changing the subject to something that wouldn't give me the creepy crawlies. "Am I just supposed to go back to school and pretend I haven't been missing for six months?"

"To Emma and the rest of the world you will not appear to have been missing. I have altered their minds. While six months may have passed they do believe you to have been a part of it the entire time."

Well that isn't what I pictured coming back to. I wasn't exactly sure how I felt about the angels altering anything in my best friends head. I would have just come up with an excuse for a prolonged absence. That would have gone over easier then what I am presented with now.

"What about Graham?" I asked quietly, unsure of whether broaching this topic was the way to go. "Where do we start looking for him?"

"I know Father said that you were to be a part of that but I do not feel right bringing you into it with the danger that may come."

Not on babysitting duty my ass.

"Well you don't have a choice. Gabe look, I know you think that what happened to him is your fault but it's not. We're both to blame. I can't let you do this on your own. It's Graham for crying out loud."

The pain on his face was evident. I hit my mark when I mentioned the blame he put on himself. I just wasn't sure how to make it stop.

"I am aware of what he is to you and the reasons you want to find him so desperately but it isn't just about Graham anymore. There is much more going on and I need to do as I am asked and protect you from it."

"You're talking about Lucifer aren't you?"

The look of shock on his face as I said the name was expected. I figured Michael had told me what he had in confidence and that Gabriel was unaware. I just hoped that in admitting what I knew that it wouldn't push the angel further away.

"What do you know of Lucifer?" He demanded, his tone matching the trace of anger that now lined his brightly lit face. "What has my brother been telling you in my absence?"

"Michael is worried about you. So spare the attitude okay?"

"What do you know?" he demanded again, completely disregarding my words.

""I know what your father believes about you and your involvement in Lucifer still being alive. I know that they think he's

45

done something with Graham which is why we haven't been able to find him anywhere. I don't know everything though so why don't you tell me?"

"There is nothing of import to share that you do not already know."

"You're lying."

I have no idea what possessed me to say it but I knew that it was true. While Michael may have told me what he thought I needed to know I knew there was more to the story. There always is with the angels.

"I have told you how I feel about lying Serenity. I am unable to do it."

"You're lying to me again. Gabriel stop it! You know what a lie is and you know how to do it. I don't know if it's because of what Lucifer did to you or if you've just changed on your own but you're doing it and I can tell. It is one of my abilities now."

It didn't take abilities to know he is holding back with me. Whether or not he was flat out lying though, that is something I could tell. I had always been able to sense the truth from people but over the last six months it's grown and there is no longer any doubt. I can sense a lie even before it's said.

"Your abilities have been developing?"

"Yes. Not all of them but there are some from before that are stronger and more apparent. According to Michael they will all begin to make themselves known as time goes on."

"That is good. That will serve you well in what we face."

"What exactly are we facing? Just tell me, you know that you want to. Why make things harder on yourself?"

It seemed I was getting through to him as his expression began to change. Even through the light I could see it. I had never been so thankful in my entire life. The last thing I wanted to do was go toe to toe with an angel.

"Lucifer has Graham. You were right; I have been keeping that from you. While I still cannot ascertain where they are located I am more than positive that they are together. That in some way Graham plays into a newer more evil plot."

"So I was right! You didn't intentionally let him live."

46

"Of course not, you saw me grieve did you not?"

He's right. I did see him grieve for the brother he thought he destroyed. It had not been a pretty sight. We all grieved in our own way for the fallen angel. Knowing he is alive now just made all of it seem like such a waste. We cared when we shouldn't have. We were all the fools he believed us to be.

"So what do you have in mind to find Graham?"

"As of this moment I have nothing. I am without my full abilities so finding my brother the easier way will not be possible."

"So we're basically going into this blind?"

"There is no we. You are going back to school. You will appear to be a normal girl while I do whatever I need to do to find Lucifer."

"Jesus! If this is the way you're going to be I almost wish Michael had been the one to come down with me."

"There is no doubt who the other half of your soul is."

"What is that supposed to mean?"

"Both you and Graham have a horrible habit of taking the name of God and using it in a derogatory nature. It is very unsettling. Please refrain from doing so."

"You're kidding right?"

"I never make jokes about this kind of thing Serenity; you should know this about me by now."

"You never joke about anything at all if you ask me but fine, I won't do it again. You're not changing the subject on me though. I will help you find Graham and if Lucifer is with him well that's even better."

"You have no idea what you are saying."

"I know exactly what I'm saying. Your asshole of a brother tried to kill me and he actually did kill Ryan. If finding Graham leads me to Lucifer then great, I've got unfinished business with him anyway."

CHAPTER SEVEN

Gabriel

There is something wrong with me. As a warrior of Heaven I am not supposed to be able to feel this much. I am built to be able to get the job done and not falter from the course at which I have been placed yet I am doing that very thing.

It should have been no surprise that Serenity's abilities were presenting themselves strongly now. It had only been a matter of time. I had not been expecting her to be able to see through me though. That was something new.

As celestial beings we have the ability to remain detached from human kind and that is exactly what Serenity was in the current moment. She is human albeit it a special one. I knew from experience that I was able to shroud my thoughts and actions from everyone but Father so her being able to see through me and know that I am keeping things from her was astounding. She is far more powerful then I first believed.

Given our connection I could not lie to her. I may have been doing it all in an effort to protect her but the one thing I should have realized about Serenity is she wouldn't accept that as a reason for a lie by omission.

She had been through so much in the eight months since I appeared to her that I needed a reminder that she wasn't the same woman anymore. That she knew what her destiny is and she is more than capable of seeing it through. I didn't have to treat her with kid gloves because she had proven herself able of handling even the worst of situations.

I knew that now which is why I had finally given in and told her everything. At least everything that I was aware of in the time we hadn't been close. She may not yet know of the devastation that I had found at Graham's place of residence but she knew that he had been taken by Lucifer. That is all she really needed to know.

Now I just had to come up with a way to keep her out of the search. Though given her attitude towards revenge where my brother is concerned that was going to be no easy task.

"You must not travel down the path of revenge Serenity for it serves no one but the very man you want to seek said revenge on."

"This isn't about revenge Gabriel…well okay, maybe it is a little but it's not what I'm focusing on."

"Then what is your reasoning for wanting to help me with Graham?"

"For one, your father asked it of both of us. More than that, if my destiny is to save the world and make it a better place for everyone don't you think coming face to face with Lucifer is going to be inevitable? In order to reach my true potential I must take on the very thing that threatens it."

She was beginning to sound like the ball of light that she is. Her time in Heaven had changed her. She never looked more like my beloved then she did in this moment.

"You need to be aware that if we do work together I am limited in what I am able to do. I will be able to protect you to the best of my remaining ability but that is no guarantee."

"I know that. I can handle myself."

I know she believes that statement but I wasn't entirely sure I could. I knew her power level is unmatched and that once she reached her full potential she would be an unstoppable force but she had not gotten to that point yet, so she was still very much the vulnerable human she appeared to be.

"Since I believe there is no talking you out of this I will agree to let you aide in the search for your soul mate but you must do something for me in return."

"Are you really trying to barter with me right now Gabe?"

"I am merely trying to reach a mutual agreement. If I am to allow you to join me then you must also do something for me in return. That is the human way is it not?"

She nodded and I watched as the smile crept across her lips. "Yes that is how we operate but since when do you choose the human way?"

"Since it has become the only real way I have to accomplish what I have been sent here to do."

"Can I ask you something?"

"You may ask me anything Serenity."

"Why did you lose your powers?"

I knew that this would come to light eventually but it isn't something I enjoy talking about. Going from being one of the most powerful angels in heaven to basically being no better than the humans themselves is nothing I want to be reminded of. I owed her the truth and for more than just her ability to see through any lie I might tell. I owed her because it all centered on her.

She told me once that anything that related to our lives as a unit should be known to her and this was no different. She deserved to know all of it.

"When I was given the task of guarding you, I went into it not realizing just what we would eventually mean to one another. I let my brother get into my head and turn me away from my care of you and essentially Graham also. I not only let you down but father as well. Something that you well know I have been unable to fully deal with in the appropriate way."

"So your father stripped you?"

"No, he gave me a second chance to make things right. I used it to call on Graham and attempt to get you out of the church. While I did not realize it at the time you had been branded so it was a fruitless endeavour to say the least. Again I had gone in believing I could change the course you were on and failed."

"Gabriel…"

"No Serenity, I do not need your sympathy in this regard. I made the choices that I did and I must live with them despite what you believe."

"You didn't cause any of this to happen though! Why should I let you believe you did?"

"It is a fact. I was to lose my powers the day that you chose to save the demon but Michael talked Father out of it. I knew it would only be a matter of time before it happened and well now here we are."

"He stripped you of your power because he believes you had something to do with Lucifer remaining alive."

I nodded in response to her statement. I knew very well what Father believed even though he could not be more wrong.

"I watched my brother walk through holy fire which alone should have told me that he was not the same brother that had been cast out. Living through the angel blade should have been something I expected given that information but it was not. I in no way helped Lucifer survive. As you know I believed him dead but until I can prove myself worthy, he will not listen."

"Then we need to find Graham and we need to make him listen."

"If only it could be that easy."

"It can be Gabriel. If you need to prove to your father that you had no part in what happened six months ago then do it. Find Graham and prove to him and everyone else that you are on the right side and you have been the entire time."

"Why do you not believe the way Michael and Father do?"

"That's easy. I don't believe them because I know you. You would never go through everything you did just to help your brother live. It just doesn't make logical sense."

"You do know how that sounds?"

"Yeah I do. It means I don't think your father is thinking logically."

"That is a dangerous statement given that it was exactly how it started with Lucifer. Questioning Father never turns out well for anyone. You would be better served remembering that."

"No, I think I'll believe in what I can see and what is real. I know what it might cost me but honestly Gabriel, I don't care. I will take whatever happens if it means believing in what's right."

Her words touched me in ways I hadn't allowed myself to feel in a very long time. She had faith in me despite everything I put her through and she was standing here now willing to fight alongside of me to prove my loyalty to Heaven. It meant everything to me knowing that even though she could have, she had never given up on me no matter how flawed I was.

51

"Go back to the college. Check in with your roommate and make sure that everything appears normal on that front. I need to know if in doing what I did, no one is harmed in a way that I cannot reverse. I will formulate a plan to find Graham and I will come to you when the time is right."

"I can do that." she agreed. "Just remember that your idea of when the time is right and mine are completely different. Don't wait too long."

I know what she is saying even though she didn't speak the words. She was telling me that if I didn't come to her as soon as possible then she would go forward without me, something I could never allow her to do.

This time I am going to do things Serenity's way. I only hope I don't live to regret it.

Lucifer

It's time.

While in my previous visits with the human I had only given him the memories, this final time I employed a much different approach. The memories themselves were enough to break his spirit and make him feel unimaginable amounts of pain but they never gave me the result I was craving.

I have never given much thought to focusing on the use of human senses before now. I always just saw it as a waste of time. It would appear though that with this particular human it is much more than that. It caused far more damage than any method before it.

Placing my hands on either side of his head and pushing the memories toward him at such a rapid pace his brain was having a hard time keeping up effectively broke his body down but going that step further and making him smell, touch, and taste the very memories I was throwing his way broke his soul.

I wanted him to feel the way his soul mate had felt as the blood was draining from her body. The way it tasted through Ryan's senses while he had been partaking of it and the way her body had gone limp right in front of his eyes. Allowing him to feel

Serenity the way Ryan did had been the thing to carry him over the edge.

Rage and jealousy were very primal emotions. They drove the person who felt them to dark places unimagined in the most pure of minds. Graham Hudson was no different. Feeling the love first hand that the human had for the other half of his very soul had built the darkness inside of him until he reached the point of no return.

While he may still carry some light within him, he also now had the taste of Serenity's blood coursing through his system. The iron like smell of her blood would flood his nostrils until he overdosed on the need for it.

Yes, the time has come. He is ready for me.

Extracting myself from the body of the useless human I possessed months before had been draining but worth it. He was nothing more than an empty shell and would be easily disposed of. Doing it in front of Graham had also been especially pleasing for me as his eyes widened in horror while at the same time displayed a look of pleasure, all the effect the sensory overload raised within him. There could be no sweeter reaction then the one before me now.

His eyes, which before had been a deep shade of green were now much like Ryan's before him and shaded in black. While he is not a demon, the darkest part of him had been contacted and was rising to the surface. He is completely at my mercy and would now be prepared for our joining.

I prepared the blood earlier, a special blend both favorable to demons as well as to the other damned creatures that walked the earth undetected. Draining the sweet virgin was easy as she had been a more than willing follower of mine eagerly awaiting the time at which I would call on her to fulfill what I had made her believe was her destiny. Now as I bent before him, the goblet in my hand at the ready I watched in delight as the body before me smiled in anticipation.

He needed to regenerate his strength. Stripping him the way I did had taken him to a level that while I may be able to inhabit easily, would not be prepared for what came next. I had to make sure that he drank every drop of the drinks prepared for him and then allow his body the time to heal to its full potential again. That would be easy as long as I could keep my eagerness in check. Tipping the goblet to his mouth and watching as the first sip began making its way down his throat I eagerly awaited what would come next and he did not disappoint. Grabbing the goblet from my hands he began drinking of it himself, gulping it down so quickly that it appeared as though he was starving, which pleased me greatly.

Yes, this is going to be much easier than I originally thought. Now that I finally found the way to break him of the light he was mine completely and would bend to my every request. I would definitely enjoy taking this man as my permanent vessel. It was only a shame that my brother and his beloved could not be here to witness the change about to occur.

I soothed myself with the knowledge that it would come in due time and when it did it would be something that neither of them would be expecting.

Taking the drained goblet back, I watched as he first wiped his mouth with the sleeve of his shirt and then using his tongue, ran it over his lips, making sure he ingested every remaining drop; an image that would appear simple to most but of which the gravity knew no bounds for me.

This is the moment I have been waiting for, finally turning the light into darkness.

"Is the drink to your liking Graham? Would you like another?"

"Yes…as much as you have."

"As you wish but Graham, you must make it quick as we have much that we need to do in preparation."

With a nod of his head I watched as he again drained another goblet of blood easily, noticing the change in his skin as it went from the dirty peach to the light pink it was now morphing into.

Yes, the time is definitely upon us now. We could begin.

CHAPTER EIGHT

Serenity

It's been a week since I've heard from Gabriel. The last time he came to me had been two days after we agreed to work together. True to his word he'd come and told me what he planned on doing and then just as quickly as he appeared, he was gone.

It's been weird going back to the way things used to be. He visits me the way he did in the beginning, coming to me strictly in my mind, as if that is somehow easier than seeing him in his actual form. I know why he is choosing to do things this way again but I still wished things could be different.

Given the way he dragged Graham into everything without my knowledge he didn't want to repeat the same thing with Emma. Having my best friend know that I heard voices is one thing but to let her in on everything despite already believing Gabriel to be exactly what he is just wasn't a risk he was willing to take.

So I had to keep our visits a secret and I hated every minute of it. Keeping things from Emma is extremely hard given the way she is but having to pretend that nothing was going on with me is even harder. It helped that my ability to speak with the dead seemed to have taken a backseat to all of the others I was gaining. It made lying to her that much easier.

Gabriel believes that when Ryan drained me in the church that night it changed my powers. Hearing voices had been my strongest ability before but now it was the weakest. I didn't care what caused it I was just thankful that this time around I didn't have to deal with it. While I wasn't the normal girl I wanted to be at least I wasn't surrounded by constant chatter at all hours anymore.

Just the way I expected the minute I came back to school Emma cornered me and wanted to know everything there was to know about Graham and Ryan. Since neither of them had appeared on campus and she hadn't had her memory wiped completely, I was her only source of information on just what happened to them.

The hardest thing I've ever had to do is lie to her about Ryan. While it has been easier to explain Graham's absence since of course I'm in love with Ryan and Emma is aware of it, I still didn't enjoy doing it. I wanted nothing more than to tell her exactly what happened to both of the men in my life.

*****

"You're a bad girl."

"Excuse me?" I ask continuing to pile books into my backpack. "How am I bad?"

"You've been holding out on me! All of the movie nights we've had and I still have no idea what happened with you and Ryan or Graham. I thought for sure I'd see him around campus but there's been nothing."

"There's nothing to tell Ems. Graham went home. He came here for me and when he realized that isn't where my head was he decided that it was better if he left. As for Ryan, well I don't know what you want me to tell you."

"He never explained what happened?"

Of course he explained but I couldn't exactly tell her that. I couldn't tell my best friend that the boy she wanted to beat the shit out of was actually a half demon sent here to take me to the dark side. Even to me that sounded crazy. I could only imagine what she'd think.

"No. I mean I've seen him around but we both pretty much go out of our way to avoid each other. I told you before Ems, I'm not his type."

"He has no idea what the right type is obviously."

That's my Emma, loyal to a fault. She has no idea that her loyalty in this case is misplaced. I hated hearing her say bad things when she had no idea how much I really cared for him. I am definitely doing a great job of being the supportive wife. Even if he didn't need or want me to be at least he would find the entire thing entertaining.

"I guess he doesn't. I always figured you two would hit it off anyway."

"Like I'd go out with him after the shit he pulled with you. Seriously Ser, what he did to you was wrong and that makes me want nothing to do with him."

"Thanks Ems."

"Do you ever talk to Gabriel anymore or did that get all screwed up too?" she asked, genuinely interested in whatever happened between me and the angel.

Being able to sense someone's true intentions is new but I found myself enjoying it. I could now tell with certainty what I had always known to be true about Emma. She cared about me and it's real and genuine. She really didn't have a dark bone in her body.

"We talk but it's not the same as it was before." I answered truthfully. It's the first real answer I can give her and I felt lighter doing it. It was as if a bolder had been taken off my shoulders. At least in this way I could do the right thing the way I wanted to.

"You ever find out who he really is?"

Well so much for being able to tell her the truth. Now I had to go back the lie.

"No. I mean I tried but he still maintains that he will tell me when the time is right. I hate it but I decided that I'm just going to take your advice."

"Wait, what advice was that?"

"You told me that maybe when he isn't with me he is somewhere he's needed more and I think I need to start believing that instead of hating on him for not being here. I was being selfish and that was wrong."

My heart instantly felt light again as I turned it around into the truth. I knew Gabriel could hear every word I was saying as well so I had no doubt that my words would get through to him if he allowed himself to believe in them.

"That's pretty good advice. I'm awesome."

"Yes Ems, you're more than awesome." I said laughing. As much as I balked at coming back to school and my life here, I'm thankful that I did. I really did miss Emma.

*****

After that first conversation with Emma I finally had answers that I hadn't even realized I'd been wanting. I wondered how Gabriel playing with her mind would work when we came face to face again and it seems that it wasn't as bad as I was expecting. She really believes I've been here with her sharing movie nights the way we used to.

I only felt bad that I haven't gotten to experience it with her. The times with Emma, whether we were in the center or out at school together have been some of the best times of my life. I always felt normal with her. I felt oddly empty knowing that she had memories of time together that I didn't. I wanted to have them too.

As easily as I adjusted back into my routine here I still found myself aching for Ryan. Given the amount of quiet time I have now that the voices have taken their vacation it always ends up coming back around to him. If he is healing up there, if they are taking care of him and if he would soon be able to come back here and join me so that I wouldn't have to go through all of this alone. It is a never ending cycle.

I may have Gabriel but that isn't enough for me. Faced with finding Graham, Lucifer and another possible life or death showdown, it would go a lot easier on me if I had him here beside me. Even before we'd gone through with our dark wedding I felt strong every time I was around him and I wanted that feeling more than anything now.

I just need to know he's really okay, something that the updates from Michael never really do for me.

It was in one of these lonely moments that Gabriel came to me, a week after I'd come back. True to his word he was back with information moving forward.

*****

"Serenity..."

"I was wondering if you were ever coming back."

"I assured you that I would."

"I know Gabe, it was a joke. Have you figured out what we're going to do yet?"

58

"Not entirely but I do believe I may have found where Lucifer took Graham and why we have been unable to reach either of them."

While I was disappointed that he hadn't come to me with a plan of action, knowing where Graham might be outweighed it. At least we would have a place to start even if what we do once we find him is still unclear.

"Where is he?"

"It is not where he is but where he was."

"Really Gabe? You're gonna be vague about it? Fine, where was he?"

"He has been in Green Haven in the old abandoned church."

The very place where I married Ryan and proceeded to have the life drained of me. Why in the world would Lucifer stay behind in the one place he could be caught in? Better yet why hadn't Michael and Gabriel known it before now?

"The warding that he did to block us originally, it appears he created it again except this time it was much stronger. He wanted to be hidden from us."

"Why didn't Uriel just break the warding spells like he did the last time?" I asked, knowing full well just what the other angels had done in an effort to save me.

"As I said it was much stronger than before and Uriel was drained from the power used during the last battle. He would have been able to find him eventually but not back then."

"So if you know where they were how come you don't know where they went?

"I do not know why I am unable to tell his exact location now but I do have a plan moving forward."

"Which is?"

"We must go back to Green Haven. I can go alone but I know how much you want to be a part of finding Graham so I am bringing it to you before I leave."

"When do we leave?"

"Two days. I know it will be hard to wait that long Serenity but I no longer have the power to alter time and mind which means we have to do it when you are not supposed to be here at school."

59

That is the most ludicrous thing I've ever heard. I was made of Heaven yet I had to sit here and go from class to class like a regular person because Gabriel couldn't alter anyone's mind anymore?

"Ask Michael to do it for you. He's been missing for six months Gabriel. Don't you think waiting even an extra two days could mean life and death for him? We need to find him and we can't wait on it."

"I have already reached out to Father and he is the reason we cannot leave any sooner. He wants you here so here you must remain. Serenity I know how much this hurts you and for that I am sorry but I cannot afford to go against him again."

He was right, he couldn't afford to go up against Heaven anymore then he already had. He already had to prove his worth again. The last thing I needed was for him to somehow bend and help me and have him sent home. I was going to have to relax and wait the time out. Two days really couldn't make anything any worse....could it?

"Fine, you've got your two days. I will do what I'm told and continue going about my life but Gabriel don't you dare think of doing this without me. I will find Graham, even if it means going against you to do it."

"I wouldn't dream of it."

*****

CHAPTER NINE

Gabriel

When Serenity went back to her human life I didn't realize just how much harder everything would be for her. I expected her to have issues acclimating back given the amount of time she had actually been gone and also the devastation she had been through beforehand.

She handled the flow of college life rather easily but the other aspects, such as her relationship with the best friend Emma were not going so easily. I had been privy to the conversation between the two where she mentioned both Graham and Ryan's absences from her life and not a word of it had been true.

Though she tried not to let it show the lying took a tremendous toll on her both physically and emotionally. She is just not cut out for the life she was now leading. Sure she is strong, there was no question of her ability to handle things in that department but she is not cut out to lie.

Having spent a life surrounded by people that did nothing but lie to her, myself included it is understandable that she draw that line early on in her adulthood. Having to be the one lying now was not something she looked forward to doing and she broke just a little bit more every time she had to do it.

I wanted to take that from her, to allow her to tell Emma everything just so that her time here would go that much smoother and in the end she would be of more use in helping me when the time came. I could not do that though. It had to come from Father or not at all.

Admitting that she had been selfish with me in the beginning did funny things to me. I spent as long as I can remember blaming myself for being manipulated by my brother and allowing Father to take me away from her that hearing she no longer held me responsible for my time away shocked me. While I knew that eventually I would come up in conversation with Emma I never expected it to go quite that way.

If Serenity could look at the situation and see her own fault in it even if I didn't believe she held any is it possible that maybe I can forgive myself for everything that I put everyone though?

"Gabriel...we must speak immediately."

"Michael."

"Are you still in Green Haven?"

"Yes. Despite Father's request I think it appropriate that I investigate everything fully before bringing Serenity into it."

When no answer came from my explanation I wondered if Michael had cut the connection off in order to deal with something more pressing. It wasn't until he appeared in front of me that I came to the realization that whatever he must need to tell me is more urgent then I originally expected.

"After the battle with Lucifer I didn't think I'd see you down here again brother. What is so pressing that you need to speak to me this way?"

"It is regarding the half demon."

"What about him? I asked, confused as to why he is here telling me instead of reaching out to Serenity. It wasn't a secret that she cared a great deal for Ryan and would want to know anything there was to know about his recovery no matter how grave it may be.

"He has awoken."

"So why are you telling me? You know I do not do so well with the hand holding that I am sure he has become accustomed to."

"Father told me to make you aware. It is then up to you to make sure that Serenity knows but only when the time is right."

I am beginning to understand why Serenity hated hearing me talk about things being done in their right time. It did seem to be the go to statement for every being in Heaven and after hearing it enough times I could see how it could become quite annoying.

"The time is right now brother. You must go and tell her. I understand what it will mean in terms of the mission down here but it will end up much worse if you do not inform her. Do not make the same mistakes I did with Serenity. I promise you will pay for them later."

Michael seemed to give some thought to what I was saying and I hoped he would take every word to heart. I made the mistake of waiting until the time was right to tell Serenity about myself and the place I had in her life and it cost me. She turned to the very side that I am sworn to protect her from. That was definitely something I did not want happening to Michael.

Having one brother screw up in a lifetime is more than enough.

"There used to be a time Gabriel where you would be the last person to tell me to disobey Father yet here you sit now telling me to do just that."

"It is not about disobeying him Michael; it is about doing the right thing in the moment. It may not be the best time to tell her that her husband is awake but there could be tragic consequences for all parties if you do not do it at all."

"Is this you believing that you speak from experience?"

"I don't just believe it Michael, I know it as fact. Go to her and tell her. Do not spare another moment here talking to me about it. Do the right thing and we can deal with Father later."

"I will heed your advice Gabriel but please while she is away do make sure to take proper guarding precautions. We don't need anyone else falling under Lucifer's spell."

I know he is concerned for my well-being but the way he made it sound is as if he wanted me to guard myself so I didn't fall victim again, which is the last thing I wanted to hear. Where I may have screwed up months ago I would not make the same mistake a second time.

This time I would see Lucifer coming.

Lucifer

Now this is what it is supposed to feel like when you possess someone.

Feeling the blood pump through my veins, my heart beating at a steady pace all the while eagerly awaiting the moment when I would come face to face with the people who had wronged me so many months before.

As I predicted Graham had been the perfect host. After breaking him of the light he was more than ready to join with me and as I walked around in his skin, I felt alive for the first time in years.

I had chosen some pretty sturdy vessels but none felt the way Graham Hudson did. Where the others began breaking down shortly after we became one he is not. He seems to accept the changes that joining brought out in him and I couldn't be more pleased.

Just as I expected, taking down the barriers I held over the church worked like a charm. Gabriel had been able to sense my location and true to his way he had shown up to try and confront me. He is aware that I have the human with me which is his prime motivation for coming to me. He was going to hate to find out what has actually happened in the short period of time that I've had the human captive.

For now I have to focus on the next step in my plan. I have to make my way back to the school and enroll again. Serenity would be my first step. Given that I am now in control of her soul mate it is now up to me to get close to her again so that the end could be reached.

This is really all about her power. I wanted it for myself especially given that she had no idea the true extent of it. If she wasn't going to take full advantage of what God himself had given her then I was going to make sure I did. Someone may as well get to reap the benefits.

In possessing as many bodies as I had over the years in my attempt to bring my ultimate goal to fruition I adapted quite easily to the human way of life which gave me more than the standard level of confidence in my ability to pass myself off successfully as Graham Hudson.

I would first gain her trust filling her with lies about where I've been and what I've been through, from there break not only the attachment she had to my old protégé but also the beloved bond between her and my brother. I had to make sure that I pulled her completely away from the very things that could take the power away from me.

This time I would not fail. It was just not possible.

Keeping myself hidden yet making my way around the main areas of the campus has been very productive. I see that Serenity has indeed made her way back to her life and along with the roommate lacking brain function I could tell she is having no trouble adapting. She would lower her guard soon and when she did that is when I would strike.

Where I had been unable to get her power in times before, this plan really was foolproof. Her connection to the human made her choice in the end obvious. In order to save the other half of her soul she would do anything and that is exactly what I wanted from her.

Until then I would watch her from afar and bide my time until she was ripe for the pickings.

CHAPTER TEN

Ryan

I feel different. I want to say that the difference is change but I don't feel that I've changed. The demon still resides inside me; I can feel it though it's much weaker than before. I'm thankful that it seems to be dormant and weak but it would have been better if it was gone for good.

The angel tells me that unfortunately it's impossible but I know that isn't exactly the truth. If they really wanted to they could knock me out again and remove that part of me completely. They have the power to do even more but for whatever reason they want to keep the darkness alive in me.

I know they don't trust me and I can't say I blame them. Yes I managed to die in my effort to protect their greatest gift but while that may redeem me it didn't exactly change centuries of bad blood. It made perfect sense that they still wanted to treat me like a leper. I'll just prove my worth to them and then their doubts will be gone forever.

Waking up to find myself surrounded by an angel rather than Serenity has been difficult. While I may have been out cold to the casual observer I was aware of what was going on around me. I could feel them working on me trying to heal my body from the battle it had been through. Bringing me back from death was no easy feat. I felt Serenity with me every single time she was here though I was powerless to let her know it.

I believe that the reason I even made it through everything the angels did to me is because she had been by my side. She refused to leave at points which only made me want to wake up and tell her how much I love her. The girl that was afraid of her own shadow and who spent her life living on the outskirts was long gone and the person that remained was exceptional.

She is stronger now proving it by going head to head with some of Heaven's most powerful beings without batting an eyelash. I'm proud of her. This is the Serenity that the world was meant to see. The one that fought for what she believed in never backed down and never gave up when things got tough.

The angel known as Michael explained to me why he is there in her place. I understood it but it didn't make me wish any less that she had been here the minute I opened my eyes. Even while my body was out my heart wasn't. It longed for her just as much as it did when we had been on Earth together. I wanted her here with me now so that not only could I tell her how I felt about her but show her as well.

It had been explained to me that I died while fighting Lucifer and in that moment I had been redeemed. I want to tell them that they would have been better off not saving me as I was ready for the end in order to save her but I just don't think it's something they want to hear. They made the choice to save me and I need to suck it up and be grateful.

It gave me time with Serenity again which in the end is all I could ever want. I finally found the person that allowed me to feel again and while being taken away from her might have been a smart decision it is also one that would have sucked. I hadn't gotten enough time with her before but with this second chance I am being given I'm prepared to take full advantage of it.

Heaven does not acknowledge our wedding. While it may have been legal with humans it is not something easily recognized by the light as it was a connection born in darkness. Every single time I look at my ring finger though and see the band wrapped around it I see it as something more than just something born of evil. We had been joined in truth, a decision both of us may not have liked at the start but one that we fully accepted. She had become mine willingly and I hers.

I wondered if she still wore her ring, if she still held me close to her heart or if Heaven had wiped out that part of her. I wanted to ask Michael but given everything they had done to save me it just didn't seem like the right thing to bring up. The last thing I needed to do was rock the boat.

While I waited for some word on when and if she would return I remembered the last time I felt her with me, the words

67

she'd spoken and the feeling that it left in me. I might question whether or not they had wiped her acknowledgement of our wedding but I never had to question her feelings and the way she had been that day proved it.

*****

"Every single day that passes it gets harder to see you like this. I want you to come back to me. None of this seems real without you. I don't know how much longer I can do this alone."

I want to tell her she isn't alone, that I am experiencing everything with her but it isn't true. When she wasn't here with me her hand placed over mine I couldn't feel her. I couldn't experience what she was going through and just what she was dealing with.

Coming back to her was the only thing I wanted to do but just from the attempts I made at trying to move I could tell it wasn't time. I couldn't move my body; open my mouth to speak or anything else that would give her what she needed. I was resigned to just continuing to heal even though it did nothing to soothe her troubled mind or my equally troubled heart.

"They're telling me that soon I'm going to have to go back to my life and I don't want to do it. I healed a long time ago but I don't think I'm healed in the way they need me to be. I know what I will face when I go back down and I don't think I'm quite ready for that yet."

There was always one thing the angel Gabriel and I agreed on during our time around her on Earth. It was that she is stronger than she realized and that she would handle any situation thrown her way. We both wanted her to see herself the way we did because if she did that then there is no doubt she would be unstoppable.

God! Not being able to answer her right now is driving me crazy. I need to tell her she can do this. That it was alright for her to leave me and complete what they believed her real mission to be and that I would be fine without her.

The last part would definitely be a lie but one I would gladly tell if it made her realize her full potential. I may not be alright without her given that she is my only real motivation to fight but I

68

would do whatever it took to make her see what I already saw deep inside her.

"Gabriel blames himself for what happened to us. It's so bad he rarely spends time here anymore instead taking every task his father throws his way in an effort to avoid me and any memory of what happened. I don't want to miss him but I do. I just wish things could go back to the way they used to be."

Gabriel is her beloved. I knew this but I wasn't sure how I felt about hearing her speak about missing him. I love her and the human part of me along with the demon hated any mention of her feelings possibly swaying away from me. I couldn't allow it to happen. I wanted to hate the angel so badly but I couldn't.

Staying away was causing her pain and I didn't want her to ever feel pain. I wanted what she did if it meant that she would be alright again. Gabriel is someone in her life that she had come to depend on at one time and if she needed that to be whole again then I would use whatever strength I had to get him back to her. He needed her just as much as she did him, it was obvious.

"Apparently it's unhealthy for me to be here every day so Michael has agreed to spend some time here with you while you're recovering and I've finally agreed to let him. I don't want to but they don't seem to want to stop hounding me about it so if you ever wake up and I'm not here please know I won't be far away."

I needed to tell her it's okay. Focusing my mind as much as I was able I pushed the words toward her and prayed that she'd be able to hear them or at least part of them. I wanted her to know that I knew she was here and that I wouldn't stop fighting when they took her away from me.

"I will be fine and I will come back to you. I love you."
*****

I have no idea if she'd been able to hear me as she left shortly after that, the angel coming to me in her place. I could only hope that as she'd been sent back down to Earth that she heard my words and kept them with her. If she did that then I know I can do this. I can heal and come back to her even better than I was before.

I didn't know what to expect when I woke up to find Michael lingering over me. I know she trusted him, that she wouldn't have

69

agreed to leave if I'd been in any danger but I really couldn't be sure that he'd be the most willing person to help me now. I wanted him to get word to her that I was awake, that I was alright and that I needed her.

Would the angel help me or would furthering their own agenda with Serenity be more important?

"She is going to be very happy to hear you have awoken."

I guess I don't have anything to worry about after all. I thought as I soaked in his words.

"Will you get her?"

"Of course I will. I made her a promise and I intend to stick with it."

"It won't ruin anything you have going with her on Earth will it?"

"How do you know we are using Serenity for anything?"

"I wasn't completely unaware while you were working on me Michael. I could hear and sense and feel I was just unable to show it."

As he acknowledged my words I realized he also seemed to have his doubts. This is where the demon side of me would always present a problem. They were trained not to believe a word I said even if I died in order to prove to them just what side I really resided on.

"I know you think I'm lying but go ahead and use your power on me, you'll see I'm not."

"There is no need for that. Despite the way I react to situations given my training I am inclined to believe in what Serenity feels. I do believe your intentions are right."

"So where is she?"

"Adapting to her life and preparing to find Graham."

Graham Hudson, the soul mate. Exactly what happened to him while I'd been out that she needed to be sent back to find him?

"What happened to him?"

"That is information you do not need to know. It is for us to handle. You need to focus on healing now."

For anyone that's ever taken a wrong step or not given much thought to their surroundings I can only liken his response to that of walking into a brick wall head on. There was no way I am going to be able to get him to break and tell me what happened to the soul mate. It didn't matter how much I wanted to know if I wasn't meant to then I never would.

Heaven only dealt in black and white. At least there is one thing Lucifer told me that remained correct.

"Well can you at least tell me if she's safe?"

He nodded his head and smiled which should have been a sight to behold but only made me even more wary. Is there more buried behind the smile or is it actually as genuine as I wanted to believe?

"Serenity is safe. She has a guardian with her and is currently adapting back to her life as a human. A unique human but still human none the less."

I could breathe easier knowing that she was safe. She had a guardian there with her who would let no harm come to her. So at least until I was well enough to go back I knew she would be protected by the highest power imaginable.

"What happened to Lucifer?"

"We believed him to have perished in the battle but it appears he has found a way around that. It is actually another reason I wanted to be the one to look over you during your stay here. I need answers."

"About Lucifer?" I asked, coming to terms with the fact that he was still very much out there and a threat to the very world he hated. That didn't sit well with me; I had been hoping that in the end they would have finished him off.

"Yes. He exuded exceptional abilities during our battle and you are the only remaining link to him that I can question in regards to it."

"Well I'll help any way I can. What do you want to know?"

"How was he able to walk through the holy fire so easily? As an angel, albeit a fallen one he should have been trapped but he wasn't. He also managed to survive the angel blade even though Gabriel himself saw his light diminish."

It was true that Lucifer and I were connected at one time. For a long time we had been thick as thieves as we walked the planet planning the eventual battle that had taken place a short time before. How he was able to do the things Michael mentioned though, I had no idea. That is the one thing he never discussed with me. If he had I might have been able to find a way around blocking myself better.

"I have no idea. He wouldn't speak to me about things like that. The only time he really ever brought it up is when he caught me trying to use my abilities against him."

"Do you recall what was said or do you need some time?"

"I remember it. I wish I didn't but I remember everything that happened. Well until the minute I died anyway. Everything after that is a blank slate."

"What did he say to you?"

"He asked me if I knew where the powers actually came from and that there is no power that I had that he hadn't created and perfected himself. They were all parts of him that he shared with the ones he believed to have the most potential. Like I said, I'm not much help. He kept the actual origin of the powers from me."

"You have helped more than you realize so I must thank you Ryan."

I helped him? How? My lack of information was actually helpful?

"I'm not sure how I helped but you're welcome."

"I will get Serenity for you now but be prepared. She was against leaving to begin with. The minute she finds out that you have awakened she may possibly jump on you and never leave Heaven again, something we cannot afford."

I understood what he was telling me but I couldn't help but smile at the thought of Serenity jumping on me and never letting me go. If that is what I have to look forward to then I really hoped we could just get on with it already. I want nothing more than for her to do that. In fact, I need it.

Serenity

Something happens when you find out your destiny is to save the world. Going to a college class just doesn't seem all that important anymore. Or at least that's how I felt sitting through one pointless class after another.

The only part that I remotely enjoyed about going through the motions this way is having Emma by my side. Spending the last seven years of my life with this girl you would have thought I would have enjoyed a break from her insanity yet I found that being apart from her for even just the six months I had been was incredibly hard.

She deserved to know the truth about me. What I am and would mean to the world. I knew I couldn't tell her per my orders but it didn't mean that I didn't want to tell her anyway. I spent the last ten years following orders whether from my mother or the center. Wasn't I due for a little rebellion?

I was thankful when I finally got to head back to my room for the day. I made it through day one of the two day wait and I survived it as expected. Now I could head back to the room, pretend to do the course work I'd been given and maintain my position as the normal college girl. Well the nerdy college girl anyway but that wasn't important.

Just as I was about to crack the first text open for the professors idea of light reading the room was bathed in light. Immediately looking towards Emma's side of the room I was thankful she still had another class to get through. The light could only mean one thing. Heaven needed to speak with me and they didn't want to wait.

Gabriel having reverted back to coming to me in my mind meant he wasn't the one behind the light this time. He knew the stakes and the rules he had to follow. It is apparent that not everyone had been clued in on Emma's knowledge level, something I am going to have to rectify right away.

"Michael, you can't just pop in like that! What if Emma had been here?"

"Emma?"

"Yes Emma, you know, my very human roommate? God, don't you guys talk to each other at all? I was told to keep everything from her and you popping in when she could have easily been here would have blown that to shit."

"I can see you are adapting to your human life easily, expletives and all."

"Funny."

"I am unaware how what I said is amusing to you but that is not of consequence. I come with news."

Dealing with angels is never boring. While in the beginning I found it more than a little annoying with how staunch they seemed to be; now it really was amusing. They really had no idea how they actually sound when they speak. If he hadn't said he came with news I might have tried explaining it all to him. His reaction would have been worth the time spent.

"So if you're here with news, tell me."

"Ryan is awake."

The words I have been dying to hear for the last six months had finally been spoken and I found myself unable to believe it. Is it true? Did I really hear Michael say it or was it all just wishful thinking?

"He's really awake?"

"Yes Serenity he is really awake. I would not waste your time or my own in coming here to tell you something to the contrary."

"Then what are you waiting for? Take me home."

"I do not think that is the right course of action at the present time. You are needed down here."

Oh I wasn't gonna let him tell me that I had to stay here while Ryan remained alone in Heaven. No way in hell.

"It is the only course of action if you want my cooperation with this supposed destiny business."

"Gabriel said that you would be this way."

"Of course he did because despite what the rest of you think he knows me and he knows what is right. So let's go. Take me to him."

I wanted to know when he had found the time to talk to Gabriel about Ryan and why it happened before coming to me but my urge to get back to Heaven and the man I love overrode all of it.

"Father is not going to like this."

'I don't care what Father likes or doesn't. You know what Ryan means to me. Do you really think I'm going to be able to do what you need me to while I know he's up there awake and all alone?"

I had him and we both knew it. In order for me to function in the way that Heaven needed me to then they had to give my way, at least with this.

"I will do as you ask this one time but Serenity it would serve you better to remember your place and who your creator is. You must accept what he wants."

"Yeah well I'll deal with that after I've seen Ryan and Michael; don't worry. None of what happens with Father will come back on you. I will take responsibility for coming home before he wants me to."

I had to make him understand that I knew the risk he is taking for me. I would not let him face the almighty wrath that would be sure to come. This is all on me and I'd gladly sacrifice myself again to prove it. Nothing from Heaven, Hell or Earth could keep me from Ryan now.

I needed to be back with him. He would not spend another minute alone while I still have breath in my body to fight it.

"You know what you must do now Serenity."

As I made my way over to where he stood I held onto him and closed my eyes, preparing myself for the full body rush that would follow as we made our way home and one step closer to the man I love.

As we disappeared from the room I felt my excitement grow. Focusing on the last time I'd seen him I sent the message and only hoped he would hear it loud and clear.

"I'm coming Ryan and I won't ever leave you again."

CHAPTER ELEVEN

Gabriel

As a warrior of Heaven I have been privy to a lot of scenes such as the one I am a part of in the church in Green Haven but though one would believe it gets easier with each one you handle, it never really does.

It may only be me that is affected by such destruction and violence but I like to believe it affects us all in much the same way. With as strong as Michael has proven himself to be I can even see him bothered by what I am witnessing now and that is no small feat.

The room is dark, cold now that the occupants no longer reside within in but more than that it is bloody. What I could only assume was Graham's blood is laced throughout the room, whether for me to find or just as proof of the violence that had taken place here I couldn't be sure.

Metal chains were strewn over the floor a foot or two away from the chair that had obviously been used to contain the human with immeasurable strength. Judging from the sheer amount of binding material throughout the room it is obvious that Lucifer hadn't had the easiest time keeping him contained the way he hoped.

It strengthened the belief that I would be able to find Graham alive. That he was still fighting this every step of the way. He wouldn't give in to what Lucifer wanted of him and he would come out of this damaged but still very much the same man I had taken as my host only a few short months before.

The light has always been strong within him and I could only hope that now it is serving him the way it is meant to. That despite whatever torture Lucifer extracted on him he would be able to fight it and remain strong in the process.

It was hard to dismiss the amount of blood strewn throughout the room. It spoke of immense violence, torture and pain.

Something I felt just as easily within me as if I had been the one experiencing it instead of Graham. I had no doubt that he was very much alive as I believe if he died Lucifer would have enjoyed letting me know but he was definitely not going to be running at full capacity if the room is any indication.

I'm thankful that I decided to make this trip alone. I knew that Serenity seeing the destruction in the room, would be her undoing. While I blamed myself for what is happening now to her soul mate I knew she would take it on even more and it would be the very thing that destroyed her. I just would not allow that to happen.

She must never see this place. I knew that if she did come back she would remember it for what had taken place upstairs. She didn't need to add anything more to the memories she would recall with remarkable detail. Lucifer draining her of her life force and knowing that Ryan had met his very death here had to be the full extent of what she knew.

The smell of the blood is overwhelming. Humans believe that there is no scent with blood but they were misguided in that belief. I could smell it as easily as I could a home cooked meal. It is that strong to my heightened sense of smell. To any demon coming across this scene it would be a proverbial wet dream, intoxicating as it was.

Judging by what I saw Graham had been a prisoner here for some time, which meant that just as I believed he had been taken almost immediately after I separated myself from him. If I only stayed with him then maybe he wouldn't have met the end that he did.

Just what Lucifer's next step is I couldn't be sure, I could only hope that I would find him before he put whatever he was planning into motion. I could not let what happened to Graham in this room make its way out into the world. I had to stop it, even if I perished doing so.

I want to see my brother for the way he was during our time at home. I did not want to see him for the pure evil he had become. Even though I was shown evidence of his darkness every single day since he had been cast out I still found myself longing for the way things used to be.

Lucifer was always the most like me. He never accepted things at face value even though it is what we were made to do. It was as if he had free will and never wanted to give it up. I always found myself gravitating more toward him then I had with Michael and the others just for that reason alone. He was interesting to me. Little had I known that I would turn out to be more like him than I ever intended.

When he fell there was a part of me that believed I would be sent with him. The two of us were always going above and beyond in our quest for real knowledge and power that once one of us was gone it would surely only be a matter of time before the other went along for the ride.

He told me to embrace the fire when it pertained to Serenity and Ryan so many months before and when he had been in Heaven he always told me to search for the truth in the light. While he may have changed sides, he had never truly changed his overall belief.

This dark side of him now, the truly torturous side could easily break me if I let it. This was not the brother I loved so deeply. This is someone or something else entirely. I need to get Graham out of this and give Lucifer the real ending he deserves even though I believe that I also deserve the same ultimate ending. Where Graham and Serenity were two parts of the same soul, Lucifer and I were much our own sides of an imperfect coin. In ending him and what he stood for it felt as if deep inside of me I would be also ending myself as well.

I knew what had to be done but I still had no idea when and where it would take place. As much as I wanted to save my fallen brother I knew that I could no longer look at that as a viable option. He is much too far gone for redemption especially given what he had done to the very being that is almost like a sister to him. Add to that the torture he had lain on the other half of her soul and he was definitely damned for the remainder of existence.

Green Haven had always been the home base for what he planned which led me to believe that even though he left the church he would not leave the place behind. No, whatever his next step is, it would eventually end up back here. He saw this as the place where it needed to begin and end. So I could stay here and wait him out or I could think like him and try and catch the next step before he put in motion.

Serenity and her reaction had to play into my next move given that at any moment she would be joining me in my pursuit. While waiting him out in Green Haven would have normally been my next step I knew that for her I had to choose a different path. I needed to think like my brother.

Lucifer would want revenge, of that I am certain. Not only would he want it on Heaven itself but also on the very people he saw as the reason his original plan failed. Serenity was in danger, as is the protégé Ryan. Both of them managed to make it out and remain alive despite what Lucifer wanted for them which meant his next step would be through one of them.

With Ryan safe in Heaven I knew that he would be spared, at least for the remainder of his time at home. Even though my brother is stronger than Father realized at first there was no way he would penetrate the light that surrounded it which meant he would make a play for Serenity. In what way he would make himself appear I was not sure but I knew that I had to step up my guardianship of her.

Nothing could come between her and reaching her destiny again. She is destined for a long life and I am going to do everything in my power to make sure that it materializes the way it is meant to. I may be weakened by loss of power but I could still fight with everything I had and I am fully prepared to do just that.

Graham would be the key. The more I put myself in Lucifer's shoes I realized exactly what he had in mind. If he wanted to get to Serenity, the easiest way to do that would be through the soul mate bond much the same way I attempted the day I had come here to stop the marriage and rescue her.

She would be powerless against it given how they both gravitated toward one another. It would take her over and she would follow it blindly not believing that anything dark could possibly be behind it. Whether he mind controlled Graham or possessed him, he would use the bond to get to her and I had to make sure that never happened.

Serenity's life depended on it.

79

CHAPTER TWELVE

Serenity

When most people think about Heaven, they usually see it as a place amongst the clouds, bathed in the brightest light where no living; breathing human can exist. That interpretation, while beautiful is completely false. It's actually much more than the way it's described. There is no throne that God sits on as he controls all of existence. The beings that inhabit it don't float around on the clouds. None of that stuff actually happens though floating around does seem like a pretty cool thing to do.

Heaven really is what you make it. It appears differently to all that end up here. While I see it as closely resembling my life on Earth, someone else might see it a completely different way. Where I see country they may see a large city. Especially for humans who enter it becomes the image their mind can handle most easily. I happen to handle seeing Ryan in a hospital when I'm here which is exactly how I see him now.

He's laid up on a bed and there are machines hooked up to his body monitoring every part of him in an effort to keep him level and more than that, alive. How it actually appears to anyone else, even the angels I have no idea but I can cope easiest with this so this is what I allow myself to see. He appears to be sleeping but as I move closer to where he lays I see that he's just resting his eyes as they open just slightly at the sound of my feet on the floor.

"Serenity…is that really you?" he whispers with the faintest hint of a smile.

"Yeah Ry, it's me."

"I thought it was but when you didn't move I just thought I was dreaming."

"How do you think I feel then? Seeing you…hearing you this way feels like a dream."

"I bet." He said with a laugh, reaching his hand out to mine.

It really did feel like I was awake in a dream. I prayed so hard, begging and pleading for him to come back to me that it almost felt too good to be true. He couldn't be lying in front of me now, wide awake and looking that good. It just wasn't possible. Yet that is exactly what is going on.

The pull between us despite our time apart is still as strong as ever as I laid my hand in his and felt him grip it tightly. The electric charge made itself known instantly as it ran its way through my arm and down the rest of my body. It was one of the things I missed most while we had both been recovering.

"I'm so glad you're here. That he told you.'

I knew who he meant. Michael had done as I asked even if he had gone to Gabriel first. I was thankful that at least in that regard I could trust in him. He was also about to deal with his father on our behalf, something I knew wasn't going to be easy for him. I had to admit my earlier assessment about him was quickly changing. I owed him.

"I don't think he wanted to live with what would have happened if he didn't tell me." I said laughing. I knew for a fact he wouldn't have liked it. I hadn't exactly gone easy on him during the last six months.

"You were giving the guy a hard time?"

"Define hard time…"

He laughed and I sighed, content with the sound of the familiar rumble I had come to adore. A sound I was beginning to believe I would eventually forget given the amount of time that had passed since I'd last heard it.

"That's my pretty girl."

"So how soon can I spring you?" I asked as I pulled up the chair beside the bed. Yes this vision of Heaven really did have its perks. It came fully loaded with everything a girl might need when her husband is recovering from death.

"If it was up to me it would be right now. I've never spent so much time flat on my back before."

"No I bet you didn't. You left that to the girls didn't you?" I asked giggling which immediately shocked me enough to slam my free hand over my mouth.

Well that was new. Since when do I giggle?

"What are you doing? Take your hand away. That was actually really cute."

"You must have gotten a head injury on top of everything else. That was not cute."

"Sorry to disappoint you pretty girl but my head wasn't the problem. I don't think I've ever heard you giggle before. It's nice."

He wasn't the only one that had never heard it because I'd never done it before. Even as a little girl I never had a reason to giggle and laugh. My life at that point hadn't been a walk in the park so I had no reason to feel light and carefree enough to giggle. Getting me to laugh was hard enough; a giggle was out of the question.

"I notice you never denied it."

"If you're talking about the girl comment I'm not dignifying it with an answer."

"Too much bullshit to swim through?"

"Yes, that's it exactly." He said laughing, recalling just as I did the memory of the last time I said that very thing to him.

Realizing what I had just done I backed away from him, the confusion at feeling me pull away evident all over his face.

"What's going on Serenity?"

"No, this can't be possible." I said more to the room then to the man sitting in the bed waiting for me to explain. I couldn't believe this is happening now. I wanted some time with him where I didn't have to focus on my abilities. Apparently they had other plans.

"Serenity baby please tell me what you're talking about. You're freaking me out."

"It's nothing, just figured out a new ability."

"Wait, what?" he asked. "What ability?"

"I can read your mind or at least your memories."

"You can do what now?"

"You just remembered the day I accused you of bullshitting me about Suzy Abramson on the quad and I saw it."

He took the information in but his face gave away nothing. I wanted more than anything for him to show me something, give me any indication of what this was doing to him or what it meant.

"You can read my thoughts?"

"Well your memories at least."

"Okay then, so let's figure out just how strong this gift is. Let me think something and you can tell me if you can read it."

I wasn't sure I wanted to play this game. We discovered abilities before and it had never gone over all that well for me. It wasn't that I had a hard time believing I had them because I didn't but I just couldn't help but feel like even more a freak for being able to do the things I could do. I didn't want to feel like that right now.

"Can you tell what I'm thinking?" he asked, interrupting my thoughts and bringing me back to what he was trying to accomplish.

"You're thinking about our wedding. The way I looked in that god awful dress." I answered immediately which only made me sit back in the chair even more, putting distance between us. How was I able to just know that when I hadn't even been focusing on his mind? What was happening to me?

"Holy shit, you can really do it." He said, his face finally showing how he felt by the smile that now lingered again on his lips.

I needed to tell him that I felt even more than just what he'd been thinking. That in addition to the memory, I'm able to feel the way his heart sped up at the sight of me walking toward him that day and how much he wanted to reach out and kiss me the moment I stood in front of him preparing to become his wife.

There is a connection between us, one that is presenting itself to be even stronger than I previously thought it to be. Due to our similarities I'd always known it was there, the ability to read him better than anyone else but I had never seen it in action until now. Is this an actual ability or one that would only work on Ryan?

"Serenity, talk to me. You're doing that thing with your eyes again."

I knew what he meant of course. I was zoning out on him and becoming caught up in my own mind. It was just another thing that seemed to happen only between the two of us.

"It's more than just your thoughts and memories Ryan."

"Explain that please. What do you mean?"

"I can read your emotions and your reactions."

"Well now that's pretty damn cool. Wait…that means you know what I felt looking at you that day then?"

I nodded and he blushed causing my body to relax and giving me the power to move closer to him again. This was Ryan, not some stranger. He wasn't going to freak out because I had abilities that he didn't quite understand. I had nothing to fear with him and in moving away I only confused him, something I didn't want to do.

"I swear to god it's not as bad as it looks. You were just really hot that day."

'Wait, you mean there's more to it than just wanting to kiss me?' I questioned playfully. Of course I knew the full extent of it but there was nothing wrong with making him think otherwise. It was actually kind of fun. Not to mention I really liked the way he looked when he blushed.

"Is that all you felt? He asked finally exhaling the breath he'd been holding. "Thank god."

Unable to hold it in I broke out in a fit of laughter. I really sucked at keeping secrets, especially when it came to Ryan. I couldn't let him go on believing that I didn't know everything.

"No I felt it all. McGregor, you're an extremely dirty guy."

Gripping my hand tightly he pulled me toward him until I was out of the chair and up on the bed where he lay, finally placing my face nose to nose with his.

"Only with you…" he said as his breath fell against my cheeks sending a shiver straight through me. Leaning in I placed my lips to his gently, taking care to watch where I placed my weight, not wanting to hurt the parts of him still healing but still needing to be as close as possible.

"Well that didn't take long." The voice said before proceeding to clear his throat. "I actually had a bet that it would take a little longer given his injuries."

Pulling back from the kiss and turning toward the sound of the voice I rolled my eyes the minute I saw who it was.

"Of course you did Michael, I would expect nothing less."

Ryan laughed calling my attention back to him again and to the reason I was here. He is really here, awake and well and I am positive it would be a matter of time before he could come back with me.

"Thank you Michael." He spoke, the smile never once leaving his face and only making me want to kiss him even more.

"It was entirely my pleasure. I think I know what everyone was talking about in terms of this girl's temperament now."

"She wasn't taking no for an answer I take it?"

"You would be correct." Michael answered before turning to face me again giving me the slightest clue as to why he was really here now. "We need to talk."

"About what?"

"If you don't mind I believe it something that we need to speak about in private. Ryan is still recovering though you would be unable to tell by looking at him and I think it best we keep this between the two of us."

That wasn't going to happen and given just what Michael was I would have assumed he would have known that before he even spoke the words. Apparently he still had a lot to learn where I was concerned.

"Anything you need to say to me you can say in front of Ryan. Recovering or not he deserves to know."

"It's regarding your soul mate. Are you sure that he wants to hear that?"

I turned to Ryan and searched for any clue in his expression that he couldn't handle hearing whatever it was. Content that there was nothing to worry about I turned back to where Michael stood.

"He can handle it so just say what you need to say."

"You stubborn human even I know it is unwise to speak of another man in front of the current man."

85

Ryan laughed again and I couldn't help but smile at Michael's attempt to figure out how the human mind operated. He was right but Ryan wasn't exactly the typical guy.

"Go ahead man. I know what Graham means to her and I'm alright with it. Just say whatever you gotta say. I'll try not to get angry and turn green."

"Humans can turn green?" Michael asked which only caused both of us to break out in another loud fit of laughter.

It was awesome knowing that there is an angel even worse off than Gabriel when it came to pop culture references. I was going to have to remember that for later.

"No Michael, it's a joke. Can you please just tell me what you came to tell me?" I asked once the laughter subsided, putting us all back on course. This was probably not the best time to be joking around with the clueless angel.

"He's been located. We've found Graham."

CHAPTER THIRTEEN

Ryan

There would never be a time when hearing about your wife's soul mate while you're visiting with her is going to be a great thing. In fact I'm pretty sure in the grand scheme of things it's probably the worst thing but since there was really nothing I could do about it I had no other choice but accept it.

Seeing her again for the first time since the night Lucifer almost destroyed us has been like feeling the air on your face for the very first time. It awakened every part of me inside and out. If it's possible she looked even more beautiful and it took every bit of restraint I had not to dive up from the bed, grab her tightly and bring her close to me, not ever letting her go.

I am alive, there is no doubt about that fact since I'd woken up but having her here with me now made me feel even more so. I knew that she affected me before all of this happened but given the reaction I am having to her now it's obvious that it has grown into something more in our time apart. I needed her as much as I needed air to breathe.

In the cheesiest way possible she completed me, making all of the parts of me I wished long dead bearable. The person I had been before I met her seemed to fade away and all that's left is the person she saw in me, the person that I want more than anything to be for her.

The way we'd been today before Michael showed up reminded me of the way it's always been since the very first day I met her. We could joke around together while still showing each other how much we cared by finding ways to constantly touch. The conversation was easy, not stilted by the weight of what we had been through together. Everything about my time with her was just easy. I didn't have to try at all, it just came naturally.

I knew what finding Graham meant. I also knew that as much as I want to be with her while she faces this I am in no way ready for it. I would have to remain here and continue to heal while my girlfriend went back down to Earth to spend time with her soul mate.

I couldn't fight it because in doing so it would only show her the insecurity I buried deep inside. While I could handle just about anything they wanted to throw at me because in the end I would have her, it didn't mean I liked it. I definitely didn't like hearing about anything related to Graham Hudson. I wanted nothing more than to voice my concerns and keep her here safe with me.

"Where has he been? Where did you find him? Are you bringing him here? Will I be able to see him?"

She fired off question after question at Michael and he seemed to hold his own, waiting until she was completely done before answering. I knew all about the bond between the two of them and I knew that is where all of the questions came from but part of me still wished I heard her be this concerned about me. I'm the one married to her after all.

"Serenity we have only just come across him. He seems to be just fine. In fact he is back at the school and awaiting the start of tomorrow's classes."

With as concerned as Serenity seemed to be where it related to Graham I found it hard to believe that he just reappeared out of nowhere and is his same old self. No one who ever came into contact with Lucifer came out of it untouched. There had to be more going on and I'll be damned if I let her go back to him without making sure she was warned.

"That all seems a little too easy doesn't it?"

Michael was the first to acknowledge it and speak. "I feel much the same which is why we have informed Gabriel and he will be vigilant in his protection of her."

That wasn't good enough for me and I knew by the look on the angels face that he knew it too. If Serenity really is the greatest gift Heaven ever created then one angel isn't going to be enough. She would need a whole lot more than him if they were to come up against Lucifer again.

"Don't send her back Michael. Keep her here until you can find out what it is she's going to be walking into."

"You know that I cannot do that. She has been given this destiny for a reason. My brother is more than capable of taking care of her during her time there and I will be watching from here. She will never spend a moment without some form of protection."

"Oh Gabriel's got this does he? The guy that listened to his daddy and walked away from her? He walked away and gave me exactly what I needed in order to get close to her. There is no way I'm going to leave her protection to him."

I could tell that my words bothered Serenity as she flinched the minute I spoke about how easily I had been able to gain her trust. I knew that she didn't hold it against me after I told her the truth but hearing it again especially with the way I'm saying it couldn't have been easy for her. I hadn't exactly been the best person when I entered her life, something I would always regret.

Michael wasn't exactly rushing to his brothers defense the way I'd been expecting which meant there is something going on that I'm not aware of. Looking to Serenity, I hoped she could fill in the blanks for me as I was sure the angel never would. To him I was still very much the enemy.

"Michael, you know Ryan's right. How is Gabriel supposed to protect me when he doesn't have all of his power?"

"Say what?" I asked, unsure if I heard her right. Since when did the angel lose his power?

"Gabriel has been stripped of his powers after what happened to us Ryan. He can protect me in a basic way but that's about it. If what you think is true and Graham has somehow been affected by Lucifer then I'm not sure his basic powers are going to be enough."

"So that settles it then, she won't be going down there until you guys sort your shit."

"I would remind you of where you are right now demon. Watch your language."

"You want me gone, I can easily leave. You've saved my life. I can take it from here." I snapped back, immediately beginning to throw the blankets back until my legs were loose and began moving to get myself into a standing position.

"Ryan, please stop. Michael, you can get mad at him about his language all you want but you know what he's saying is true. Gabriel doesn't have the power of Heaven anymore because none of you want to trust him which means he's going to be ineffective against Lucifer when the time comes. Sending me down would be the same as what I did a few months ago when I made my choice. You will send me to slaughter."

I stopped as she spoke making no further effort to get from the bed. I knew it wasn't in my best interests anyway but I knew when I wasn't wanted. With as easily as I handled Gabriel calling me a demon, hearing it from Michael angered me in ways I wasn't used to. Just when would I become more than just the demon that didn't belong?

"As I said, I will be monitoring things from here. I would go to Earth but given that Ryan is still not fit for the transport back I think it better that I stay to guard him."

"I don't need a babysitter."

Serenity laughed and I looked at her confused. I wasn't aware I'd said anything funny.

"We're a lot more alike than I thought." She said in way of explanation.

"What do you mean?"

"That's exactly what I said to Gabriel when I realized he would be guarding me."

"Alright, so someone want to explain to me what all this Gabriel mess is?" I asked, putting Serenity's words out of my mind. As much as I wanted to focus on how alike we were; that wouldn't serve any of us with what we had to deal with now.

Serenity turned to me and smiled weakly. "That's easy. Gabriel is basically being treated like the black sheep because of everything that happened to us. They don't trust him and they believe that he intentionally wanted to keep Lucifer alive."

"How is what we did his fault?" I asked, genuinely confused. I had no idea how the decisions we all made could have landed him in so much trouble.

"Good question. Michael's the only one that can answer that."

"I know you believe me to be on the same side as my father in this regard and in some ways I am but I do not believe that Gabriel intentionally kept Lucifer alive. I only mentioned it to you because it is something Father is handling."

"Alright well you still haven't convinced me that it's safe for Serenity go to back down and face Graham. If he's powerless he's useless. She deserves better than that."

"Gabriel is not useless Ryan." She snapped angrily before again backing away from me. I felt the distance between us even before she moved away, that's how deeply her words affected me.

"Serenity will be guarded to the best of our ability and while I do concur that Graham may not be exactly as he once was, I see no cause for any obsessive concern right now. In order to know the full extent of his time with Lucifer we must make contact with him and Serenity is the best way to do that."

I hated all of this. I knew I was pushing her away with the extent of my concern as well as the bleeding over of my hatred for the soul mate connection. She had every right to pull away from me but it still hurt watching it happen. I just didn't want her in any situation that I wouldn't be able to help her out of. I love her; it's my job to protect her.

"As much as I hate to say it, he's right Ryan. I have to go back and I need to be the one to get close to Graham. The bond between us is strong and with or without it I know he wouldn't hurt me. If there's something else going on Michael can come if Gabriel can't handle it but I won't write Gabe off."

I couldn't win here and I didn't want to ruin any more of the time I had with her before she left. All I wanted the minute I woke up was to be with her and now that she's here I wanted to focus on that and not the fight that was happening now. I am going to have to concede.

"Michael, keep eyes on her every second you can. I'll trust in Gabriel's ability to protect her but if anything happens I don't care if I'm well or not, I will go down there."

"How much time do I have before going?" she asked quietly, again turning my attention back to the damage I had done in allowing myself to get so riled up.

91

"Enjoy a few more hours here. I will come to you when it's time."

Michael vanished and I turned my body toward Serenity who stood as far back from the bed as she could manage. It was just the two of us now and I needed to get back to the way it had been before the angel interrupted. I could not let the last few hours here with her end this way. I never wanted to argue with her, let alone push her away in the process. All I wanted was to keep her safe always.

"I'm sorry."

"You have nothing to be sorry for Ry. I don't know what got into me."

"I do."

"Then would you mind sharing it with the rest of the class because I really have no idea. All I know is that I couldn't handle hearing what you had to say."

"Do you remember our conversation before Michael showed up, about your ability?" I asked and as soon as she nodded her head I continued. "You were so quick to anger because of what you felt from me. Serenity your emotional state feeds off of mine."

"So because you got angry, I had to get angry too?"

"You didn't have to but you did. So you are the one that doesn't have to apologize. This is all on me. I'm sorry."

"I know you only want me safe. I actually agreed with everything you were saying but I couldn't handle you downplaying Gabriel and his abilities. You have no idea but I swear I saw red when you did that."

"You saw what?" I asked, swallowing the lump that was building in my throat. I knew exactly what she was talking about; it is something I felt on more than one occasion while I am in my demon form. It was just not something I was prepared to hear coming from her mouth. Not when she is made of pure light.

"I saw red. I was angry Ry."

I knew what I have to do but it would break me. She is getting too close to me and now that she is feeding off my responses it was even more dangerous. Serenity needed to do as Michael suggested

92

and she did need to go back down to Earth alone. I didn't want her to leave but I knew if she stayed it would only become worse.

She was latching on to the demon side of me and her abilities were adapting themselves to it. Yes, she definitely needed to leave and soon. I just couldn't tell her, not until I learned as much as I could about it. Considering she is leaving me with an angel powerful enough to give me the answers I want I knew that the minute she left I'd work to figure it out. Only when I had the answers would I tell her.

Until then, I needed things to go back to normal. I needed to hold her and I needed to feel the way she felt when she was nestled in my arms. I wouldn't be alright again until I did.

"Let's drop all talk about Graham and Gabriel and what you need to do. How about you come over here, climb into bed with me and we can just enjoy our last few hours together?"

"I thought you'd never ask."

CHAPTER FOURTEEN

Graham

"Mr. Hudson, I have been made aware of your family problems which resulted in you pulling yourself from your classes but that is not the way we handle issues of that nature here. While I realize you must have been lost in an immeasurable amount of grief it is still customary to inform us if you plan on taking a leave such as the one you did."

As much as I didn't want to deal with this idiot I knew that in order for this to work I needed to do it. I had to play on his sympathy and get him to agree to let me return to classes, despite the six months I'd been gone.

It seemed that in terms of Serenity the angels had taken care of her absence quite nicely by altering the perception of time to suit their needs. Something that could have easily been done for me but not something I wanted. If I was going to do this I would do it the right way. At least as right as using the passing of my mother as an excuse is anyway.

"The situation was out of my control. My mother's sudden passing required immediate action. I did what I believe to be right in leaving campus immediately and heading back to Green Haven. I know that you do not believe that it was right but I was given no other option."

"There is always another option Graham."

I really didn't want the lecture. I just wanted to get back into my old routine. I had to do it. It was required of me and I would not let him down.

You are not letting me down. Just continue down this path and he will bend. Do not lose your cool this early. We need to remain under the radar until the time is right.

It had been a last minute decision, him allowing me to control my body but one that in the end he made for the greater good.

While he had taken me as his vessel and was fully prepared to override my basic human instincts with his own, he decided against it. He was still with me, making sure that I did as he said but he would let me make the final calls in terms of how to go about things.

I had no issue with doing things his way; in fact I realized I enjoyed it. I had memories of going through life in a more backseat capacity before but I could now do things differently and was jumping at the chance. The Graham Hudson I'd been before him is long gone, replaced with a much better model.

"At the time I did not believe that to be the case sir."

"I will allow you back into your courses under one condition."

I was paying for this education so of course he's going to let me back in. Turning away money is something I had to assume would be frowned on considerably by the institution. Putting conditions on it was only going to make it worse but I would do what he asked. Whatever got me out of here and closer to my goal.

"What's the condition?"

"Should you need to leave again for any reason you must come and speak to me. I need to be your very first stop. You can't go running off the way you did the last time, no matter what the reason. Am I making myself clear?"

Yeah he was making himself perfectly clear and he sounded like a father, something I hadn't had in years and I most definitely didn't need now. The anger was building in me just listening to his tone and it took everything in me not to lose it.

"Crystal clear sir. I won't go off again without letting you know."

"Alright, I guess all that's left now is to welcome you back."

"Thank you for giving me another chance." I said as sweetly as I could manage without making myself sick. Plastering the weak smile on my face for added effect, I rose from the chair and held out my hand.

Accepting and shaking it the Dean motioned for the door. The meeting was obviously over. I am free to go.

"I believe you've got classes you need to get to. If you have any further issues today don't hesitate to call me."

95

That wouldn't be happening. I had only come to him to begin with because it was the only way I could get back into the school routine without calling undo attention to myself. In order to move forward I had to appear like the studious college student even though that was the last thing I wanted.

You handled yourself perfectly Graham. We are now one step closer to our goal.

Yes, our goal. The one in which I would get closer to Serenity Richards again, earning her acceptance and trust easily the way I had before. I didn't know all of the details of why I had to do it but I was more than willing to go along with it if it meant having his approval.

I wasn't sure how it all began, only able to remember the day the two of us joined together as one. He told me that it is imperative that the past remain hidden from me because it had the ability to compromise everything that we had to accomplish in the here and now.

"Are you clear on where we must go from here Graham?"

"Yes."

"You must go back to the school and go back to your old life only in the way that it pertains to Serenity Richards. The two of you have a connection that cannot be broken and you must use that to gain her trust again. When you have succeeded in your goal I will then take over."

"Why is it so important that I get close to her? From what you've told me there are a lot more willing women on the campus that would jump at the chance to help you with this?"

"You are correct. There is no shortage of women that would be sympathetic to the cause but Serenity is different. She is the one and you must do as I have requested in order for this to work out."

"I will but how do I handle the hunger that grows inside of me?"

"You must fight that hunger Graham for it is only the darkness growing inside of you. The more you fight it the more it will grow. It is only when you give into the impulse that you will fail. You must not fail."

Nothing he told me made a lot of sense but I would do as he asked. I would find Serenity again and I would befriend her, getting as close to her as was humanly possible and then when the time was right I would let him have control.

"Do I need to go find Serenity so that we can begin?"

"It appears that she is not on the campus so you must go about settling into your classes and I will inform you of when we begin. You must remember to remain as normal as possible. Any change in the way you appear to her will only hinder what is to come. So Graham, be yourself."

If only he understood that I didn't remember exactly who I am. While he knew of me and the way I'd been before, whatever had taken place between us before is a blur. I am supposed to act in a way that I couldn't even remember. I had never known myself to be that great of an actor before but I suppose it was time to find out.

I was about to put on the show of my life.

Gabriel

It would seem that I had been right in putting myself in my fallen brother's shoes. I had no idea what he is planning in the long term but it looked as though I had read his short term goals easily.

He was definitely going to use Graham Hudson to further his agenda. As I watched Graham make his way across the campus like a man on a mission it all became clear to me. I was thankful that for the moment Serenity was still locked safely away in Heaven. With the reappearance of Graham it meant that she was going to be in danger and I needed time to prepare.

I heard the conversation between him and the Dean. He was using his mother's death as the reason for being away as long as he had been. It is cold but a move that would garner the most sympathy so I couldn't argue against the use of it. If Lucifer wanted Graham to infiltrate Serenity's life then the easiest way to do that would be to immerse himself back in the college experience. Using the death of a parent to do so was wrong but right for his long term goal.

97

I wanted to make myself known to Graham but knew better. I had to remain in the background, watching and waiting for any sign of what was to come. Showing myself before the time is right could do damage that I would be unable to fix but it didn't stop the urge inside me. I would know within seconds of being in his company what happened to him. If only I could get close enough to him I might be able to see what is to come and help in more than just the way I had been tasked to.

"Gabriel…"

As expected it was time. Michael was contacting me to let me know that Serenity is about to make her descent back down.

"Graham Hudson is on campus as expected brother. You must prepare Serenity for what she will find when she gets down here."

"She has been told Gabriel. She knows what to expect though she is not completely on board with it."

Of course she isn't. She was the other half of his soul; she wanted to believe that he is the same person she had known before Lucifer had gotten his hands on him. While we all seemed to realize that it was impossible she couldn't allow herself to totally accept it.

"Leave that to me Michael. I will make sure she understands the gravity of everything that has taken place. "

"Have you been able to ascertain any more information about our brother's end game?"

I wanted to be able to give Michael more to go on but I had come up empty. Other than realizing that Serenity and Ryan would be targets I hadn't been able to figure out what the end game would be. With Lucifer it could be just about anything and even stepping into his shoes, thinking the way that he would helped very little.

"I have nothing new to report. He seems to be using Graham in the way I expected. Further exploration is needed and I am afraid that only Serenity can do that."

"You want her to get close to the human?"

"Yes. It is the only way that we can ascertain just how Graham is being used and proceed accordingly."

"Be at the ready brother. Serenity is saying her final goodbyes to the demon as we speak. It will only be a matter of time before it is to begin."

Hearing what Serenity was doing left a bad taste in my mouth. While I am doing everything I could to block the beloved bond we share it still found ways to get past my defenses. I am happy that she seemed to be leaving Ryan behind in order to come back down here and I wanted nothing more than to make it stop. I could not let the bond and my reactions control what came next.

I have to keep her safe. I could not allow anything else to override my task.

CHAPTER FIFTEEN

Serenity

Something is wrong. I'm trying not to let it get to me but I can't help it.

I thought that when Michael left and we were finally alone together that everything would go back to normal between us. That the tensions that had torn us apart earlier would fade away and we could get back to being us again but that wasn't happening at all. In fact it just seemed to get more awkward as time went on.

Ryan is hiding something from me and I have no idea why. I know that the way we started off had been based on a lie but he had come clean pretty quickly about it. This time though it didn't seem that he was willing to come clean and tell me what was going on.

He did everything right in our last few hours together of course. He held me tight, stroking my back while I lay with him on the bed and just enjoyed the feel of his hands on my body but it wasn't quite the same way it had been the previous times we've been this exact way.

I have a habit of reading too much into any given situation especially when it has to do with him but this time I really didn't think that was the case. He might have been doing everything right but it almost felt robotic. He would fade off the way I did as if lost in thought and it was actually a struggle to get him to come back to me.

The first thing that came to mind is that with my abilities appearing he was having a hard time coping but if that's the case I figure it would have shown itself a whole lot sooner than now. They had appeared before Michael had shown up yet his reaction was only happening after the angel left. I wanted to enjoy the time I had left with him but am finding that harder to do with every passing minute that he remains blocked off from me.

Is he different because he realized that I was able to feed off his emotions the way I had earlier? I know I found that strange and had to assume that he might too. It wasn't exactly a common thing to be able to have this much of a reaction to each other. I really didn't think a lot of couples had this problem but I wasn't exactly the pillar of knowledge.

I have a choice to make, I can either let it eat me alive or I can just ask him about it. It was an easy choice. I couldn't keep doing things the way I always did before. I have to be different now.

"Ry, can I ask you something?"

"Anything Ser, you know that."

"You said that I'm feeding off your emotions because of this ability I have. You haven't exactly been right since you said that."

"Was there supposed to be a question in there?" he asked, shifting his body on the bed and pulling me up with him.

Tilting my head up so that I could see his eyes and exactly what he may be thinking I was met with a concerned look and I instantly knew I'd been right. The way I reacted to his mood had been the problem.

"Does it bother you?"

"You're going to have to be more specific Ser, I'm not sure what you mean."

"My ability to read your thoughts and feed off your emotions the way I did when Michael was here."

I could tell by the look in his eyes that he wanted to lie to me, to tell me what I wanted to hear because it would cause the least amount of upheaval. I couldn't let him do that and prayed that he would tell me the truth no matter how much it might bother me to hear it.

"Yes."

"What exactly about it bothers you?"

Running his fingers through his hair with a sigh he looked down at me and the lock on his face made my blood run cold. I wasn't going to like what he had to say and he knew it.

"You could just read my mind and find out."

Well that wasn't what I expected to hear but damn did it hurt. Hearing him say it reminded me of the time in the church when I thought he was able to read my thoughts and how bothered by it I'd been. I had been wrong but now the roles were reversed and I'm able to do what he can't.

"I won't do that and you should know that."

"Truthfully Serenity I don't know anything anymore. I know how I feel about you but I know next to nothing about you. The real you and not just the girl I met the first day in Psych. I have no idea what you'd do."

Why is he acting like this? What is he holding onto so tightly that he was giving me attitude to try and hide?

"That's bullshit Ryan and you know it. You know deep down the type of person I am especially after everything we've been through. You're just using that as excuse not to tell me what you're actually feeling."

"You wanna know the truth that badly Serenity? Even if the truth puts you in even more danger then Graham and Lucifer ever could?" He spat out immediately, not even registering my words.

"Yes I do because I don't like the way it changes you keeping it from me the way you are."

"You're connecting to the demonic side of me! Are you happy now?" he shouted again, the stress of what he had been holding obviously getting to him in ways I couldn't begin to understand.

"I'm what?"

"The anger was the tip off. You fed right into it and that's not me. I don't get angry and you know that."

"So I channeled some of your anger. I don't see the big deal. How does that mean I'm connecting to the demon side?"

"I don't have the answers Serenity. I didn't want to tell you any of this until I could talk to Michael about it. While he may not exactly like me I knew he would want answers because it has to do with you and your role here. All I know is that you're at risk every moment you're around me now."

"How?"

"The more of my emotions you channel…" he choked out with a sigh "You will embrace my darkness. I really don't think that works well for your plan to save the world from Lucifer."

He had a point. If I really am connecting to the demon side of him then it wasn't going to do anything good. I instantly regretted pushing him the way I did. He wanted to get answers before bringing this to me, which meant he wasn't lying to me the way I thought. He was hiding it but only because he knew how I operated.

"I'm sorry."

"You have nothing to be sorry for Serenity. You asked me if this bothered me and I should have just told you why it did. I just didn't want to tell you without knowing everything there is to know."

"Why do you think this is happening to us?" I asked, genuinely wanting to know. We might not have all the answers but he had to have some idea of why he believed we were going through it.

"You and I are not supposed to be together. I may have been redeemed Serenity but I am still a demon. I am still inherently dark inside and you are the brightest form of the light that there can ever be. We are just not meant to be."

I knew this but it didn't mean I accept it. While my head told me that the two of us together was trouble my heart wouldn't listen. It is the same way it had been when Gabriel told me that Graham was my soul mate. I hadn't wanted to believe it then either. It was just unacceptable.

"I don't care about whether or not we're supposed to be together or not. We are together and I refuse to walk away just because it might be a little hard to handle."

"It's more than just a little hard to handle pretty girl. I'm already an abomination. I'm not even supposed to exist and yet here I am. Falling in love with you the way I have only makes it that much worse. We are not supposed to be doing this. It goes against both the laws of the light and the darkness."

"What are you saying?"

I didn't want to believe what I was hearing but there is no way I could deny it. The way he was making it sound, he didn't think we should be together anymore. I would not let him give up on us just because things were changing.

103

"I'm not saying anything, other than giving you the facts." He stated simply turning his eyes away as he spoke the words which only made my heart hurt more.

"Sounds like a lot more than just stating facts to me. So why not just spit it out Ryan. We're not supposed to be together so we should just end it right now before things get worse. That is what you want say isn't it?"

The pain in his eyes at my words ripped at my heart but I couldn't back down. Not when based on his very actions I knew that was where he is allowing his mind to go. While he might not want to let me go he was definitely thinking about it.

"That…is…not…what…I…want." He said spelling every word out for me in an effort to make me believe him. He had done it before so I knew immediately what his intent was. I just wasn't sure I was buying it this time. He still couldn't look at me.

"It's not what you want? Then look me in the eye and tell me Ryan. Prove it to me because until you do I'm going to trust my gut."

He looked at me then and I waited with baited breath for the words to fall from his lips. The words that would prove to me that he meant every word of what he was saying. When after a few minutes they didn't come, I knew I had gotten my answer.

"Well at least I know where you stand now." I said, immediately sliding myself out his embrace and sliding off the bed until I was back in the chair across from him.

As painful as it is moving away from him the way I am, I know it has to be done. He is giving up on us even though I heard everything and am still prepared to fight.

"I'm sorry Serenity."

"No Ry, you're not. What you are though is a coward. What you said is probably true but even knowing that I'm still here ready to fight for us just the way I did when I made the choice to go against my true destiny in order to save you. All you want to do is accept it and walk away before it gets too tough. So I'm the one that's sorry."

I stood and made my way to the very place Michael had vanished from only a few short hours before. It was only a matter of time before he appeared again to take me and I found myself praying for the interruption now. I had nothing left in me to say to the man lying in the bed before me. If he's willing to give up so easily then I have to accept it.

"Don't leave like this. Please…"

The pleading in his voice got to me. It attached itself to my heart and I wanted nothing more than to go to him and just forget about everything that had just happened between us but I couldn't.

If he really believes that we aere better off apart, that we aren't meant to be then there is no sense wasting any more breath trying to change his mind. It has to come from him and that isn't going to happen right now.

Michael appeared right in the same place he disappeared from and he placed his hands on my shoulders, whispering quietly as he did.

"It's time Serenity."

"I know. Let's go."

"Have you said your goodbyes?" he asked gently. If he knew any of what had taken place in here since he left he didn't show it, something I was thankful for. I wasn't sure I wanted to talk about it, especially with an angel.

"Yeah we have. Let's go."

"Serenity…wait!" Ryan called out one last time.

Not trusting my voice to speak, knowing that at any given moment the strength I was trying so desperately to contain would shatter around me, I chose instead to speak my final words to him in the only way I could. Focusing my mind and leveling my gaze straight on his face I said the only thing I could say.

"Even though you can't see it, I love you and despite what you believe, I will never give up on us. Goodbye Ryan."

CHAPTER SIXTEEN

Ryan

Well that didn't go the way I wanted.

I knew that I wasn't acting like myself and I knew better than anyone that she would pick up on it. I wasn't exactly doing everything I could to hide it. Even if I wanted to block her from being able to tell something is wrong, I'm still lacking full control over my body and any attempt I could have made would have failed. The problem is I didn't even try.

Instead I sat here like a chump and let her drive herself crazy over it before finally asking me what was going on. I made her believe I had issues with her abilities when in reality I don't. Yes there is a concern about her picking up on the demon side of me and changing because of it but it isn't enough to scare me away. Her abilities are part of what made her perfect for me. There is no way I could be afraid of them.

I have no idea what I just let happen. I gave in and told her my fears which should have been enough but no, I had to go and word it the way I did and now she believes I want nothing to do with her. At the very least she thought that I was too afraid of what we might mean to the world that I was pushing her away. I didn't want that but once the opportunity presented itself, I found it hard to turn away from.

She would be safer being as far away from me as possible right now. She could focus on what she needed to do with Graham and not worry about letting the dark parts of me overtake her. When she fed off my anger I knew I had to do something but I tried not to read too much into it before speaking to Michael. I knew he would be able to help me figure out what was going on but now we might never get to that point.

I'd done the one thing with her that I never wanted to do and there wasn't a damn thing I could do to fix it. At least until I am able to get the answers I need. If I tried anything right now she would see right through it and it would only make things worse than they already were which I definitely didn't want.

Though how it can get much worse than having your wife call you a coward before disappearing is beyond me. Instead of just doing what I wanted to and enjoying the time with her now that I'm awake, I had to go ahead and push her away.

Brilliant job you did there asshole.

I needed to heal because the only way I could even remotely make up for what I'd just done was to go to her and make her see that I was wrong and I couldn't do that in the present state I'm in. As much as I wanted answers to my concerns I wanted to fix this more. I could not handle her believing I didn't believe in us.

I am no better than Gabriel with the way I'm acting now. While he had taken off on her and given me the opportunity to get close to her, I was throwing her to the wolves. If Graham really has been changed by Lucifer then Serenity is going to be walking straight into it and she wouldn't be in the right state of mind to handle it. She's going to be easy prey and unless Michael got her to talk then there was nothing I could do to stop it.

I basically just handed her over to them.

Nothing I told her at least in terms of cold hard facts had been a lie. I am definitely the abomination I claimed to be. While it isn't unheard of for an angel to sleep with a human it is more uncommon to hear of demons doing so, at least in the sense of creating life from it. I knew my father took like a kid in a candy store when it came to women, my mother wasted no time in telling me that but as far as I could tell I was the only demon hybrid that had been created from such a union.

I shouldn't exist. Lucifer himself told me that on more than one occasion though he embraced it easily enough. Once I showed a power level previously unknown to him he'd taken full advantage of just what I am. He pulled me in close, trusting me with things that he hadn't spoken of with any other demon of our kind. I had grown secure because of that treatment and had eventually stopped believing myself to be the screw up in the Devil's design.

She is much better served being with her soul mate or even the angel she is bound to. They were both better matches for her and wouldn't go against the very laws of Heaven in order to happen. Graham and Serenity could be free to love one another on Earth until they were joined in Heaven and no one would bat an eyelash. It would be looked at favorably where I am the complete opposite. I was born with a dark side and it is one that even the brightest light in Heaven can diminish.

I can't stop thinking about the way her face looked when she realized what I was trying to tell her. The agony that appeared there even while she tried her hardest to appear unfazed by what I dropped in her lap. There is no doubt about her love for me, her final words proving it but I had no way to stop it once it began.

Aching for her every second since she left with Michael was going to be the death of me I'm sure of it. All I wanted was to turn back time and have her back in my arms where I could hold her tight and tell her that there was nothing wrong with me and be so convincing that she wouldn't have cause to doubt me.

"You and I need to speak."

Looking up I realized that Michael had come back while I'd been throwing myself the most epic of pity parties. His words for me didn't come as a shock. I knew it was coming the minute he arrived to pull her back down.

"Yeah we do."

"I remained silent where it pertained to Serenity before leaving but I need to know what happened in here before I arrived. If it's something that could affect what happens on Earth then I must know so I can warn Gabriel accordingly."

"She didn't tell you?" I asked searching his eyes for some clue that he was as clueless as he appeared to be.

"She refused to speak to me the entire trip, at least when it pertained to the both of you. I was able to get her to speak openly about Graham but that is all."

"I screwed up and I think it may play out a little down there with her so you might wanna warn Gabriel."

"You need to give me the facts. How did you screw up?"

108

There it is. This is my chance to open up to Michael and pray that he was able to help me or that he'd even want to help after everything was said and done.

"How much do you know about Serenity and me?"

"If you are speaking of your actual relationship I only know what she has told me in past conversations, which is really quite little."

"No, I mean about the two of us, the darkness and light issue."

"I know a great deal about that. Why do you ask?"

"We're not meant to be together are we? What I mean is, we're completely wrong and that isn't accepted right?"

Michael nodded curtly before speaking again. "It is true that what the two of you share is against the laws of Heaven but that does not mean that it is wrong. You have been redeemed. I realize that you do not see how that can matter given what resides inside of you but it does count for something."

"So we're not completely damned then?"

"No not in the way you seem to believe. While it is unheard of for a host of light and one of darkness to be together as one unit it does not mean that it cannot exist. Heaven stands to gain infinite amounts of knowledge from your union if we are allowed access to it."

I couldn't believe what I was hearing. Serenity had been right the entire time when she said that she didn't care how it was seen, that she would fight for it because it's what she wanted. I had been going solely based on Heaven's disapproval and been wrong in my assumptions. I had chased her away for nothing.

It didn't sit well with me. If I was trying to lift the shitty feeling I felt off my shoulders I was doing a piss poor job of it.

"Does this have to do with what happened between the two of you earlier?" Michael asked, again breaking through my thoughts and bringing me back to present.

"Yeah it has everything to do with it. I know what I am and I know what she is and what is expected of her and I didn't want to hold her back from any of it. I pushed her away because I thought what we shared was so god damned wrong and now I'm hearing it's not. I screwed up Michael."

"The two of you are already joined and have been for some time. What would possess you to push her away now? You have always known deep down what the two of you shared may not be right but you accepted it. What changed?"

"She can read my emotions. Well no…she can read my mind and my emotions. When she went off at us about your brother she was feeding off my anger."

"I still do not see the problem."

"The anger resides in the demonic side of me Michael and in connecting to it, I'm afraid that it is going to do her more harm than good. That it will eventually change her. The last thing any of us needs is for Serenity to turn dark."

"You do not give the light of Heaven much credit for all the love you claim to have for her."

He was right. I didn't give her the credit she deserves. As much as I said this was about her it had everything to do with me and my own stupid fears. It's just another way I royally screwed things up pushing her away.

"Yeah you're right I haven't given her much credit. I just don't want to be the reason something happens to her."

"You will not be. I know that it is not engrained within you yet but you must trust in us to take care of our gift. I am aware that she is your wife and I also know that Heaven does not want to recognize it but Ryan, you have my word that she will remain safe whether you are there to protect her or not."

I had no idea what to say to that. He's right in that I wasn't exactly the most trusting when it came to her, well anything really. I hadn't been given many chances to see the good that can come from trusting in something more powerful than your own self. I was swimming in unfamiliar territory.

"Well there's nothing I can do about it now, I can't give her what she needs in order to believe me which means I'm officially screwed."

"We will figure this out. In the meantime I must inform Gabriel of everything you have told me so he can adequately help her should she need it."

"Just do me a favor would you Mike?" I asked, deciding then and there to go for broke. I knew I didn't exactly deserve his help but I had to try anyway.

"As long as it is not a dark request I will do what I can to help you."

"Make sure Gabriel keeps her away from Graham if she appears to be hurting. The last thing I need is for him to step in before I've had my chance to make this right."

Michael only nodded in agreement which immediately gave me the peace of mind I needed. If he agreed with keeping her from Graham and would do as I asked and make sure his brother knew then maybe things might not turn out so bad after all.

It would give me the calm I needed to be able to heal and get back to the life that was moving on without me. I could put my entire focus into making sure I'm ready and when the time comes I could go down and make things right with Serenity once and for all.

I only hope that when I did go back to her, I wasn't too late.

CHAPTER SEVENTEEN

Serenity

"You and I are not supposed to be together. I may have been redeemed Serenity but I'm still a demon. I am still inherently dark inside and you are the brightest form of the light that there can ever be. We were just never meant to be."

No matter how much I want to block those words from my subconscious I can't. Even if he was speaking nothing more than facts it still didn't make it hurt any less. I knew all about the facts but I had chosen to ignore it and go my own way. It seemed Ryan just didn't feel the same way. It ripped me apart inside knowing that we weren't on the same page anymore, that everything we had been through together had divided us in the end.

I meant what I said when I told him I would never give up on us. I wouldn't do it not even if he didn't believe. It just wasn't something that I had ever been able to do. Even now if my father came back into my life I would gladly accept him back. Yes I'd be mad but I would still hear him out and get his side of it before making a final decision on what was best for me. It is the exact same way with Ryan.

If being a part of the light caused something to happen between him and me then I didn't want any part of it. It wasn't worth it to me. We had both sacrificed our very lives for each other, no power higher or otherwise would change it. I just needed him to believe in it as strongly as I did because without it there was nothing to fight for.

I can only compare it to that of a person who is lost in addiction. It doesn't matter how many times you go at them trying to get them to see the light and change they can't do it until they're ready to face it and beat it. It takes a tremendous amount of strength and right now that is something Ryan had in low supply. He needed to focus on healing and then maybe he would see what I have been trying to tell him. That no matter what comes at us; we will rise above it and stay together.

It had not been an easy road home. I knew Michael wanted to know what was going on with me as I wasn't exactly trying to hide my hurt but I just couldn't bring myself to talk about it. So I did the only thing I could actually manage. I turned the conversation to Graham and what I needed to be prepared for once I got back.

*****

"Serenity, I know that it is none of my concern but the tension in your body is hard to ignore."

"I'm not tense."

"You may not believe you are but I assure you that is exactly what runs through your body."

"Whatever. I'm not tense. I'm upset but I'm definitely not tense."

"Maybe it would help if you spoke about what is on your mind."

"Not happening Michael so just drop it."

"Is that really what you require of me?" he asked, causing me to actually acknowledge his concern for me, something I hadn't come across much in the times we had been together.

"Yes, it is. I don't want to talk about what happened with Ryan. Why don't you tell me what I'm going to walk into once we get back?"

"You need to prepare yourself for the inevitable meeting with Graham."

"Yeah but have you been able to learn anything more since you talked to us earlier?"

I really wanted to know exactly what I was walking into. In the same way that I wanted to know Lucifer's plan the day of the sacrifice the need is just as strong now. If I knew what I could expect I would be able to handle it that much easier.

"I have not learned anything new other than that he has since returned to the college and seems to awaiting your arrival."

Great so there is going to be a welcome wagon when I got back. Exactly what a girl wants to hear after a blow out with her

113

husband that left her out of sorts. I was definitely not going to be in the mood to deal with this, at least not this quickly. I needed time to decompress.

"Is there any way to avoid that for a while?"

"I am afraid not Serenity. You must engage with Graham. It is the only way we can ascertain where he stands and what may be coming next."

Fabulous, there's no way out of this.

"So you have no idea if he's under Lucifer's influence?"

"Not yet."

"So I just go in and act normal then?"

"Yes, that is currently the best course of action but please keep your guard up, even if only a little."

*****

I don't know how to act normal with Graham anymore. It was like in knowing what I did about where he had been the entire time he'd been missing that I am unable to see him as anything more than Lucifer's pawn now.

Michael left me quickly the minute we safely touched down and I found myself longing for Emma or hell even Gabriel so that I wouldn't have to be left alone with the thoughts in my head. In moments like this one I wished that I could still hear the voices of the dead. It had always been such a steady stream before Gabriel chased them off, something I could really use right now.

I didn't trust myself alone with my thoughts anymore. I wanted to fill my head with noise so that the pain of what had taken place earlier could be erased from my memory but there was no sound to be had. So focusing my mind on the area around me, I made my way toward the dorm fully prepared to knock myself out the minute I stepped into the room. If there wasn't anyone around to help me with the quiet then I was damn sure going to help myself.

Too bad I wasn't blessed with the ability to have super speed. At least then I would have been able to get started on my plan sooner. Until then I guess I was stuck with the memories.

The logical part of my brain knows that I am in too deep where Ryan is concerned. Where normal couples took their time getting to know one another, we had been forced into it without much time to adapt to the way we were. We were similar in so many ways that it would have seemed that moving at that speed would be flawless for us but I'm finding out the hard way just how difficult it really is.

Ryan was right when he said that he really didn't know me. I didn't really know him either at least in terms of the everyday things that seemed important. While he couldn't be sure I wouldn't read his mind, I didn't know if he was entirely truthful with me about being unable to read mine. I just trusted where he couldn't. It is one of my fatal flaws. As much as I tried not to, I always deviated back to the way I was as a young child and trusted certain people without reason.

The difference is, in the short time I had known Ryan he had more than proven himself worthy of my trust. He had come to me when it went against his very nature to do so. He accepted my decision when it came time to make the choice even though he didn't agree with it. Even facing death he had done the right thing by me, sacrificing himself in order to make sure I could be saved.

I had been under the assumption I did the same for him but it's obvious by his lack of faith in us that it isn't the case. I was completely and utterly alone. Where I had been the weaker one of the two of us before, I was now standing strong while he is breaking down and there is nothing I could do to change it. I could only hope that in separating myself from him that he would come around.

I wasn't sure how I am going to handle it if he didn't.

"Serenity…"

Gabriel. Thank god.

"It took you long enough. I've been dying here."

"You seem perfectly healthy to me."

"It's a figure of speech Gabe, god."

"Well I am here now, how can I be of assistance?"

"I need noise and a lot of it until I get to my room."

"Is there any particular reason why?" he asked and I found myself searching him for any sign of knowledge of the earlier incident. Finding none I carried on as if I hadn't just used my power on an unsuspecting angel.

"I just can't handle my own thoughts right now."

He began humming and much the way it used to, I felt my body instantly respond to the sound, my muscles relaxing instantly.

"Thank you."

I continued making my way across the campus while he hummed in my head completely unaware of anyone or anything going on around me. As I made my way through the door of the dorm, fully prepared to take the stairs at a run to reach my bed faster I heard a voice from behind me.

The humming ceased and I knew why. I recognized the voice almost as easily as I did my own and Gabriel going silent only proved that. Turning around, I came face to face with the very man I'd been sent back down here to connect with and was met with the brightest of smiles.

"Serenity…I was wondering if you heard me calling you."

"Keep your guard up Serenity; do not let him know you suspect him."

Guided by Gabriel's voice I looked up into his eyes and smiled. If they wanted me to put on a show then they better be prepared because they were about to get the performance of a lifetime.

"Graham! Hey!" I squealed before throwing myself into his arms. "I'm so happy to see you."

Gabriel

I have to hand it to Serenity. Coming face to face with Graham could not have been easy for her yet she still somehow managed to handle it as if it didn't affect her at all. She was never much of a liar but she could definitely put on a show when she needed to.

The minute he appeared behind her I had felt the darkness. He was bathed in it which meant my worst fears had been realized. Lucifer had indeed broken the man down and turned what had

116

once been a very bright light within him into total darkness. I was definitely going to have to prepare myself to protect Serenity. I only hoped my powers stood up against whatever flowed through him.

Given the way she reacted to my appearance in her mind, asking me to fill her head with noise I knew this couldn't be easy for her. Something happened in Heaven and while I may not know exactly what it is, I knew that it was getting to her and she needed to shut down for a while.

It had been months since I sang to her and feeling the response from her body at the sound filled me with a happiness I hadn't felt in what seemed like forever. I am unsure if the bond she shared with the demon would change the way she reacted to me and am more than a little pleased that it didn't seem to. I enjoy being able to help her even though I had to remain controlled at all times.

Even the momentary interruption in her mind seemed to do wonders for her. She seemed stronger than ever, able to handle whatever Graham was here to throw her way. Watching the way she stood her ground now even though she was acting pleased me. This is exactly the way she was always meant to be. It had been a long hard road to get her to this point but now that she was it seemed there was no turning back.

"Gabriel I need to speak with you immediately."

Given that Michael had only been here with Serenity a few short minutes before I was confused as to what he needed to speak to me about so urgently. Had he found out more information about Graham?

"What is so urgent brother?"

"You need to do whatever you can to separate Graham and Serenity. New information has come to my attention and it would do her no good to interact with the soul mate right now."

"What new information Michael? Have you learned more about what has happened to Graham?"

"No this pertains to the other man in her life."

Ryan? What would her speaking to Graham have to do with him? He is safely tucked away in Heaven without a worry as to his own personal safety.

117

"Ryan and Serenity had words before she made her way back down there. In a misguided attempt to protect her from something he believed he was causing he said unforgiveable things to her which we fear will leave her wide open to whatever is going on with Graham."

Now it all made sense. Ryan upset her and in doing so is now concerned about how it would play out down here. While I was unable to stop their inevitable meeting, I could find a way to get them apart so that I could inform Serenity of what was going on, at the same time doing what I had been told and protecting her.

"What did he say to her?"

"He believes that she is able to tap into the darkest parts of him. He is severely misguided where her real strength and power are concerned so he did what most humans do and he pushed her away."

"How would she connect with the demon side?"

"It appears she can read him brother, every facet of him. While she chooses not to read his mind without his consent she can feed directly off the emotions without the same protocol. It is a concern that we most definitely have to look into but it is not of high importance. Father has agreed with me in that regard."

So Serenity is able to read Ryan. That was definitely something new. I couldn't help but wonder if it would work the same way between the two of us now. Is it an ability that spanned across multiple plains or was it just something she shared with the demon alone?

"I will do whatever I can from this end. I cannot stop what has already been put into motion though."

"Then stand guard and be at the ready for every possible situation."

"Is there anything else I need to know?"

"It would seem that Ryan also told her that Heaven has an issue with the two of them being together so it seems that he has done even more damage to her already fragile heart. You must not overstep your boundaries Gabriel but you must take care of her in any way possible so that it does not manifest itself while in the company of the soul mate."

118

As hard as I tried not to be affected by what my brother just told me I couldn't do it. Not only had Ryan pushed her away based on her ability and its relation to him but he also made her believe that they were better apart which meant she was hurting in the worst way imaginable. She was still very much human and would be affected greatly by the man she loved telling her that they were doomed.

I immediately thought of the ways I could take care of her in his absence. She is still very much my beloved and now that the door has been swung open in my direction I can't resist the urge to find out just what could happen between us.

"Gabriel did you not hear me? I can feel your intentions from here. You must remain focused on the goal and leave the beloved bond in the background or you will end this before it begins."

I wanted to heed my brothers warning but the more I focused on the ways that Ryan had slipped up I found it harder and harder to do. He is right of course, I need to keep my mind focused on the task at hand but I am greatly affected by the news as it pertained to the demon and the girl I happened to care for.

"Don't worry Michael; I will remain focused on my goal. No matter how I feel about Serenity I will keep it under wraps until the time is right."

Or at least I would try to.

CHAPTER EIGHTEEN

Graham

When he told me she wasn't on campus it had been a tremendous let down. I'd been looking forward to getting a jump start with the plan. Imagine my surprise to see her walking across the quad in the direction of the women's dorm. It was as if the sky had opened up for me. I was going to get what I wanted after all.

Of course I had done everything to the letter as I was expected to. I made my way to my dorm and gotten myself settled back in. I even made it to one of my classes but the minute that let out I made a point of heading right to the quad to search for her. Appearing to be a regular college student may have been part of the plan but it is definitely not what I am in it for.

I was not looking forward to repeating it all the next day, whether Serenity was back on campus or not. Though seeing her as she travelled at an alarming speed across the quad had lifted my spirits considerably.

You are aware of what you must do now Graham. Do not let me down.

Yes, I'm very aware of what I need to do and I plan on following through with it. I understood the importance of getting close to Serenity Richards again and I was not prepared to fail.

Her jumping into my arms in the manner she did took me off guard. I had no real memory of knowing the girl before now so I found her reaction strange. She seemed more than a little happy to see me and my bodies reaction to it was more off putting than the act itself had been. Just what was the relationship I had with this girl before and why it's affecting my body this way now?

My heart rate increased the second she came into view and while I easily ignored that, it was impossible to ignore what is happening to me now. I liked the way her arms felt wrapped around my neck and the way my heart was still racing, I found myself powerless to the burning need that was making its way through my system. Whatever the connection between the two of us, it definitely had its perks.

She's cute no doubt. Some would even say she's beautiful which made going into this blind to our history that much easier to take. If all I had to do is stand around and look at her while she reacted to me this way then it is definitely going to be a very easy job.

Her hair smelled of vanilla, a scent I was not a fan of but found myself easily intoxicated by and her hazel eyes when they met mine appeared to see into the deepest recesses of my mind. Just what is it about this girl that got to me and was my reaction bound to cause a problem instead of being useful to the end result?

Your reactions to her are expected Graham. Embrace them and the fire that they bring to the surface, it will serve you well in the long term.

That is all I needed to know. If he believed them to be legitimate and useful then I would do as he said and embrace it along with the wave of emotional reaction they brought.

"It's good to see you too Ser." I said, using a variation of her name that felt foreign as it rolled off my lips. "I was beginning to think you didn't even go here anymore. You're a hard girl to find."

Laughing awkwardly she began to extricate herself from my arms and I immediately felt the chill as the space widened between us. I knew I was supposed to embrace everything that was happening between us but was it really necessary to embrace the sensations I didn't enjoy too?

"Yeah I know. I've had so much going on lately even Emma calls me a ghost."

Emma. Why did that name sound so familiar to me? I realized immediately that if he wanted me to do this job affectively then I was going to have to know more about my life before the change had taken place. Going into this blind isn't doing me any favors.

Emma is the best friend. They currently room together in the dorm and yes Graham you know her. Tread carefully.

"Well then you need to stop hiding away so much. How is Emma anyway?"

This was definitely not a subject she seemed to enjoy. The way her face contorted at the mention of how Emma was meant that there is more going on here than even I am aware of. I was pretty sure that she didn't know how Emma was.

"Honestly, I haven't talked to her today so I have no idea. I've been off campus all day. I should probably go up and see her though. I'm sure she's got tons to tell me about her latest conquest."

She was rambling in her effort to cover for the lack of real knowledge she had. I would have found it cute if I didn't want to know more. The way her cheeks turned pink led me to believe that she didn't do so well with lying, especially lying as it pertained to me.

Let her go for now. It is obvious you will not be getting any further with her this evening. We will try again in the morning.

"Yeah, I'm sure you've probably had a long day. I should let you get some sleep and give you and Emma your girl time. Wouldn't want to keep you and end up asleep in her bed again would I?"

Where the hell had that come from? I knew it had to be a memory but given that he hadn't given it to me how was I able to recall it so easily?

"She actually liked that though so I don't think she'd mind it all that much." Serenity replied with a small laugh which did nothing for the quickening of the pulse under my skin. I am beginning to see exactly why he wanted to use me for this particular job. I seemed to have a connection stronger than most when it came to her.

"Alright well I'll get out of your hair. Do you think we could maybe grab a coffee before class tomorrow?" I asked, not at all knowing where it was coming from but fully prepared to see it through and use it to my advantage.

"Uh sure Graham Cracker. You wanna meet at the same place as last time?"

Same place as last time. Well I couldn't very well answer that question with no recollection of the place we had previously been to. When no sound came from the man inside my head I decided to just fly by the seat of my pants and answer her.

"Yeah sure thing, that sounds perfect."

I watched her as she smiled one final time before turning and making her way slowly up the stairs. Watching the way her ass moved as it sashayed its way up the stairs hadn't been my intent but I found myself unable to look away. She really was a beautiful creature and while I didn't understand exactly what was going to come next I knew that I was going to enjoy spending my free time around this girl.

Maybe college isn't going to be so bad after all.

Serenity

When I came face to face with Graham again I wasn't expecting it to feel the way it did. I had been prepared for him to be different, in some way scarred from his time with Lucifer but talking with him only proved one thing to me.

If he'd been affected by his time with Lucifer and even if he is under the angels control now it wasn't obvious. He seemed exactly the same as the last time I saw him. He is the same old Graham, which only made talking to him that much easier. I didn't have to put on an act the way I started to in the beginning.

When Gabriel alerted me to his arrival only seconds after my brain registered his voice I'd been afraid to turn around and face him. I knew I had to do it and I was determined to put on the best show possible and while I think I had done a decent enough job I stopped acting the minute he spoke to me. I just fell back on our history together and let it control what happened next.

I knew that in order to find out what is really going on I need to get close to him but I accepted for a completely different reason. I genuinely wanted to spend time with him. I know it may have been wrong given everything that happened between Ryan and I but I couldn't help myself.

Taking a breath as I finally made my way to my room door, I mentally prepared myself for what was waiting for me on the other side. I knew I was going to run straight into my best friend and that she was going to level me with questions about where I had been, questions that I would not be able to answer. Where the conversation with Graham had been easy this was about to get a whole lot harder.

Exhaling one more time I turned the knob and made my way into our bedroom, letting my eyes immediately go to her side of the room. Where I had assumed she would be chomping at the bit the minute I entered, I was sadly mistaken as the look she threw my way proved the opposite.

"Hey Ems."

"Where have you been? I tried calling you like a hundred times today and shocker, no one picked up."

I had been expecting this question but the look on her face was not at all what I had been waiting for. She didn't look interested. Emma looked pissed. This was definitely not going to be good.

"I went to Green Haven."

When no change appeared on her face I continued. "I got a call from my mother. Apparently something happened to Graham's mom and well we were close before so I went back to find out what was going on."

"Why turn your phone off?"

"I didn't turn it off Ems. It probably just died. Look I'm sorry. I didn't think you'd be all that concerned considering all the parties you've been going to lately."

I know it's a long shot but I have to take it. She is the party girl of the two of us and if I had to use it to throw her off what was really going on than that is exactly what I'm going to do.

"You're lying."

"I am not lying."

"We've known each other a really long time Ser. You get this look in your eye when you're not being honest with me and it's been happening a lot more lately. You might not be lying but you are keeping something from me. So just stop."

Damn. The brilliant job I thought I'd been doing was a fail. This was the story of my life. I wasn't a liar and I definitely couldn't keep things from Emma. No matter how hard I tried I always broke and told her everything. This had been the longest

124

time I'd ever held something from her and it looked to be coming to an end.

"Fine, you're right. There is something I haven't told you."

"Serenity, you must not reveal—"

"Yeah Gabe I know. Just trust me please."

"I knew it! What the hell is going on Serenity?"

This is it. I'm about to tell her the truth, well at least as much of the truth as I could. There was a small amount of comfort in knowing that at least in this regard I wouldn't be lying to her.

"Graham's back."

There was a few seconds as I watched her where I wasn't sure she believed what I told her, which only added to the growing anxiety I felt. I wasn't sure why it affected me so much but I had to make her believe this because for once it wasn't a lie.

"Well that explains everything. No wonder you've been so weird lately. Why didn't you tell me sooner?"

The relieved breath I was finally able to take felt amazing. She believed in me. Maybe I could get through this after all.

"I didn't want to lay any more shit on you Ems. I mean it seems like that's all I've been doing lately. Between the Ryan mess and well Graham up and leaving the way he did, I mean I've been a pretty big basket case."

"Says you."

"Really? You're telling me that you've been totally okay with the way I've been moaning on your shoulder?"

I was never more thankful in that moment for Gabriel and the information he'd given me about the memories he implanted in Emma's mind. I knew everything that had been put there in order for her to believe that we'd been together the entire time. The angel really spared no expense, though making me into a blubbering mess may have been a bit extreme.

"Isn't that what best friends do? I mean when Cody screwed that other girl behind my back weren't you here doing the same exact thing for me?"

She had me there. Emma met Cody our first semester and had quickly fallen head over heels for him even though it wasn't something she normally did. When she found out that he'd been screwing around on her with other girls it ripped her apart and I had been the rock she needed to stay on the straight and narrow. I'd done everything in my power to make sure she didn't let it take her down the dangerous road she'd been on during our time in the center.

She was right; we really were a rock for each other.

"Yeah Ems, I was here for you when that happened. I guess I'm just not used to having all of these stupid guy problems."

"I'm just happy you decided to finally join the human race. I was beginning to wonder if you were even human at all."

I knew she meant it in a joking way but she was hitting way too close to the truth now, which only made me want to tell her everything even more. This is not good. I need to steer her off this topic now before I do spill my guts.

"Well glad I could finally dispel the myth of my actual heritage for you Ems."

"Okay so get over here, sit and spill." She said patting the empty spot on the bed beside her. "Graham being back, how are you handling it?"

Doing as she said and planting myself on the bed beside her I answered her the only way I could. I told her the truth.

"I'm not sure Ems. I mean I'm glad he's back and that he's alright but something just doesn't feel right about it ya know?"

"What doesn't feel right?"

"I mean he seems like the same old Graham on the surface but there's something more going on. I can feel it."

"Well you know there's only one way to find out for sure right?"

I wasn't sure what she was getting at but given that I made a coffee date with him for the next morning; it wasn't as if I didn't have options.

"What do you mean?"

"Go out with him. Look, before you say that you can't do that because of whatever the hell happened between you and Ryan, hear me out." She said, holding up her hand in the air for emphasis. "The only way to know for sure what's going on with Graham is to spend time with him and not just time between classes. Time alone and away from other people."

She's right which is exactly why I made the coffee date to begin with. Well that and wanting to genuinely spend time around him again but she didn't need to know just how far gone I was in that department, at least not yet.

"He asked me to grab coffee with him in the morning."

"Well, what did you say?"

"I said yes."

"Then there you go Ser, you've got your chance. I know you're not looking for a love connection but given the history between the two of you, I think coffee might be the perfect chance for you to see just what's been going on with him since he took off."

"You're right, it is."

"Great! Now that we've settled that uncomfortable bit of business, you in the mood for a movie marathon before your big date?"

"I thought you'd never ask."

CHAPTER NINETEEN

Graham

It had taken most of the night but I finally found the place I believe Serenity had been talking about when she mentioned us going there the last time we'd been together. It is amazing how many actual coffee bars there are surrounding the college. It appeared that what they said about students needing their coffee fix had been true. There was no doubt this city catered to the all-nighter.

Dressing for this pseudo date was more difficult than locating the right coffee bar. It seemed that while I didn't recall buying any of it I owned a great deal of plaid shirts and blue jeans. While this may have been my acceptable form of dress before the change it's definitely not now. I was going to have to make time to shop after meeting with Serenity. I could not live with this wardrobe any longer.

You must remain as close to the way you were in order for this to work. While the wardrobe does leave something to be desired for a man of your talents I must insist that for the time being you continue using it.

"Fine, I'll do it but for the record I won't be enjoying a minute of it."

When I had taken on this assignment I knew that I would have to stick to a code, one that only the man inside of me knew the full extent of but in agreeing to not change anything about myself even though I desperately wanted to, I realized that I needed answers in order to continue. I needed to know who I was before everything happened.

"Do you think you can tell me more about myself before I meet with her?"

That would depend on what you want to know.

"Well other than the knowledge that Serenity and I have a past and that I need to use that past to get close to her again I know nothing. Well other than my horrible choices in clothing. I think if this is going to work I need to know more."

For two years Serenity Richards was your next door neighbor. The two of you connected almost immediately and forged quite the strong friendship. You fell in love with each other over the course of those two years together though neither one of you had the gumption to tell the other. So until recently that went under the radar as it were.

So that explained the connection between the two of us. I knew from previous conversations that she was important to me but now I'm being informed of just how important. It explained the ease at which we spoke to one another the night before. It explained a whole lot actually.

You two are connected as I have said previously and that is why you must move forward with her and earn her trust again.

"You might need to tell me a bit more than that. If she brings up things we've been through how am I supposed to answer?"

That you will figure out as it appears. I cannot prepare you for that which I do not know Graham. You just need to know that she ultimately loves you deep down even though her heart has been guided in a different direction as of late. I want you to remind her of that fact in your time with her.

That's easy enough to do. With the way the girl had jumped into my arms less than twelve hours before it would be a cake walk getting her to do it again. With the way she looked this is the part of the job I was going to enjoy the most. Getting her under me was a goal I could definitely get excited for.

You must stop thinking that way. Serenity is not that type of girl and any step you take in that direction will compromise what I am hoping to accomplish. You must think with your heart and not your dick.

That was easy for him to say. While he may be inside of me and calling the shots he didn't have to be around the girl and the very hunger it provoked inside of me. No, I had to do that all on my own and it's hard as hell to think straight when I'm overcome with need. It had been there last night and I had no doubt it would be there again when we met for coffee.

129

Graham you must remain focused on earning her trust or this will fail. Now the only real things you need to know are basic information. Emma Daniels is her best friend and has been for the last seven years. They are extremely close though it would appear young Serenity hasn't been telling her friend everything there is to know.

"Yeah I got that last night when she mentioned the friend. Is that something you also want me to handle?"

No you must not get close to the friend. She is not a part of this.

"So what else is there that I need to know?"

She likes her coffee with a lot of sugar something that if you order for her you will need to know. She will tell if you give her the wrong one. The most important thing you need to know though is that she believes herself to be in love with a half demon named Ryan.

"She…what?"

He was to be my greatest gift to the new world but in the end turned out to be just another useless human. None the less she fancies herself in a marriage of sorts with him. You must rise above that and conquer her heart.

"Oh, so nothing too difficult." I answered sarcastically. There was a familiar feeling inside of me at the mention of the other guy but I couldn't figure out why and where it was coming from. Is it possible that I had come across him before?

You are correct, you have met the man. He shouldn't present too big of a problem since he is not here but you must be on guard regarding it. It is the only thing standing between you and her.

So I was going to have to compete with a non-existent boyfriend. I could handle that. Out of sight and out of mind. While I knew Serenity was not that type of girl just based on the few minutes with her I could still make it happen. The boyfriend really didn't present as big of a problem as I first thought.

"Well I guess I'm good to go then right?"

Yes Graham you are. Remember to keep things light and not give her any reason to doubt the changes within you and this will go smoothly.

Right…go have coffee with a girl like any ordinary guy would be doing this early in the morning and remember, don't give yourself away. Yeah, no pressure there at all.

Serenity

Why do I feel like I am making the biggest mistake of my life meeting Graham for coffee?

I tried to focus on what Emma said to me before I left this morning but I still couldn't help feeling like I was betraying not only myself but Ryan even agreeing to a simple coffee.

*****

"You can't wear that."

"Why not?" I asked as I zipped up the jacket and gave myself one final once over in the mirror.

My choice of standard blue jeans complete with knee holes from extensive use and the white spaghetti strap shirt now buried under my bomber jacket seemed just fine for what I was about to do.

"You're meeting a guy that you've been in love with for the last four years Ser. You can't just show up wearing that. The weather's not so bad outside; wear that sundress I bought you."

A sundress I absolutely hated. Yeah that was definitely not happening. I had no real fear of dressing up but only when I absolutely had to and right now, coffee with Graham is not the time.

"I am not wearing a dress for coffee Ems. This outfit is fine."

"Maybe for you it is but I know guys and he's definitely gonna wanna see you in the sundress."

I wanted to tell her about Ryan and that I couldn't wear the stupid sundress because I wouldn't wear it for anyone but him. I couldn't do that though given where he actually was. Which meant the only way to get her to drop it was to wear the dress.

"You know I'm right. You're gonna change aren't you?"

"If I change will you drop it?"

"Yes."

131

*****

So of course I conceded and changed even though I hated every second of it. So here I sat outside Java King waiting for Graham in a sundress that had way too much yellow in it and wishing I was wearing anything else. So lost in my own hatred for being a pushover I didn't hear anyone approach until they spoke.

"Wow."

Looking up from the table I smiled weakly. Some things never change. It was the school dance all over again as I locked eyes with the man in front of me.

"Blame Emma."

"The last thing I'm going to do is blame her. I think I need to thank her." He replied sliding easily into the seat across from me and pointing toward my cup.

"Sugar with a side of coffee?"

"You know it."

"Mind if I have a taste?"

In all the years I've known Graham he never once asked me for a taste of my coffee. I knew I was supposed to take signs like this as proof he was different but I couldn't. It was coffee for crying out loud; maybe in the years since we hung out his tastes had changed.

"Go ahead but be warned, it's pretty sweet."

"Just the way I like it." He said with a smirk before lifting the cup to his lips and practically draining the remainder of what was left.

This isn't the first time Graham talked to me this way and where I used to be able to ignore it before I am finding it more difficult to do now. He's flirting and while I didn't exactly have a lot of experience with it, it seemed like the most natural thing in the world and something I wanted to be a part of even if it was wrong.

"You always did have a sweet tooth Graham Cracker."

"Only when it came to you." He shot back, placing the now empty cup back on the table, his eyes locked on mine.

I felt the heat in my cheeks immediately and forced myself not to react by covering my face. I had to remain in control here even

132

though within the first two minutes of being around him I seemed to be travelling back in time. I could not let him see how affected by him I am.

"So what have you been up to?" I asked, changing the subject and hopefully taking his attention away from the blush that was now deep across my face.

"After everything that happened I just needed to get away for a while."

I saw the change now, the very thing that Gabriel and Michael warned me about. The answer he gave I'd been expecting and while he had hidden the answer behind what he believed to be the truth his body language spoke volumes.

The faintest line of sweat is breaking out across his forehead and his heart was racing. I didn't wanted to read him but he was making it too easy. His answer was truthful yet his body language spoke openly of a lie. What am I supposed to do with that?

"I'm sorry about your mom. I can't imagine how much you're hurting right now. She was a great woman."

I couldn't let him know I was on to him. I just had to keep things as normal as possible, though knowing that my abilities worked on more than just Ryan was almost too much to take. I didn't want to be able to do this and worse have no control over it, especially not with Graham.

"Yeah, she was. I swear most days it feels like I'm just floating around in a daze. Like I'm watching a movie of myself."

Again he gave another truthful answer and this time his body matched it. Now I really didn't know what to make of what was going on.

Reaching across the table I placed my hand on top of his. It was the most natural of moves and one I didn't give a whole lot of thought to before doing it. I just knew that if he was telling me the truth about his mother's passing and how he is dealing, he needed support and I want to give it to him.

"God Ser Bear, I've missed you so much." He said placing his free hand on top of mine and squeezing gently.

"I missed you too…" I whispered. "I'm so glad you're here."

I don't know what bothered me more about the exchange between us. The fact that I meant every word I said or that I enjoyed the way his hand felt wrapped around mine. Whatever it is I knew it wasn't going to end up good because it just brought to light what I had been trying so hard to deny.

Graham Hudson still held a very large piece of my heart.

CHAPTER TWENTY

Gabriel

There's a process that takes place when a host of Heaven or a demon from Hell decides to take a vessel. While they differ in what actually takes place before it happens they do have an alarming amount of similarities. When I had chosen Graham to be my vessel I had not done it in the traditional way other than securing his acceptance.

When we decide that we will need a vessel the most important thing is making sure they are accepting of it. From there we then inform them that we will take over their entire being leaving them unable to do anything themselves. We essentially become the person and usually we try to stick as closely as we can manage to them as to not arouse suspicion in those people that are most close to the vessel we have chosen.

When one born of darkness decides to take a vessel they also have to garner acceptance but they can do it by any means necessary. They can torture, maim and break down the person until saying yes is the proverbial light at the end of the tunnel. They also have the choice of doing things the way that I had with Graham except most enjoy the art of actually taking the being over and leaving them broken when their use is complete.

Watching Graham as he enjoyed coffee with Serenity I realized the signs instantly. I am also privy to their conversation as per the agreement between Serenity and myself. In agreeing to let me listen in it would help me in discerning just what Lucifer had done to the man I once called my vessel.

Serenity was right in her immediate assessment of him. He is different and had been deeply affected by his time with my fallen brother. While the changes weren't obvious they were there and easy to see to someone who knew the person as well as Serenity did. I had seen the changes in him the first night, my light being diminished by the heavy amount of darkness that surrounded him and now Serenity herself was seeing further evidence of it.

Her confusion is valid though as his body seems to be the only thing that betrayed his words. If not for that reaction there would have not been any cause for concern and I would have told Michael as much. He had given himself away though which meant I wasn't going anywhere quite yet. I had to take advantage of the chance I am being given and investigate further.

I am trying not to be affected by the way Serenity responded to his words. Having access to her mind only seemed to make everything I am already dealing with that much harder. I was determined not to let our bond affect me but the way she put her hand on his was not helping me. I am again reminded of Ryan and how he would react in this same situation. If he could see what I was now baring witness to I knew he would be none too pleased. Something we agreed on.

It took everything in me not to reach out to her and remind her of her true purpose in meeting with Graham. I could easily tell that she was doing what is expected of her but I am also privy to it being so much more than that. She felt for this man and she had every right to. He was her soul mate after all but she had to remember that he wasn't the same guy he had been six short months before. He is more than that now.

As much as this bothered me I knew I would not do anything to change it. I needed answers and the best way would be for her to get as close to him as possible even if she is risking her own heart in the process. I just had to be at the ready if I felt her falling in a way she would not be able to pick herself back up from.

"I should have done more for you Ser. When you told me about your feelings for Ryan that day I shouldn't have run you off."

"To be honest Graham," she said pausing getting her thoughts straight. "You had every right to react the way you did. I just didn't want to lie to you."

"I know you didn't. I should have seen it for what it was. It's been eating at me a lot. I just want you to know I'm sorry."

Damn him. He is being sincere and breaking through the guards she placed around herself. If he kept this up there would be no doubt he'd break through completely and she'd forget what she is here to do. I couldn't let that happen. No matter what I felt for her I would not let her fall victim to whatever it is he is trying to accomplish.

"Serenity, I know you believe him to be sincere but please do not forget what we suspect. Please do not fall for a few sweet words."

"Oh you mean the way I did with you?" she responded immediately, her face betraying nothing to Graham that she was indeed speaking inside her mind.

"One is not the same as the other. You would do well to remember that."

"Consider it noted Gabriel, now I'm gonna get back to Graham before he realizes something's up."

"You don't have anything to be sorry for Graham. It happened but it's in the past now."

"You really mean that?"

"Yeah, I do. I get it and I don't hold any of it against you."

I have never heard her sound as sincere as she did now. She meant every word she was telling him and it didn't sit well with me. Where I may have had the power before to stop this before it began I was powerless to it now.

"So…I guess you're married now huh?"

The minute the words fell from his mouth I knew I had him. While I had used him to try and persuade her to get out of the church before the wedding had taken place I hadn't gotten around to telling him that it happened. He had gone missing before I had gotten the chance. He knew though which meant that someone else had filled him in and I knew who.

Lucifer.

There is really no doubt now. He is behind all of this and turned Graham into whatever is sitting across from Serenity. I couldn't let it continue, there is no way.

137

"There is no way he could have known about the marriage unless Lucifer himself informed him. Serenity you need to get out of here and you need to do it now. I need to inform Michael."

"Do whatever you have to Gabe but I'm not leaving. I know what he just did and I'm not leaving here until he tells me how he did it."

"I cannot leave you with him."

"Looks like you need to make a choice huh? I am not leaving. If Lucifer has my friend under his control then I am going to do whatever the hell I can to stop it."

I know there is no argument I could make that would change her mind. Serenity had always been this way, headstrong to a fault and while it was a trait I admired in her, it is becoming a severe pain in the ass now. I needed to inform Michael of what I believe to be happening but I couldn't leave her with him to do it.

She is right I did have to make a choice. I only hope I'm not about to make the wrong one.

Serenity

When I agreed to let Gabriel access my thoughts so that he could be a part of this meeting with Graham I never believed he would become this much of a pain. I know he is only doing what he was told but it didn't mean I had to accept the consistent intrusion.

I know what's up with Graham, I wasn't a complete idiot and all he was doing with the constant talk of guarding myself and remaining focused is reminding me of what happened between Ryan and me the day before. Something I really don't want. In the same way Ryan had gone off about Graham and Gabriel both, believing me to be a complete idiot now Gabe is doing the same thing and I'm officially sick of it.

If he needed to talk to Michael so badly then he could just screw off and do it. I would be more than fine here with Graham. Even knowing that he knew about things he should have no knowledge of I know that he wouldn't hurt me. If he wanted to he would have had more than one chance by now. I was giving him

138

the benefit of the doubt until he slipped up so badly I had no other choice but deal with it.

"Ser, did you hear me?"

"Sorry, what did you say?" I responded focusing again on the man in front of me and putting the one inside of my mind out if it the way he belonged.

"I said…you're married now?"

"I guess I am yeah."

"That's pretty crazy I bet." He replied, his lips lifting into a smile. "Can I tell you a secret?"

"You can tell me anything Graham."

Waiting for him to respond I watched as he began fidgeting in his chair, his eyes averting mine. Whatever it was he wanted to say, it was obvious he wasn't feeling the most secure about, which only made me wanna know more.

"When I pictured you married I always assumed it was going to be to me."

Holy shit! I thought as the words tumbled from his mouth, complete with him pulling his hands from mine and immediately rubbing over his face. Yeah this is definitely something he was uncomfortable talking about. He wasn't the only one.

I blushed deep and following exactly what Graham had just done seconds before, I put my face in my hands. I wasn't sure how I was supposed to respond to that. There's flirting which I seemed to handle alright but then there was this. This was in a whole other ballpark.

He really pictured us married?

"Say something Ser. I can't stand you hiding your eyes from me like that. I wanna know what you're thinking."

I didn't know what to think. This is almost too much. I was here to find out what Lucifer had done to the first guy I ever loved. I wasn't here to listen to admissions like this. This threw me completely off course. The angel that seemed to always know the right time to interrupt would have been perfect right now but as usual is remaining silent.

Removing my hands from my face but keeping my eyes level with the blue table in front of me I sighed.

"I don't know what to say to that."

I felt his hand then, reach out and take a hold of mine and before I could react he intertwined his fingers through mine, locking us together.

"Don't say anything. I just thought you should know."

Shit...Shit...Shit...Shit...Shit.

This is definitely not good. Graham telling me not to say anything only made me want to say something that much more. I couldn't do this, not with as scattered as I already felt. Gabriel was right the entire time. I needed to get out of here and away from him and I needed to do it right now, because truth be told if I stayed then something is going to happen and it just can't.

"I need to go…"

I start to stand, trying to break my hand from the grip he now had on it in the process. Before I could completely break free he stood to his feet and made his way around the table, his hand still locked in mine, a look of determination in his eyes I had never seen before and one that sent chills straight down my spine.

With no idea what he was going to do next I prepared myself to fight him off. I would kick him in the balls if I had too. I normally wasn't the go to girl for that but with the way this situation is beginning to make me feel, I was willing to try anything once if it gave me the result I needed.

"Don't go." He choked out, the sound instantly pulling my eyes to his.

"I can't do this with you Graham, please let me go." I pleaded and secretly prayed he would hear and abide by. If he was still my Graham inside then he would let me go much the way he did that day in my dorm. I didn't want to focus on what the other result could be. He just had to be the same Graham.

"Ser, please help me."

At the tortured sound of his voice as he asked for my help my body immediately went limp and I felt his free arm reach out quickly and come around me steadying my now wavering frame.

"What did you just say?"

His strangled response was hard to hear but I managed to get the gist loud and clear.

140

"Help me please."

CHAPTER TWENTY ONE

Gabriel

It is a lot worse than I originally feared. Graham hadn't just been affected by Lucifer.

He is being controlled by him.

I should have recognized this immediately and it did nothing for my ego to know I had again let something this large go unnoticed. While the darkness that seemed to surround the man wasn't the strength of what I would assume a vessel of Lucifer's to be there really could be no doubt now given the events taking place before me.

While I had gone silent with Serenity I had not left her. I had just taken a step back the way she requested and was now able to get a clear picture of what we were all dealing with. I needed to inform Michael but given how we had been communicating as of late, I wouldn't have to leave her to do so.

"Michael please tell me that you're witnessing what is happening."

"Yes brother it is worse than we imagined."

"Have you made Father aware?"

"Gabriel you know our father, there can be nothing above or below that he is unaware of though there are dark entities able to block his all seeing eye. He is more than just aware. He is beginning to formulate a plan."

As much as I would like to say that this is the first time I heard of Father doing such a thing, sadly it was not. Having the ability to see and know everything that happens both above and below has always made him appear as though he never has to do much planning because it seemingly plans itself in his response to the issue at hand but there are rare occurrences where he is unable to predict, which is what is happening now.

He was going into planning mode which meant he wanted to rise above whatever it is Lucifer's end game will be and put a stop

142

to it with an end game of his own. We may not be on the best of terms given what he believes about me but I felt more secure knowing that he is aware and focused on it. I wouldn't have to sift through this sea on my own even though I had been prepared to do just that.

"His responses especially now seem most sincere and I know that Serenity feels the same way. Could it be that he is trying to break through the vessel bond?"

That very well could be what he is attempting to do or it could be something far more sinister Gabriel. We do not know the full extent of the power that our fallen brother now wields. This could be just a large form of manipulation.

"How do I make her see that?"

I'm afraid in this regard that you may not be able to. If Serenity truly believes that it is Graham fighting for control of his body you know there may be no talking her out of it. You must stay with her Gabriel until we can figure out what to do.

We were agents of Heaven but with the way we were always trying to figure out what path to take next it seemed as if we were nothing more than your garden variety human. It is a fact that irritates me greatly.

"There is something that you're not thinking about brother. There is one sure fire way to break her out of this bond she shares with Graham."

You are not saying what I think you're saying Gabriel.

I was implying exactly what he thought I was. If we wanted to break Serenity out of the bond with her soul mate, neither one of us would be able to do it on our own. I shared a bond with her but not one strong enough to defeat the soul mate bond. There is only one person alive and breathing that would be able to do that.

"We need him Michael, even you must see that."

I am very much aware that he could be of use right now but he is not ready for transport. Something far worse could happen to him doing this and then we would be no better off than we are now. It is too big of a risk.

143

"If we do not risk it, then Lucifer will get his way and something far worse than Ryan could be at stake. Do you really want to deal with the fallout if we do not do this?"

I thought this through as much as possible. I knew there was a great deal of discord between the demon and Serenity and that in bringing him down here I would be sacrificing him as well as her very state of mind but it is a risk I am willing to take in order to save what is left of the man Lucifer was now in control of.

Being a vessel for my fallen brother is not Graham's destiny and if it meant bringing down the person Serenity cared for even more than she did the world than so be it. I would do it.

"You know that I do not want to give our brother any more of an advantage Gabriel but we require more time. I do not trust our chances if we take this step right now."

"Then talk to Ryan and get his opinion and let it be his call. If what I believe of him is correct then he will want to come down here and he will want to stop this before it goes even one step further."

"As you wish brother but in the meantime keep eyes on Graham and your charge. Do whatever you can with the power you still control to make sure nothing happens to her until I get my answer."

I could easily do as Michael asked. I would find out if what Graham is putting her through now was just a ploy to bring her closer and I would react accordingly.

My only hope is that Ryan did not take too long making his decision because if he did then Serenity's very existence may hang in the balance.

Graham

Something is wrong with me, seriously wrong.

I had one goal. I was to get close to Serenity again and earn her trust but things have been happening since the minute I sat down with her and now I can't focus on what I need to do. All I can see is her.

It started with an overload of memories flooding my mind so quickly I was almost unable to keep up with them. Then I began experiencing the emotions that came along with them and since then I have been completely lost. I did have a connection with this girl, one so strong I am unable to control what came next.

I could still feel him in me fighting for control but he wasn't able to win. This is something so big that even someone as powerful as he was is unable to combat it affectively. It seemed to be even more pronounced when Serenity and I were in close bodily contact. As long as my hands were on her in some way I am able to remember things I had previously forgotten and experience them all over again as if it was the first time.

Just what the hell is happening to me?

He was angry now. It was obvious that not being in control of what was happening is pissing him off but whatever is building inside of me is so strong that I couldn't bring myself to care that I would probably pay for this later. I had control of myself and while I had no idea how to handle that, I was going to try anyway.

"What's going on Graham? How can I help you?"

The serene sound of her voice broke through and hit straight in my heart. Yes I definitely knew her and in a way that no one else would ever be able to. She is the better part of me and she was the only one that could help me.

I knew it was only a matter of time before he was able to combat what was taking place so I wanted to remember as much as possible. I had to. I couldn't let him take this from me again. I knew I had a past before the change had taken place and now that I was recalling very vivid points of it I never wanted it to end.

"I remember you…"

"Of course you do Graham Cracker."

There it is again, the sweet sound of her voice. Her tone serious yet melodic at the same time, causing my stomach to tangle itself up in knots at the sound. I wanted her to keep talking to me forever. It was the only thing that managed to tame the beast inside of me.

God what was happening to me?

145

"Graham I want to help you but you need to tell me what's going on…" she said, breaking through the overflow of my mind again just the way I wanted her to.

"He did something to me; he's still doing something to me. Serenity you need to help me please."

I know how I sound; I could hear the echo of my own voice in my head. I was pleading with her, almost to the point of begging because I just wanted it all to stop and somehow I knew she was the only one that could do it.

I am beginning to remember it all. The cold and dark basement of the church and the way I had been chained to the metal chair, jagged edges from the binds cutting into my flesh causing my blood to spill to the floor beside me.

I could see his hands on the sides of my head as if he was doing it right now in the moment. Flooding me with memories of what he said was her death and also the death of my mother. Showing me happier times with both of them and then torturing me with their individual death scenes.

Closing my eyes tight I tried to block out the images that seemed to still come at a pace I am unable to handle. I need to get a grip and I need to do it soon before he took over and all of this was lost to me again. I couldn't let that happen, not before making sure she knew everything.

"He tortured me…he's still torturing me Ser…"

Her body melted into mine then her arms wrapping themselves around my back and pulling me as close to her as she could manage. Raising herself up onto her toes she whispered towards my ear, the heat of which flooded through my body like an electric charge.

"Fight him Graham, fight it. I'll get you out of this."

"I'm…trying…"

God I could smell it now, even while I stood in her arms. The blood. The golden goblet that he handed over to me willingly and I drained, making me no better than all of the other dark creatures before me. Just where the blood came from I wasn't sure but I knew that with the way I am remembering my own torture, it most likely hadn't come willingly.

146

He'd broken me down until I had let him have his way with me. When he'd been torturing me he promised he would do it and he had. He'd officially taken me over and I'd let him.

'I'm so sorry Ser…I tried to fight it…"

I could feel it. He was forcing his way back through. I knew it was only a matter of time before he made his way fully back to the surface and I was lost to her forever. I needed to warn her before he got the chance to take back over. I only hoped that when I did it made sense. I knew she was the only one that could stop this.

Serenity was what he wanted and I had given him free access to it. I needed to finally do what I should have done six months before and help save her.

"You have nothing to be sorry for Graham; I'm going to get you out of this…"

"I'm his vessel. He's angry. He wants you and Ryan and he wants you dead. I don't have much time so please listen. Stay away from me."

I watched her eyes go wide in my arms and I knew she was getting what I am trying to tell her. Now when he took me over again I could be sure she would do everything in her power to stay away from me at least until they could figure a way out of this. I had done what I couldn't do all those months before. I protected her, at least in the only way I could.

"Go now Serenity, he's about to break through and if he sees you I don't know what he's going to make me do."

When she made no move to walk away from me, I stepped backwards and placing my hands carefully on her arms just below her elbows I pushed her, hating it the minute my arms made contact.

"Go! Now! Get the hell away from me!"

As she turned to run I felt it, the overpowering sense of hate within me and things began to get hazy. I knew what was happening, he is ready to take me over. I only hoped as the world went dark around me that I had gotten through to her and she was going to get the hell away from me as fast as her legs could take her.

Our very lives depended on it.

147

CHAPTER TWENTY TWO

Serenity

It's been almost a day and a half since the incident with Graham and I still had no idea what I'd been a part of. I witnessed him in a full breakdown and been pretty much powerless to stop it. The brightest light in Heaven is powerless. How ironic is that?

I wanted to be able to help him but given what he is fighting off inside of him I knew I couldn't. At least I couldn't do it alone. I needed more than just my own growing powers to be able to take on Lucifer and with Graham being his vessel even if I had been strong enough I wasn't entirely sure I could have gone through with what needed to be done.

He may only be the vessel for the King of Hell to the angels and even the Almighty himself but he is still the same Graham Hudson to me. The boy who had taken me to my first school dance, the one who spent countless hours alone with me watching movies in my room and the first boy I'd ever allowed myself to have feelings for. It wasn't something I could just shut off.

That only meant I wasn't the right person for this job. They needed to get someone better. I may know him better than anyone which gave me the advantage in getting close but that was really all I was good for because if push came to shove I wouldn't hurt him and I knew it.

I am pretty damn sure Lucifer knew it too which is exactly why he planned everything the way he had. He had used my own heart against me.

I managed to dodge Emma the entire time, taking off from Graham and wandering around campus until my classes took me under. I finally made it back to the room the night before and just passed out in the bed and hadn't even heard her when she'd come home later that night. The only proof that she even made it home at all was her sleeping form in the bed across from me as I got ready to head out for more classes this morning.

I was thankful she was safe. If what Graham told me is true then there is no telling if Emma would become a target or not. If Lucifer had been itching to get to me in the worst way possible, choosing Graham had been the perfect way to go about it, the last thing I need or want is for Emma to be next. I could not let anything happen to my best friend.

It was a struggle going to class today. I wanted to go against what I knew I needed to do for my own safety and instead go searching for Graham. Or at least what is left of him now. I know I needed to stay away but I couldn't. If being around me at all had triggered his ability to fight through the strength Lucifer held over him then I wanted to do it again. I wanted to keep him fighting.

Gabriel had been with me ever since and when I expressed my need to him, expecting him to be completely against it, I'd been shocked to my core when he actually agreed.

"What are we supposed to do about this? I mean I know Graham said to stay away from him in order to protect myself but he's in there Gabe…I can feel him. I can't just sit around and do nothing."

"I had my doubts to the validity of what he was telling you when he asked you for help. I thought it a ploy by my brother to bring you even closer to him but I was wrong."

"So what do we do?"

"Father is putting together a plan that will have us all dealing with Lucifer but in the meantime I do believe it's best if you go to Graham again. If what you believe is right then you are the only one that is able to break through Lucifer's stranglehold on him."

"Is the soul mate bond the reason he was able to break through?"

"It would appear to be that way yes. I told you before it is the strongest bond ever created. There are no limits to its reach. It appears we are seeing that firsthand in the way the two of you interacted."

"I want to find him. I know that it's not him anymore but I can't just sit around here pretending to be something I'm not while he's fighting a losing battle with a fallen angel."

149

"Then work with me and do that. I understand what you feel you must do and while I am here as your guardian I intend to help you do that."

"You really want to help me?"

"The only alternative is sending you back to Heaven where you can be guarded twenty-four seven by the highest order of angels while we face Lucifer once and for all."

"I don't want that. Hiding me away isn't going to do anything and in the end you're killing Graham too if you go after Lucifer while he is the vessel."

"I will not let anything happen to Graham. While I may have been sent down here to guard you I am also here to do right by that young man and I will do that before my time here is done. The best way I can accomplish that is to help you in your pursuit."

"So then where do we start? Would he really go back to the dorm with everything that happened yesterday?"

"No. I am pretty sure that if my brother is indeed controlling him again he would have taken himself virtually underground but Serenity, before we begin I think there is something you need to see."

When Gabriel told me there was something I needed to see, I had no idea it was going to be this. Going back into my old hometown again and facing the church where I almost lost my life. I wasn't sure how I felt about being here. The wounds of that day were still very fresh in my mind. It hadn't just been the place where I almost died, it had been the place where Ryan did die and I wasn't sure I could face it, even with the time that had passed.

"Why do you want to show me the church?" I asked as he appeared in his true form beside me.

"You recall me telling you that I found traces of Graham here previously?"

"Yeah, you said that he spent some time here but that they moved on by the time you found it."

"Yes all of that was correct but what I didn't explain to you or show you before now is exactly what I found when I arrived. I think in order to move forward you need to know everything."

"How bad is it Gabriel? What am I going to be walking into?"

150

I could see the struggle he was going through all over his brightly lit face. I wasn't going to like what I saw when we walked through the doors and he was trying to find a way to prepare me.

"It is a sight at which even I am sickened by. I have always known my brother to be truly evil but the level of destruction that he left in his wake, both here and at Graham's childhood home have rendered me speechless. You must prepare yourself for the worst."

No amount of preparation could have prepared me for the scene that we appeared in the middle of. The lingering smell from the blood alone was enough to tie my stomach up in knots until I was unable to contain it.

Turning away from the sight and running to the corner of the room I emptied the contents of my stomach, more than a little thankful I hadn't eaten before we decided to make the trek here. If I had then it only would have made what I was going through now that much worse. Running my sleeve over my now fully watering eyes, I turned back around and locked eyes with Gabriel.

"He really was telling me the truth. Lucifer tortured him."

"Yes Serenity, he did. It is the only way he could have broken him."

"All this blood, is it his?"

"Not all of it no, it would seem there is blood of another victim in the room as well."

Another victim. As I let Gabriel's words sink in I realized the full gravity of what had been taking place during my stay in Heaven. While I had been sitting by Ryan's bedside after healing, Graham and another helpless person had been down here fighting for their very lives and losing.

"Do not blame yourself for the scene that lies before you Serenity. There is nothing you could have done. Lucifer has powers that we haven't seen for millennia and he was able to successfully block us from the horrors of which he created down here."

It was easy for him to say that. Well okay fine, maybe it wasn't easy for him given that he is still blaming himself for everything that happened to me but I couldn't just let the guilt go. I

151

was at least partially to blame for all of this. If Graham hadn't been a part of my life then he never would have been here to begin with. I couldn't help myself. I had to take the blame.

"Have you been able to figure out how he was tortured? Was he just beaten or was there more?"

"With Lucifer there is always more Serenity. I can only assume that he used a plethora of torture techniques in order to garner his end result. My guess is that he went in through his mind first and when that proved to be ineffective then he moved on to the physical."

"I can't believe this…" I said as the tears began falling from my eyes. Graham had gone through hell on earth and he had done it all because he'd known me. All of this happened because of the connection we shared and no matter what happened next I knew I would never be able to make up for any of it.

"I believe it is time for us to go. With as difficult as this is for me to witness I can only imagine it is dragging the very human parts of you into despair, something that I cannot let manifest."

He was right. I wasn't handling this. I needed to get out of here before the pain dragged me down. I wanted to close my eyes and will the sight away but I knew that was impossible. As long as I lived I would never forget what I saw here. Graham's torture would live with me forever.

"Before we head back to the school there is one more stop we need to make. Are you sure you can handle it?" Gabriel asked, bringing me away from the sick feeling in the pit of my stomach and back to the issue at hand.

"As long as it's nothing like this then yeah, I can handle it."

"It is destructive but not to the extent that this room is, of that I can assure you."

"Then let's go. Let's see what else Lucifer's done. I need to know it all if I plan on getting Graham out of this alive."

Gabriel

I admired her strength. In the situation I put her in she had been able to stand her ground even when the very human part of her wanted to break.

Seeing the devastation in the church basement brought about the very basic of human reactions, one that I could not fault her for. If I had been able to react that way in what we were witnessing I would have been right there with her. It was a scene still so horrifying it had the ability to turn stomachs.

She needed to know what she is going up against. It is imperative if I am to protect her while she made her decision to go back and face Graham again. If she knew what had been done, everything that he had been trying to tell her the day before then she would go in with more than enough knowledge to handle herself.

The soul mate bond had indeed been the thing that changed Graham. It had given him the ability to break through Lucifer's hold on his body and warn Serenity. It pleased me to know that even though my brother believed himself to be in control he was nothing of the sort. Graham still had the final control and was not against using it. He only needed the right motivation.

I would do everything in my power to get him out of this. Now that I knew exactly what I am dealing with I could work on my own plan alongside of Father's that would indeed work to a healthy result for everyone involved. I needed to do this; I owed the man that was now fighting for his life under my brother's control.

Most of all I owed it to Serenity.

She was not to blame for any of this; it had been her lot in life from the moment she had been placed on the earth. While she had been an eager participant in Heaven, wanting nothing more than to help save the world she had not asked for what is taking place now. She was no more aware of what was going to happen then I was when I agreed to guard her. If we had known every single thing going in then we surely would have chosen different roads all in an effort to protect the very people that were now in danger.

"Are you sure you are ready for what comes next?

"I don't have a choice here Gabe. I have to be ready."

I couldn't let those words go. I had been trying to tell her for as long as she'd been aware of me that she always had a choice and that wasn't going to change now. I would never put her through something she didn't first agree to handle.

She would always have a choice with me.

"You do have a choice. You have seen the worst of it. We can go back to school and we can find Graham and go from there. You do not need to choose to see anything else."

"I know Gabe; I just meant that I have to see it. I don't have a choice because I won't allow myself one."

"As I made you aware in our private talks, the scene you are about to appear before is the one in which Graham's mother was lost. I need to be sure that you can handle that given your relationship with the woman."

"I haven't seen her in years Gabe. I can handle it though I'm not gonna lie, I hate that she had to die because of me."

I was beginning to understand her upset in regards to me blaming myself. I wanted nothing more than to tell her again that this was not her doing. Lucifer had chosen to do what he did and we were all just victims of it.

Grabbing a hold of her and waiting as she prepared her body for the change of transport I let myself enjoy the feel of her body connected to mine. I tried to put it out of my mind but with the closeness we were sharing it was becoming increasingly difficult. I could deny it all I wanted but we were connected even if she was unwilling to acknowledge it. I just needed to be sure that in my enjoyment of the feel of her next to me that I didn't become lost in it. I could not afford any mistakes, especially now.

"I'm ready when you are." She whispered, bringing me back to the present. Closing my eyes I focused on the place at which we were destined to stop next and before I knew it, we were landing and the moment was over. She moved away from me immediately and took a step toward the damage that now awaited her.

"Jesus Christ."

"Serenity is there no other word you could use?" I asked lightly, not wanting to upset her but instantly becoming annoyed at the use of our father's name.

"You're telling me you came here, saw this and that wasn't the first thing that came to mind?" she asked turning to me with a frown.

"That is not of import. I am unable to handle your use of the words so please refrain."

"Gabe I think the least of our problems is my potty mouth."

"You are correct."

"Of course I am." She replied before turning back toward the leveled ground where Graham's house once resided. "So did he kill her before he blew the house apart or was she just a part of that?"

"It was before."

"He tortured her too didn't he? The same way he did to Graham…"

"Not in the same manner but yes Serenity, he did not go easy on the mother."

"Son of a bitch!" She cried the upset from earlier replaced in her tone with a hint of anger. An emotion I could easily identify with as it had been the same for me.

"They find her body?"

"No…This leads me to believe that Lucifer is still in possession of it. A fact that I am sure he has kept well hidden from his vessel."

"You said that he would have tortured Graham with memories right? Is it possible that this was a part of it?"

"It's more than just possible. I believe it to be a fact that he used this death to torture Graham into accepting him."

"Then why hide the body?"

"Future torture I can only assume."

"Sick…son of a bitch." I heard her whisper before she began taking steps toward what remained of Lucifer's handiwork.

"Yes he is."

I likened myself in so many ways to my older brother and even felt at times that I should have fallen with him but his level of anger and torture I would never identify with. Those were the parts of him that I would never understand. He is indeed what Serenity

155

believed him to be in that regard though I couldn't bring myself to say the words.

"We need to go. I want to get back to Graham...or Lucifer. Whoever is in control. I can't be here anymore. I've seen all I need to see."

Pushing down the happiness that was building in me at the thought of getting to place my hands on her again, I motioned with my hand for her to come back.

"Then let's go. There's no time to waste."

CHAPTER TWENTY THREE

Ryan

"She's doing what?"

I can't believe what I'm hearing. I thought that when I allowed her to go back and interact with Graham that she was going to do everything she could not to get caught up in Lucifer's web and now I was learning she is doing exactly the opposite.

Serenity is playing right into his fucking hands.

"She's determined to use the bond between the two of them to save her soul mate."

Did he really have to call Graham that given the way I feel about her? It's ripping me apart inside hearing it which was doing nothing for keeping the darker side of me at bay. I wanted nothing more than to end Graham's very existence as it is.

"She is aware that he's only a vessel now right? That the Graham she remembers is no longer there."

"She is but it would appear that she doesn't seem to care. She is determined to help him no matter what it may do to her."

Jesus Christ!

The minute the words came to mind I immediately looked up to Michael to see if he heard them. I knew the way taking the Lord's name in vain worked around here and I wasn't exactly looking to get in trouble for my use of it. When no reaction came I breathed a silent sigh of relief. Looks like I'd be living for a little longer.

"I know what you are feeling but there's only way we can prevent her from immersing herself entirely with the vessel."

"You need me." I stated, knowing immediately that I was the only real option they had. Sure Gabriel had a connection with her but not one that could sustain the soul mate bond. Serenity and I may not be soul mates but we did have the one thing that the soul mate bond and that of the beloved didn't. We were in love with each other despite the way we left things. I had no doubt about that.

"Gabriel and I concur on that yes. We need you. I just do not think we can use you."

"Why the hell not?" I yelled angrily. "What the hell am I here for if not to help you?"

"Ryan you must calm yourself. I am not denying your need to help us but you are still healing from a very real human death. I do not believe that you would survive if I were to bring you down there at the present time."

I didn't care. If he thought for a second I was going to stay here laid up like the weak human he believed me to be while my wife was down on Earth facing certain death then he was going to be sadly mistaken. There was no way.

Over my dead damn body.

"I'm going. I don't care if I live or die but I am not going to sit back and let her deal with this alone."

"I assumed that would be your response."

What the hell?

"Well if you knew that I was going to say that then why even bring up all of the other stuff?"

"It is something that I am required to do. I need you to realize the gravity of the situation from every angle. You cannot just focus on yourself and your needs but also those of Gabriel, Serenity and Graham."

"I could care less about Graham."

"I am aware of that as well but the woman you claim to love cares a great deal for the human as her actions are proving. This is where I do not think you are prepared to be of use to us."

So I had to just get over the fact that my wife, the very woman I pledged to love for the rest of eternity has a bond with a guy that I can't exactly compete with and that she is down there getting closer to him as I sat here trying to heal?

That wasn't going to happen anytime soon.

"I can be of use to you no matter what I might feel for Graham Hudson. Your own brother has a bond with Serenity and he isn't the biggest fan of the soul mate bond either yet he's down there

158

with her right now. You know that doesn't matter. You just don't want to take me."

If his face any indication then Michael was about to give in to me. If Heaven really was worried about my reaction to the soul mate bond and to Graham himself then they needed to worry about that with Gabriel too and they weren't.

"That is not the only concern here demon."

"Then just spit out what is because I've got all day to argue it."

Seeing an angel becoming irritated is not something I enjoyed but found myself unable to care about. I didn't care how pissed off with me he got or how many times he wanted to call me a demon, I wasn't going to let him off easy. He either gave me a valid reason I shouldn't make the trip or he was going to lose.

"I already explained to you that moving you in your current state could result in the very human part of you that we saved passing on again. You are not strong enough in that regard." he stopped as if thinking of what to say next in order to further his failing argument. "How do you think Serenity is going to respond to learning of your passing again, especially if we are unable to bring you back this time?"

He'd done it. Shit. He'd actually given me a reason that I couldn't argue with.

If something did happen to me in my haste to get down there to help her she would never forgive me, herself or any of the angels. She loved me; she made that perfectly clear before leaving me days before.

I just couldn't sit here and do nothing either. It wasn't the way I did things.

"Talk to your Father, or figure something else out but you find a way for me to get down there without dying Michael. If you don't then I'm going to take the risk and go down myself. I don't want Serenity hurting but I'd rather she be hurting over losing me than herself."

Just like she was destined for better things over six months ago when we'd been thrown together she is meant for more now and I would be damned if I didn't do everything in my power to

159

make sure that came true for her. I didn't care about my own life, human or otherwise. All I cared about was her and I was going to make sure I did whatever it took to get down there and prove it to her.

"I can see why she loves you the way in which she does." Michael stated finally after a few minutes of silence.

"Why's that?"

"You two are very much alike and I fear it will be this very thing that gets the both of you killed."

"You wanna tell me what you mean by that?"

"You're both stubborn and all about the ultimate sacrifice. As noble as that is, it will be the very thing that ends you both."

Michael was right. Serenity and I were very much alike in a lot of different ways but none quite as big as the one he just mentioned. Both of us had proven that in spades already. Her willingly giving herself up to Lucifer in an effort to redeem me and then me following suit in giving up my very life to ensure hers remained. It seemed we were junkies for it.

I'd known it before but until being confronted with it never realized just how pivotal a role it played in our very existence. She is doing it again now, walking into the lion's den to face Lucifer in order to save Graham while I sat here willing to face death again to save her.

"Would you rather I just laid down and accepted everything?"

"No Ryan I would not. You were redeemed because of your extreme sacrifice for the side of good. It is what makes you the person that you are. While you may have been thrown into the side of darkness you have always longed for the light as your prayers as a young boy have proven."

Wait…what?

"My prayers?"

"You reside in Heaven the way that you do and you have not yet realized that we are aware of everything?" Michael questioned immediately making me feel like the biggest idiot on the planet. Of course they had heard my prayers. They were all knowing.

"You heard those?"

160

"Actually it was Father and Gabriel that heard them. I was just informed of them at a later date but yes Ryan we are all aware of what you prayed so desperately for."

He knew…hell they all knew that I prayed for Serenity even before I realized it had been her that I'd been praying for.

"I can't believe this…" I said, the words getting caught in my throat as the shock told hold.

"Everything does have a way of coming full circle doesn't it?"

"Yeah I guess it does. Look I need to know, is what I'm thinking right here? Are you trying to tell me what I think you are?"

"You were put in Serenity's path because of the dark road that had been given to you. She was put in your path by the light."

There it was.

"I don't get it."

"You are not meant to 'get it' as you say. You are only meant to live it."

"Look, I'm taking on a lot here. Do you think you could for once take it easy on me and just give me information straight with no riddles attached?"

"Serenity was meant to come to you before you came to her. We had no idea Lucifer had gotten his grips into you. We only learned of that once you appeared on scene at the college. We could tell there was a darkness surrounding you but we could not figure out just what that was. It is because of your ability to block us and also Lucifer himself."

"She would have come to me even if I hadn't been a part of the plan to end her?"

Michael nodded and I felt the world start to spin around me. I was hitting information overload. Everything I had ever known and believed about what happened back then was now turning out to be wrong. There was so much more that I still had to learn.

"Life is a learning experience Ryan surely you learned that by now." He stated simply as if it's something I should have just known all along.

"Yeah I mean that's what everyone says but I don't exactly listen much."

161

"You might want to start."

"No kidding."

Serenity, the fierce ball of light that I'd met and fallen head over heels for had been meant to be with me from the start. Maybe not in the way that we were but at the very least she had been sent to me as an answer to my prayers. They had taken their sweet ass time with it though.

"There is an answer for that as well Ryan." Michael said interrupting my thoughts.

"To what?"

"To why she appeared when she did and not sooner."

"Alright man I'm all ears."

"She had to come to you when you needed it the most, which is around the time at which you ended up coming to her. Your motivations were not pure but hers were."

"She had spent her entire life living with her abilities and staying away from people Michael. How could she be the answer to my prayers?"

"You really know nothing of the situation do you boy? I guess that shouldn't come as a surprise."

I had no idea what he was talking about. He had gone back to talking in riddles again which is just making my head hurt. I am trying to come to terms with everything he just told me and failing. It looked like there was even more he wanted to tell me and I wasn't entire sure I could handle hearing it.

"Are you making an assumption about humans again?"

"Of course but that is not what is of importance here."

"Just say it." I said, hoping that in asking him to spit it out we could end the spinning feeling that's going through me. At some point I'm going to reach my tolerance limit and I want to be sure I know everything before it happened.

"Serenity was just like you. You were not the only one that sent us multiple prayers for the exact same thing."

"She prayed for someone too?"

"Yes. We were willing to answer her call in the form of her soul mate but as it would appear that wasn't enough. So we put her on your path. As I said we had no idea of your true nature at the

162

time, only believing you to be the fragile human we had come to hear a lot from. That was our first attempt at answering two prayers at once."

Wow.

"I don't know what to say."

"I figured as much. I have never experienced levels of quiet this large since you were brought here. I rather like it."

"I've been out cold the entire time I've been here. So you may wanna rethink that man."

"Your body may have been out cold as you say but you most definitely were not. Your mind never shut down and neither did your heart."

"So I've been driving you crazy huh?" I asked with a grin.

"Like no other human before you. I much prefer the quiet."

"Well I'm sorry to disappoint you but you won't be getting much more of that."

"I figured as much. It was enjoyable while it lasted."

It wasn't lost on me that we had travelled far off from our original conversation and while I was still processing everything I had learned I knew we had to get back to it. Given what Serenity was about to face on Earth with Gabriel, there was no time to waste.

"I'm coming with you." I said; the finality more than evident in my tone.

"I figured that much as well. So let's prepare you as best we can."

CHAPTER TWENTY FOUR

Serenity

I wasn't sure what would happen when I saw Graham again. I just knew that it had to happen but before I could think of doing any of that, I had classes I needed to go to and a life to pretend to live. Neither of which I was looking forward to.

Gabriel, true to his word had left me only to find out where Graham ended up. Otherwise he was with me every second, almost to the point where the mere sound of his voice in my head was driving me crazy.

While I would have been more than happy to wait until the end of class to find out what he learned it appeared he didn't feel the same. So appear to me in my Psych class he did. The irony of which was not lost on me. No better place to appear crazy then the class that was teaching us about it.

"It would seem that Graham has not left the campus the way we assumed. He is still very much here though his activities leave something to be desired."

I knew that Gabriel's wording of the situation would never match up with any image I may be able to conjure so I just decided to ask him what the heck he meant. If I didn't I knew it was going to take me ages to get a straight answer and that's something we didn't have. Not to mention getting caught talking to a voice in my head might look a little suspicious.

"What activities are you talking about?"

"It would appear he has quite the appetite for the college females."

Oh god. I didn't need to know anymore. I knew exactly what he was getting at and hearing any more was sure to turn my already fragile stomach even more. After the way I reacted at the abandoned church I wasn't exactly itching to repeat the experience.

"Okay well thanks. I'll figure it out after class."

"Does this not bother you Serenity?"

164

Yeah it bothered me in more ways than one but I wasn't about to admit that to the nosy angel. I wasn't even sure I wanted to admit to myself. If Lucifer really was in control now then the way Graham is acting shouldn't exactly be a surprise. I had to focus on that and not on the fact that it actually hurt knowing he was with other girls.

"No. If that's what he wants to do instead of coming to class that's up to him. Now can we talk about this later?"

"You do not seem happy about it."

"Gee thanks Gabe. I couldn't tell that on my own or anything."

"I have upset you with this news. I apologize."

"You didn't upset me but if you don't get the hell out of my head right now you're gonna see a whole lot more than upset. You wanted me to come back to classes and appear normal so let me do that already."

"As you wish."

Thankful that he is going to respect my privacy and stay out of my head for the remainder of the class I turned my attention back to the front of the room. It was then that I realized a lot had changed while I'd been talking to the angel. The class was practically empty and I am still seated.

"Ms. Richards, can I have a second of your time please?" the professor called, causing me to immediately raise myself from my seat and move toward him.

This was not going to end well. I'd been absent from the class since I returned and I bet he was starting to notice my total lack of interest while I was here. Where he had gone off on Emma before for being late all the time, he's about to do the same with me and I deserved every bit of it.

"What can I do for you Professor?" I asked calmly, shutting away the events of the last few days to appear as normal as possible.

"It's come to my attention that you may be the person to give me the answers I need."

Well that isn't what I expected. It still might have to do with me and my lack of interest in the class but from the sound of it; he

165

actually just wanted information about something else entirely, which only made me think of Emma. Had she gone and done something I was going to have to cover her for?

"Sure, I'll help anyway I can. What's up?"

"It's regarding Ryan McGregor. A few of the students told me that it appeared as though the two of you were growing close. I realize that this is quite personal but I need to know if there is any truth to the talk."

He wanted to know about Ryan? What the hell?

"Ugh…I guess we're close. I mean we were."

"But you are not any longer?" he pried gently which only put me even more on guard then I already was. Given how Lucifer had basically broken Graham, I had no idea how far reaching his power went. I wasn't entirely sure I could trust the man before me now.

"No, he moved on."

"It would appear as though he moved straight off the campus if his attendance is any indication. You wouldn't happen to know anything about that would you?"

All I could do was shake my head in response. "No sir. I have no idea where he went."

"Well alright then. If you do come across him or he contacts you in any way, can you please have him come see me immediately? If he doesn't I am going to have to grade him accordingly and up until recently he had been such a good student I would hate to have to do that."

After promising the professor up and down that I would do what he wanted if Ryan did contact me I made my way from the class. I needed to head to my room for my other course books and it was the perfect excuse to have a little bit of alone time. Hearing Ryan's name again had gotten to me.

I couldn't afford to let what happened between us to do that right now. I had to focus on getting Graham out of the clutches of a bunch of women.

"Psst…Serenity!"

Hearing my name I immediately began looking around. When I couldn't see anyone calling out for me, I began making my way

166

toward the dorm all the while praying for something to happen to silence my mind.

"God you really are deaf lately. Serenity stop!"

Spinning around again at the sound of my name I ran straight into the very red face of my best friend. Of course the voice I heard had been hers. She bailed on the class again and needed to hiss at me in order to not call attention to herself.

"You're going to end up flunking Psych Ems."

"Yeah well that may not be such a bad thing. I only took the class to hang out with you anyway. You know the last thing I wanna be is a doctor like the ones at the center."

I did know that. She hated her time there and was still cursing every doctor in the place whether they helped her or not. While I was able to put that time out of my mind for the most part Emma had a hard time. She hated the fact that I wanted to pursue medicine and wasn't silent about it.

"Then just drop it. It's that simple."

"Yeah, maybe, I'll think about it. Anyway that's not why I've been calling out to you."

"So why were you?"

"Have you actually seen Graham since that day you two grabbed coffee?"

Oh god. She knew about Graham and his newest pursuit. Of course she was here to tell me all about it. As much as I didn't want another repeat of Gabriel and the way he had told me in class, I was thankful for something else to think about. I could officially start putting Ryan in the background again.

"No actually I haven't. Why?"

"I thought he came back for you."

"He didn't come back for me Ems. I told you that before. He came back for school. He's pursuing his art dream."

"Yeah well we all know that is just a bullshit excuse."

"No, you think it is but why are you talking about Graham?"

"I saw him earlier. I thought at first it was you that he was with, that you'd decided to blow off class again so the two of you could be alone but well here you are."

167

Yeah she was definitely going to tell me about Graham and the other girls.

"I only blew off classes with him once Ems and that turned out to be a very big mistake. So you saw Graham with another girl and thought you'd hunt me down to tell me?"

She blushed instantly and I couldn't help but laugh. "Yeah Ser, I thought you should know what that sleazebag is doing."

Sleazebag wasn't even the half of it. If only she knew what was really going on she might not be so quick to jump down his throat the way she was. I knew she was doing it to be a stand up friend to me but knowing everything I did, I wasn't in the mood to hear it.

"Look Ems, I love you for thinking of me but Graham is not the same guy that left here six months ago. Something changed him. He's free to make out with whoever he wants."

"Why don't I believe you?"

"I have no idea, because I'm telling you the truth. Just like the other day when you told me to wear the sundress I was telling you that same truth. It was not a date and there is nothing between Graham and me. All we share is a past together."

"Yeah, a past that had the two of you waking up together in my bed if I remember it right."

If I didn't love her as much as I did I would curse her memory. I remembered that morning quite well all on my own, having her recite it back to me was not going to help. I had forgiven Graham for his words that day but it didn't mean the entire experience didn't sting, even now.

"That was a mistake."

"Didn't seem that way to me."

"Emma I'm gonna say this as nicely as I can because I love you but you need to focus a little less on my love life and more on your academics. It's bound to create more excitement then I ever could."

Just as I expected I watched her tense at my words and I instantly felt like shit. Not telling her everything was killing me and now I was coming across as a grade A bitch because of it.

"So it's like that really?"

168

"Emma you know I don't mean anything by it but yeah, it's like that."

"All I've ever wanted to do is look out for you Serenity. When you told me about kissing Graham all those years ago I wanted to kill him for it but you stopped me because for whatever reason you loved him still and didn't want to make anything worse. Ryan comes along and does the same damn thing to you and takes off and again, I want to go to bat for you. No guy ever treats my best friend like garbage. Graham is back and he's on the other end of the quad sticking his tongue down another girl's throat and instead of being upset with him, you're basically telling me to screw off again. I'm done."

"Gabriel if you have any words of wisdom now would be a good time." I spoke in my mind, praying he would hear me and tell me the right thing to do here. With as upset as Emma is, I either needed to tell her everything or give her a reason to believe I wasn't the bitch I appeared to be.

"Just apologize. Pretend to be angry about Graham but do not tell her anything. With Lucifer in control again, anything you tell her will put her at risk."

Of course he would give me the logical response. He would tell me the things I already knew and yet also give me my way out.

"Emma wait!" I called as she began to turn and walk away from me.

"What Ser? You gonna tell me again how Graham doesn't bother you and that I'm just wasting my breath?"

"No…"

"Then what?"

"It does bother me alright. Of course it does. I've loved him since I was 16 years old. When he came back he told me he did it for me, the first time anyway and he's back again and this time it's not for me. He's different Ems. As much as I want to say it doesn't bother me, you seeing him with another girl, it bothers the hell out of me. I want him to be here for me."

I was doing everything the way Gabriel said but where it should have felt more like a lie, it wasn't. I really did feel everything exactly how I'm saying it.

169

"I don't want things to be different. I want to go back to the way everything was before he showed up and screwed with my head and my heart. I just can't let myself go there because if I do then I'm going to end up running and I'm tired of running."

As Emma wrapped her arms around me in acceptance of everything I said I heard Gabriel's voice in my head again, his pitch low and his tone relaxing.

"It feels good to tell the truth doesn't it?"

Graham

God that felt good.

She had been so eager, the girl with the sparkling blue eyes and lengthy blonde hair. Hair that was almost as long as those smooth delicious legs that only a couple of hours before had been wrapped nicely around my neck as I'd gone down on her just the way she begged me for.

Yes she was delicious and satisfied the hunger deep inside of me nicely. The ache in my body after my time with Serenity was now sufficiently dormant though I had no idea how long it would last before I'd have to find another willing female.

It had been this way for the last two days. Finding random women all across the college campus and taking them back to my room, feeding on them as only I could. Learning of their deepest sexual fantasies and making them all come to life. God life is good. If I had known it could be this way I wouldn't have stayed celibate as long as I had.

The burning began again as I kissed the latest distraction goodbye. Beginning at the base of my feet and travelling straight up until it hit my groin full throttle. I need it again.

Graham you must tame the desires within you. Now that I have you back the way you were meant to be, you need to focus on the task at hand.

Of course he's going to ruin my fun. He had no idea what it felt like for me, seeing all of these bodies travelling back and forth from their rooms to classes, all of them more than a little eager to spend some time with me.

170

I didn't have to wine and dine these girls. No, it would appear that when you sent your little girls away to college they took it upon themselves to change and embrace a wilder side. I had never given it much thought before but I was definitely going to take advantage of it now.

"I know what you want me to do and I'll do it but I can't just ignore this craving anymore. I need it."

You need to focus on Serenity!

"No man, I need to have another one of those beauties over there underneath me." I replied spying a group of what appeared to be very eager women with their eyes locked on my body. Yes, I definitely needed one of them, maybe even all of them. I was up for anything.

"Besides, you saw the way I reacted when I was around her the last time. You really want a repeat performance?"

How much do you remember of what happened with her?

"I don't remember much of anything other than the way you screwed with my body when she ran from me. I ain't itching to repeat that, you get me?"

Then stop screwing your way through the campus and focus on the task at hand. You will obey me or I will be forced to come up with an even darker technique to get your cooperation. Let me handle any further reaction you may have to Serenity.

Walking around with him originally seemed like a dream come true but the more time he spent bossing me around I found I want nothing more than to kick him out. He is seriously ruining my fun. Placing me on a college campus and telling me not screw around with very willing females was like putting cookies out on a counter and telling kids not to eat them. It was damn impossible.

"Fine, I'll do what you want but I'm going to need it again soon."

He knew what I meant. Other than sex with very willing coeds it's second on my list of things I desperately needed. Right from the first taste I had fallen under its spell and the second taste had been much the same.

The blood of a virgin is an acquired taste but one that I took to quite nicely. I knew it pleased him to no end the way I had taken to it, so I had no doubt he would help me out. This was definitely a win-win deal. I had only taken one virgin since I landed back here and the amount of blood during the act had not been enough, so he'd taken over and gotten me more. Well if he wanted to keep me going along with this plan, he was going to step it up again.

I will get you what you need when you do as I ask.

"Then tell me where you want me boss. I'm all yours."

It's time we made acquaintances with the roommate.

I recalled what I remembered of Serenity's roommate and immediately my spirits began to rise. Maybe this wouldn't be a total waste of time after all. If he wasn't permitting me to sleep with random women than I guess it was just time I grabbed one that wasn't so random.

CHAPTER TWENTY FIVE

Gabriel

Well it is official.

Ryan has been informed of everything that is happening down here and is going to begin preparations for his return back to the planet.

The right thing to do here would be to inform Serenity of it immediately but given how hard she is trying to keep him out of her mind the last thing I want to do is be the reason he appears there. She needed the break. It is more than a little obvious that what she had gone through with the demon had taken a toll on her.

She wasn't quite as focused as she wanted me to believe but I wasn't going to call attention to it. Thus far in our arrangement she had made good on everything I wanted and needed of her and I would continue much the way I had been. I would watch her, guard over her but most of all I would stay out of her business.

If we were ever going to be more to one another when the time is right then I had to remain as far away from her personal troubles as I could manage. She was more than a little aware of what is between us, having at one point felt it herself so I had no doubt that in doing things the way that I was planning to, she would respect me more in the end.

Admitting to Emma how hurt she had been hearing about what Graham had been up to since their time together had affected me deeply. I wanted to shield her from the things Lucifer was making the boy do but if I did that then I wouldn't be giving her all the information she would need in order to move forward with her plan. I knew it is breaking her heart even though that same heart belonged to another man. It was the soul mate bond at its finest.

While Serenity and Emma had been going through the motions of becoming close again I felt him across the campus. He was only a few hundred steps from where they stood and it had taken everything in me not to let Serenity know. She wanted to get closer to him and now would be the perfect chance. Given what she had admitted though I knew she needed the time alone more.

So as soon as the two girls broke up their emotional bonding experience I followed them both back to the room, Serenity there to grab her books and head to her next class and Emma to rest. I had gone through the room prior to their entrance in an effort to be sure that nothing awaited them on the other side. Once I am secure in the knowledge that everything is as they left it, I watched as they made their way inside shutting the door behind them.

I had the ability to be able to listen in and be a part of what would take place between the girls but chose not to. Serenity trusted me in more ways than just the obvious ones and while I may still be keeping things from her that she would be better off knowing, I am determined to honor her trust in me.

As the door opened a few minutes later, bag securely thrown over Serenity's shoulder I prepared myself to again follow her to class to ensure her safe arrival. As I stood waiting for her to move, she stuck her head back into the room.

"Hey Ems…movie night when I get back?"

"You know it. I'll have them ready for ya." I heard Emma call back before the door shut and Serenity began making her way to the stairs.

"Are you sure that a movie night is what you should be focusing on right now?"

Her reply came back almost immediately, sarcasm ever present which only caused me to smile. It is moments like this that I lived for, even with everything that had happened.

"Yeah actually Gabe, it's exactly what's needed given the level of shit I'm sifting through today. Why do you care anyway? You jealous you weren't born a girl?"

"I assure you that I am more than pleased I turned out the way I am thank you."

"Of course you are." She replied with a snort. A noise I had never heard her utter before which surprised me. Is she really that affected by what Lucifer had Graham doing or is there more going on that I am unaware of?

"You think you can do me a favor?" She spoke again her voice raising as she asked the question.

"I will certainly try."

"For the next two hours, can you stay out of my head? I think my Psych professor might already think I'm a few bricks short of a full load, I don't need anyone else believing it too."

"Radio silence Serenity. It will appear as if I'm not even there."

"Thank you…"

"You're more than welcome Serenity."

As I prepared to make myself as invisible as possible the way she had asked of me, she shocked me again as her voice came to me loud and clear.

"Gabe?"

"Yes?"

"I know I owe you a whole bunch of explanations about what's going on with me but I just…"

"You owe me nothing."

"No Gabriel I do owe you something. Just…thank you for not pushing it."

When she had spoken to me again I had not expected it to be the way in which she is now. In fact I was waiting for more admonishments in regards to the fact that I never seemed to leave her alone. This was a welcome change though I wished it didn't come attached with the sadness I could hear in her voice.

"I will never push you Serenity. When you are finally ready to speak to me about what is troubling you so deeply, you know where to find me. Until then free your mind of the worry that inhabits it. Everything is fine."

I couldn't bring myself to tell her that everything she believed she owed me I am already aware of, either learning of it by watching and listening to her conversations or from my brother who had been privy to what I had not. I knew that it was wrong but with the strain in her voice, the way all of this seemed to be taking its toll the last thing I wanted to do is make it worse. Even if the only person it would be worse for is me. I had to keep things this

175

way for now and let her come to me in her own time. Until then I just had to be okay with feigning ignorance.

"Thanks…I guess I'll talk to you after class."

As she walked with purpose toward her next class, my eyes glued on her body as it maneuvered its way through the flow of other students, I only hoped that I was doing the right thing keeping Ryan's impending visit from her. That in the end it wouldn't damage what is already beginning to look more fragile by the second.

I had to make sure that no matter what, Serenity did not fall apart.

Graham

Well this is turning out to be the shittiest idea ever.

Just what the point was in showing up here and trying to feel out Serenity's best friend was beyond me but I'm growing bored with it all. I want nothing more than to get out of here and back to a woman that didn't look ready to spit on me and claw my eyes out.

You will do nothing of the sort. If you want me to give you what you've craving then you will do as I have asked. You are only here to scare sense into Serenity anyway. The roommate is to remain off limits. I have no use for her.

Well it was great that he's telling me that now. With the way he made it sound we needed the roommate in order to make our next move on Serenity and then she would cease to exist. No one that knew of him ever made it very long. It was just the way things had been since he'd taken over.

She does not know of me. She may remain alive. While Serenity may trust her and care for her deeply she brings nothing to the table where the plan is concerned.

"She may not bring anything to the table for you but I wouldn't mind bending her over it."

I couldn't help it. Despite the fact that I knew nothing about this girl, I'm drawn to her in the most primal of ways. She was

176

smoking hot and I just wanted one small taste of her. Having her naked beneath me would just be an added perk.

Calm yourself Graham or you will be punished.

"Punish me like the way I want to punish this hot little number right now?"

ENOUGH! I am not going to tell you again. I do believe letting you have your way with the blood has made it go to your head. You must remain in control of your faculties or you will pay for your disobedience.

"Did you hear me? She's not here and even if she were here I wouldn't let you anywhere near her. I'm on to you buddy."

I liked Emma. She was a fighter and when she believed in something she went straight at it. In this case she was going straight for me and it was entertaining.

Flashing the biggest smile I could manage I made my way over to Serenity's bed and made myself comfortable. She may not be here right now but I'd wait it out. She had to come home eventually and I couldn't wait. Until then I'd just let Emma entertain me. Who knew where that could lead?

"I know I screwed up with her Emma. Why do you think I'm even here? I'm actually shocked I got through the door."

"You wouldn't have if I realized sooner that it wasn't her coming back for her keys. Speaking of which, you need to leave. I don't want you here when she gets back."

"Sorry princess, I ain't going anywhere."

"I'll call campus security and then you won't have a choice."

"Threaten me all you want. I'm still not moving until I get to talk to Serenity."

She made good on her threat by going straight for the phone on her bedside table and realizing the seriousness of what she was about to do and not wanting to call any undue attention to myself, I dived across the room grabbing her wrist tightly until the receiver dropped from her hand.

"Good girl. You really don't want to do that anyway."

"I…don't?" she stuttered as I leaned even closer into her body. I could smell her fear the minute my body touched hers and I'll be damned if it didn't turn me the fuck on.

"That's right princess, you don't. Now why don't you just sit back down and relax. As soon as Serenity gets here you'll see this nonsense was for nothing."

God I'm talking out my ass but it seemed to work. Either my calm tone is relaxing her or she is so filled with fear that she wanted to comply in fear of her life. Whatever way she was dealing with it was irrelevant to me. As long as she calmed down I was fine.

"She's right you know."

"Who's right about what darlin?"

"Serenity...At first I didn't believe her when she told me that you changed but it's obvious."

"We all gotta grow up sometime love. From the looks of it though you've already grown up enough."

She covered her chest the minute my eyes fell which only caused me to break out in laughter. Yeah she was afraid all right and I wasn't making it any easier on her by pushing her the way I am.

"You know," I continued, smiling "That day you found us in your bed, I always wished it was you with me instead of her. I think the two of us would have had a lot of fun together."

"You sick bast—

"No need for name calling sweetheart. Just stating facts. I distinctly remember your hand slapping my ass so I bet you've given it some thought too."

"You're delusional."

"No actually I'm a realist. Why don't we just skip all the bullshit and admit it."

"Admit what?"

"You want me."

"I want you out of here."

Pulling her to my body again I hit pay dirt. She may want to pretend she didn't feel anything towards me but I knew different. The hard buds of her nipples peeking through her shirt spoke the truth where her mouth could not.

"You forget...I can feel it. You wanna try lying to me again?"

178

When no response came I released her and watched as she tumbled backwards onto her bed. The way her body is placed now it would only take one step for me to be on top of her, burying my face into her very needy chest.

Graham do not make me warn you again.

Son of a bitch!

"Seems like it's your lucky day sweetheart, I'm not going to touch you right now but you can be damned sure I'll be back and you won't be able to say no."

Before I could decide on my next move I heard the sound of the door behind me and turning toward it I waited patiently for who was about to walk through.

"Emma! I don't have my keys, can you let me in?" I heard the voice call through the door and immediately my heart began to race. Yes, I would definitely have to deal with Emma later because now I was going to get what I had come for.

I was about to get Serenity and this time I wouldn't let her slip away quite so easily.

She was going to be mine.

CHAPTER TWENTY SIX

Serenity

I can't believe I'm so stupid. When I'd gone home earlier to grab my books I left my keys on the nightstand by my bed, which meant that now I was going to have to hope that Emma was home and could let me back in. I wasn't in the mood to deal with campus security. All I wanted to do was crash and watch movies with my best friend.

Banging my fist on the door I waited for a response. When none came I called through the door and hoped that Emma would hear me. Who the hell is asleep at this time of day, even if you had been up the entire night before?

"Emma!" I called loudly with a bang of my fist on the door. "I don't have my keys, can you let me in?"

I heard what sounded like voices from the inside but before I could react the door swung open and I was confronted with a red faced Emma. Just what the heck had she been doing before I showed up?

Better yet, who had she been doing it with?

"Oh hey Ser, sorry about that. Heard the first knock but was kind of caught up with something." She said motioning with her hand behind her.

So she was here with a guy? Jesus what happened to putting the damn scarf on the door the way we agreed? The last thing I wanted to walk in on is my roommate mid screw.

"I can make myself scarce if you need some more time." I managed to choke out though the words on my tongue sounded wrong. I didn't want to leave my room for crying out loud. All I wanted to do was sleep this god awful day away.

"No! I mean you don't need to go anywhere. It's nothing like that. Actually the person's here to see you."

"Someone's here to see me?" I asked, actually confused as to who would be coming by for me. It wasn't exactly news that I had very little friends.

"Yeah." She said pushing the door open further and giving me a full view of the room and just who was waiting for me inside of it.

Graham.

Shit, this is definitely not what I'd been expecting when I made my way home tonight. The last thing you think about when all you want is a hot shower and your bed is your first love showing up in your room even though you're supposed to be out finding him. Talk about timing.

"Hey Ser…" he said, his voice as smooth as velvet instantly making my body go numb. Damn soul mate bond, I was actually beginning to hate the reaction he seemed to give me.

"Graham what are you doing here? I asked as I made my way into the room letting Emma finally close it behind me. Just how long had he been here and why did my roommate look like she'd been caught with her hand in the cookie jar?

Oh no. She looked that way because something had been going on between the two of them. Feeling the bile begin to form in my throat I turned my gaze back and forth between the two looking for any clue as to what I realized. Emma couldn't lie to save her life so I knew that I'd get my answers quicker from her.

"Nothing took place between the two of them Serenity. Remain calm."

I have never been more thankful for Gabriel then I was in that moment. He had known where my head and heart wanted to go and he immediately put a stop to it.

"Thank you."

"I actually came by to see you." Graham answered with a smile making his way toward me.

After everything I'd heard about him today I wasn't sure if I could stand having him near me. If what he really wanted, Lucifer control or not is other girls then he could gladly leave and get them. I would save him but that's all he'd get from me.

181

"I would have figured you had better plans." I snapped, failing in my ability to keep my real feelings in check.

"So you heard about that?"

"Yeah Graham I heard about that. The last time I see you, you're begging me for help and then the next I'm hearing about how you're off screwing other girls. You'll excuse me if you're the last person I want to be around right now."

I motioned toward the door but he was having no part of it. He came even closer to me and I saw Emma's eyes go wide in horror. Something had obviously happened in the room before I'd gotten here for her to have that much fear in her eyes and I wanted to know just what that was.

"Stay where you are. If you know what's good for you, don't take another step toward me until you tell me why Emma's so afraid of you."

"She's not afraid Ser, she's just pissed off and wants me nowhere near you."

There was lie number one. I wondered just how under the influence of Lucifer he was at the moment and how many more lies I'd catch him in before he broke again. If he wanted to play the lie game then I'd play along…for now.

"Well that makes sense."

"Of course it does sweetness." He said moving dangerously close to me again. "Now that you're here though, you mind if I steal you for a little while? I kind of want to talk to you in private."

As soon as his arms wrapped around mine bringing me into the hug I felt my body which had been tense every second leading up to it begin to thaw. Even knowing he wasn't himself couldn't change the way my body reacted to him. It was infuriating.

"Anything you have to say you can do it in front of Emma and then you can leave." I said pushing my reaction from my mind and trying to keep myself composed. "If you haven't guessed, you're not exactly wanted around here anymore."

Leaning his mouth close to my ear he blew into it gently, my body instantly reacting with a shiver causing him to chuckle. "You know you want me here."

Well with all the lies he was able to tell I wasn't expecting any truth out of the conversation but there it was. He knew I wanted him there and no amount of denial on my part was going to convince him since my body had decided to betray me by going practically limp in his arms.

"Come on Ser, at least let me explain everything. I think with our history I've earned that much haven't I?"

Catching Emma's eyes I saw her motion her head no, giving me even more proof that something horrible had indeed happened before I'd gotten here. If she was that frightened for me to be alone with him then maybe I better start listening.

"We don't need to go anywhere." I answered as I continued to look straight at Emma. "Ems doesn't mind giving us a couple minutes. Do you Ems?"

"Are you sure Ser?" I don't exactly feel right leaving you with him."

"I'll be fine Ems, no worries. Graham here wouldn't hurt a fly. Would you Graham?" I asked, turning back to him and flashing the brightest grin in his direction which I hoped would have the result I desired.

"Serenity is safe with me Emma."

After another string of looks between the two of us, Emma sighed and made her way toward the door. Turning around one more time before making her way out into the hall, she spoke.

"You've got fifteen minutes. If he's not out of here by then I'm calling campus security, for real this time."

Seizing the opportunity at her words I manoeuvred out of the hug he had me stuck in and made my way over to her bed. I needed distance if I'm going to go forward with this. Having Graham that close did nothing but screw with my brain and that is the one thing I needed more than anything right now.

"Man she really hates me huh?" He said with a laugh, turning towards me and following suit until he was sitting beside me on the bed.

"Gee I wonder why she hates you Graham."

"Seems like someone else might hate me too?"

"I could never hate you but I don't like you very much right now. Let's just leave it at that."

"If I ask you to hear me out, will you do it?" He asked and as I looked up into his eyes I saw the same look I'd seen two days before. The pleading look that was borderline begging. Where he seemed almost cocky a few minutes earlier, now he seemed like his old self again. Just another way my head was all screwed up by him.

"Yes I'll listen."

"What you heard it's true. I'm not going to tell you I didn't do those things but Serenity you gotta understand."

"Understand what exactly?"

"I'm in love with you. I've been in love with you since we were sixteen. I was stupid enough not to tell you back then but when I finally did I wanted you to feel the same way. You're married to another guy now and well I'm alone. As much as I want you to be the one I'm with forever it's not possible."

His words hit me and they hit me hard. I knew he felt this way, at least the real Graham felt this way. I had gotten that much from him the day he'd come to the church to stop me from marrying Ryan. He wanted me to know how he felt about me and that he wanted to fight and I just turned him away. I had no choice at the time given Lucifer's branding but I would have made the same decision regardless. Saving Ryan was the most important thing to me.

If I'm completely honest, even with the way I felt about Graham it still is the most important thing to me.

"So you decide since you can't have me you'll screw your way through the campus?"

Where I expected him to laugh he just bowed his head. What the hell is going on? Where is the cocky bastard from earlier? Is this Lucifer's way of fucking with my mind so I'd be vulnerable enough for him?

"You think I'm proud of it? I'm not alright. I screwed things up even more."

"Yeah Graham you did."

"Where is Ryan?"

184

I don't know how to answer this. If Lucifer really is in control of him then he knew exactly where Ryan is and didn't need me telling him but if this was the soul mate bond at work again and really my Graham then I needed to tell him the truth. Not admitting everything to him is just not something I am prepared to do. Where hiding things from Emma had become easier with time it would never be that way with him.

"He's gone." I answered quietly, hoping that would be enough of an answer for him.

"For good or just for a while?" he pushed.

Tell him what he wants to hear Serenity. You wanted to get closer to him well here is your chance.

"Am I talking to Graham or Lucifer?"

"Graham. While my brother is deeply engrained inside of him he is not controlling the output again. It is your Graham as you say."

"He's gone for good."

As much as I hated the words that fell from my lips I knew that they were true. As much as I loved him and wanted to be with him he couldn't let himself feel the same way. He couldn't get past how wrong we were for each other.

"Shit! I can't believe this!" Graham shouted pushing himself away from me on the bed, more than a little affected by my news.

"Yeah…" was all I could manage in response. He'd come here for answers and well now he was getting them even though I wasn't being the most truthful in my responses. There is a whole lot more to the story that he didn't know.

"Serenity I need to make this up to you. Please let me make this up to you!"

Again he pleaded with me only this time he was using his body to do it as well as his words. His hand immediately locked with mine and I could feel his eyes all over me, searching me for the answer he desperately wanted to hear.

"Graham…"

"No don't say anything yet. I've got something else I need to say."

185

"Fine." I answered motioning with my hand for him to continue. "Say whatever you want to say."

"Every one of the girls I was with, they didn't mean anything."

"Graham if you want me to forgive you, telling me about sex with other girls is not going to get you anywhere."

"Let me finish please." He pleaded again, causing my mouth to close and just listen. "Every time I was with a girl it wasn't them I was with. I know that makes no sense but you have to believe me. Yes I wanted to get laid and yes I didn't give a shit who it was with but every single time I closed my eyes it wasn't them I saw. All I could see was you."

Jesus Christ. I really didn't want to hear this now.

"You saw me while you were screwing other girls?"

"No…yes…I don't know. You are all I ever see Serenity. God I can't even take a step without thinking about you, seeing you in my head and wanting nothing more than to find you and—

"And what Graham?" I ask as his voice cuts off leaving me hanging.

"Do this." He said breathless.

Using the hand locked in mine he pulled my body to his and pressed his lips hard onto mine with a desperation I haven't felt since he asked me to save him two days before. Recalling the way it felt two years before when we found ourselves in this exact situation I closed my eyes and allowed myself to embrace it meeting his lips with as much desperation as he had.

Parting my lips just slightly as his tongue pushed for entrance I moved my body even more into his until I was practically in his lap. Not opening my eyes for fear of the reality of the situation setting in I wrapped my now loose arms around his neck and deepened the kiss, crashing my tongue into his as we became hungry for each other.

Pulling back just slightly I began sucking on his lips, feeling the dry cracks begin to go soft under the wetness of my mouth. As I sucked on him hungrily, his lips answering my need with one just as strong I felt my body being slowly pushed backwards on the bed. Graham positioned his body in perfect contrast to mine, our

186

bodies melding perfectly together, the kiss never once breaking as neither one of us was willing to come up for air.

Lost completely in the moment, the smell of his cologne filling my nostrils and fueling the hunger inside of me, the wetness of his tongue as it met with mine again sending a fire through my body, I didn't realize anyone had entered the room until I heard the sound of a throat clearing loudly across from the bed.

Finally pulling back from the moment and opening my eyes I took one last look at Graham his eyes giving nothing away before turning to face the person who had just walked in on the two of us. Fully expecting to come face to face with my angry best friends face I was shaken to the core when I realized that the person that had caught us wasn't her. It was someone far worse.

The cloudy blue eyes staring back at me didn't belong to Emma at all. They were Ryan's.

CHAPTER TWENTY SEVEN

Graham

When he told me we were going to scare Serenity I didn't think for one minute things would go the way that they were now. She was angry with me but she saw through my attitude. Whatever the relationship between her and the roommate she was smart enough to see that something wasn't right the minute she walked in.

She closed herself off to me and now I was going to have to work twice as hard to get her back. I just couldn't figure out whose motivation I was following in getting her back, mine or his.

He wanted me to scare her of course, having her find me with Emma; she would instantly be worried I told the girl something she wasn't ready to hear. That hadn't happened though, all she had been was pissed which is when everything started changing again.

I realized too late that the change in me is what his ultimate goal was. He wanted to figure it out so he made no effort to stop it or change me once it began. I felt the strength begin rising in me the minute she told Emma I wouldn't hurt her and within just a few minutes he was completely pushed into the background and I was the one in control again.

It seemed to begin with touch. Whenever I was close enough to her for us to be touching she seemed to reach into the darkest parts of me and give me strength I hadn't realized I had until that very moment. From there it just became stronger the more we interacted with each other. With the way she was gauging my reactions I'm sure she knew what she was doing as well. I was pretty sure just like he is; she was doing it with a purpose too.

The difference was I knew she was doing it to save me. When I asked her to help me at the coffee shop she had taken it to heart and was going to do whatever it took to succeed, even after I told her that she needed to stay far away from me. Even being with other girls didn't deter her. She is still here and fighting for me, whether she's scared or not.

I don't know if it's the connection between us or if it's something more but the minute our lips touched I was lost completely. It was like everything that we'd been through together in the last five years came flooding to the surface and had taken a hold of me and wasn't letting go. I was intoxicated with her scent; her breathing seemed to be what kept me doing the same. The beating of her heart matched mine and in that moment there wasn't a thing in the world that could touch us.

In that moment I was completely alive.

When I pushed her back onto Emma's bed I expected her to stop me. She would tell me that she wasn't ready for this and that we needed to stop but no argument came. She just continued kissing me and I continued to enjoy the feeling of the way her body just fit perfectly in sync with mine.

At least until I heard the door open. Serenity hadn't sensed it and my body immediately tensed in preparation of what was to come. Where I could have stopped it then and there I continued. I wanted every bit of what she wanted to give me, no matter who was in the room. It's only when she finally took notice that we both broke apart and realized just who walked in on us.

Ryan McGregor.

The last person I was expecting to see and judging by the look on Serenity's face the last person for her as well. Given that she told me he was long gone, what he was doing here now was lost on me. Though with the way I felt for her, I could only imagine that the broken man before us now could only be here for one reason. He wanted her back.

I shouldn't feel sympathy for the guy given what he is but I felt nothing but. I had been where he was, watching as she moved on with someone else. Seeing or hearing about her moving on is like a million knives being shoved in your chest at exactly the same moment but in a dozen different places. It would hurt all over and judging by the pain on the guys face now, there was no doubt about it. He is definitely destroyed with what he just witnessed.

189

The minute I released myself from her body and she moved from the bed I felt the change again. He was beginning to take back over. Without the connection between us I would be lost again. Reaching out to her quickly, I pulled on her arm until she turned back to face me.

"He's taking over again. I need to get out of here."

I expected to hear some kind of response but all she did was look away, leveling her gaze on the other man in the room. Whatever I thought was taking place between us had obviously been a delusion because there was no doubt about where her real loyalty was. She would always leave me for Ryan.

It was only when I began to make my way off the bed that I heard it but as I took in the situation in front of me I realized that it wasn't something that had been said aloud. Instead it was her voice in my mind, quiet but very clear.

"Do what you need to do Graham. I'll come find you but do me a favor?"

"Anything." I answered back hoping that I would do as she had done and keep it between us. When no reaction came from the other occupants of the room I realized it worked.

"Stay safe and keep fighting until I can get to you."

I couldn't promise her that given that the minute he took over my body again I would be lost but since every time I was with her I felt even stronger than the time before I would do everything in my power to keep him at bay even if it was a losing battle.

"I'll try." I whispered. *"Serenity are you sure you don't want me to stay? I mean as long as we stay connected in some way touching I can stay here with you and Lucifer won't break through again."*

"No. I've got this. I need to face this on my own but thank you."

Accepting her answer I made my way to the door and with one final look back in her direction, sadness weighing heavily in her eyes, I ducked my head and headed through, leaving her alone to deal with the fallout of what we had just done.

Any feeling I may have had for her in that moment quickly disappeared as the strength of the darkness began to overpower me again, bringing me to my knees in her hallway.

My last thought as he took me completely over was one of hope. I hoped with everything in me that when it was all said and done, she'd keep her promise and come back to me because I wasn't ready to face what came next without her.

Ryan

For as long as I can remember I have never been able to truly feel anything other than emptiness. I am devoid of emotion. Where one might feel an emotional upheaval in certain moments of their life I have gone through it all feeling next to nothing. It was why no one could ever get close to me because they could sense the disconnection and would back off, some even running as fast as their legs could take them.

It could have been because of the part of me that wasn't entirely human but I like to believe it is the most human part of me. Growing up with a mother that didn't know the first thing about real love and actual feeling to then being recruited by the man with no heart himself I had never been exposed to real and genuine feeling so I allowed myself to be cold inside. Disconnected from the rest of the world and until this very moment it served me well.

Everything changed for me the day I walked into that Psychology class. Not only did my world turn on its axis but so did the emptiness inside of me. Even with a clear goal in front of me I still somehow managed to allow myself to be changed by the bright light that is Serenity Richards. Not only was I no longer empty but also filled with that light and a hope for a brighter tomorrow, not only for my own life but for everyone around me.

Serenity broke through the empty shell that I had been and brought me to life. She allowed me to feel real love for the very first time something that while I wished for it, had never until that moment materialized. I thought of love as fleeting, something that I was too good to actually experience and Lucifer had no problem

191

helping with that belief. I was always better than the silly human emotion, which is why I had never felt it.

Until I did feel it and it forever changed me.

When I agreed to come down and help the angels with Graham and Serenity I never thought for one second it would have gotten to this point. That I would witness the very person that had given me love locked in a passionate embrace with another man. She was too good to do something so primal, so very human to me. She was a light from Heaven itself for crying out loud. The basic human impulses would have no effect on her.

I was dead wrong. My eyes hadn't deceived me; she was indeed locked in a very intimate embrace with Graham Hudson and given the amount of time it had taken for her to break away once I entered the room spoke volumes to how deeply she had fallen.

Graham wasn't just some ordinary guy though. He was the one guy that had the power to take her from me and while I wanted to believe that he would never do it, I'm being faced with the knowledge now that anything is possible when it has to do with the bond they both shared.

God this is killing me. I needed to say something and there were no words that would come. There was something else deep under the surface though and with each passing second it was building and soon there would be no way I'd be able to control it. It would unleash and the minute it did no one in the room was safe. Not even Serenity herself.

The one thing Lucifer loved about me while he had been grooming me had been my anger. There were no boundaries on the level it could reach and he loved to watch me when I was under the control of it. It was the darkest part of me and the one thing that made me more than just a regular human. It is also the very thing that caused me to leave so much death and destruction in my wake during my time with him.

My anger made me what I really am inside. A demon. All I could see now as I watched her stand before me, Graham making himself scarce almost immediately was red. Yes the anger is indeed reaching a level of which I had never known before.

I needed to get it under control. I wasn't alone in the room. I had to remember the innocents that surrounded me. While Serenity may be guilty of doing what I believed to be the unthinkable she was still just as innocent as Emma who was behind me standing still as a statue. Michael is also with me though keeping his presence hidden given that until only a few minutes before his fallen brother had been in the room. I had no doubt he would destroy me if I let the anger take complete control.

It wasn't entirely a bad idea, having the angel end the torture I was currently experiencing. This was a vision I would never get out of my head.

"Looks like I didn't have to call campus security after all." Emma spoke up, filling the silence that had taken over the room.

"Emma…" Serenity said, the sound of her voice finally calling me to her face and the pain that I now saw clouding over her normally bright hazel eyes.

"Yeah I know, you've got a lot to deal with obviously. I'm gonna go to the library, give you two time together."

"Thank you." I heard her whisper as I just nodded my agreement, still not entirely trusting my voice to speak. I was still having a hard time getting her kissing Graham out of my head.

We all stood in silence while Emma grabbed her jacket and made her way out so I thought about what I was going to say to her once we were alone. While Michael may still be in the room with us, I didn't care whether or not he heard any of it. She may belong to Heaven but until five minutes ago I also thought she belonged to me. He is going to let me say whatever I'm feeling or I'd find a way to make sure he never made it back here again.

Shit.

Why didn't they take this away from me? Why heal my human body, bring me back to life but not take the very thing I wanted rid of most of all. I didn't want to have this darkness inside of me, it was clouding my judgement. I wanted to be able to think clearly, deal with this rationally but as long as this is inside of me, I never would. Speaking about killing an angel wasn't me at all.

With as angry as I was, I didn't blame her the way my heart wanted me to. I couldn't blame her because if I hadn't said the things I said the last time we'd seen each other she never would have put herself in this position. As much as I believe that you need to take responsibility for your own actions and that she was deserving of some blame I couldn't let her have it. I had to take my own responsibility here. I caused this, at least partially.

"I don't know what to say…" she admitted once the room was clear. While I had been waiting for her to make some excuse for what I walked in on, I hadn't banked on her saying something I could completely agree with but she did.

"Yeah, me either." I managed to choke out.

"If the two of you won't speak then maybe I should speak for you." Michael interjected, immediately bringing our attention back to the elephant in the room. Well, annoying angel anyway.

"You want to speak for us?" Serenity asked as her eyes went wide with the realization that we were not as alone as she first believed.

"Well it is quite obvious both from your body language, your thoughts and the fact that neither of you is able to actually speak that you may need an interpreter."

"Go ahead Mike. I can use all the help I can get." I answered him, thankful that he was able to sense what was going on with us and wanted to help.

"Why don't you start by telling me just when he became well enough to travel?" Serenity snapped.

"He is not well enough for transport. It is a miracle we made it here in one piece if you must know but he is most persistent as it pertains to you, so here we are."

"Oh…"

"What is happening between the two of you now is what the humans call miscommunication and in order for all of us to move forward appropriately, the two of you need to speak and get on the same page. So let me help you both out."

Michael motioned with his hands, one hand pointing at each bed before he spoke again.

"Ryan, go sit on Serenity's bed, and Serenity, please take your seat back on the bed you just exited off of."

"You want us to sit apart?"

194

"Do you really believe that the two of you given what just happened can be trusted to sit near one another?" Michael shot back, causing Serenity to follow his command and take her seat on the bed with no more argument.

As he turned to me I did as he said and followed suit, making my way over to Serenity's bed and taking a seat. If he wanted to play it this way I was most definitely not going to stop him.

"I want the two of you apart because what you do not seem to realize Serenity is that the darkness inside of Ryan was triggered by what his eyes witnessed and I do not trust him near you or you near him because of it."

She covered her face with her hands and I heard the sigh through the cracks in her fingers. She had no idea what she had done to me and with the realization coming from Michael it was obvious that she was getting the full impact of what her choices had done. I wanted to feel bad for the way she was feeling but I couldn't. I needed her to feel it, the same way I did.

"I know everything that happened when the two of you last spoke and I feel that I need to clear a few things up for the both of you. Ryan was wrong in everything he said. While Heaven does not agree that the two of you should be together we are intrigued by it and we want to study it. A being of light being emotionally attached to one of such darkness is a new experience for all of us. What he did in pushing you away was not right."

"As for what we all just witnessed, Serenity I know the pull between you and your other half. I know how powerful it can be and that once locked in its embrace it is impossible to walk away. It has been that way through each of your shared lifetimes. You have the ability to weaken Lucifer's hold on the boy because of it. While I do not think it is wise that you get into bed with him I do understand where it comes from."

"You're making excuses for what I did. Don't do that Michael; it doesn't seem like your style."

"I do not know what you mean by style but I am not making excuses for your behavior. I am only stating factual information."

"Gabriel…oh never mind."

195

"Yes my brother is the soft hearted one of us. That is no secret but as I said, I am not doing it because I care for you; I simply state the facts as I see them. As for my brother…Gabriel you may make your presence known now."

The room lit up immediately as Gabriel made his appearance in the room causing both Serenity and I to block our eyes from the magnitude of it.

"Why did you let things progress as far as they did brother?" Michael asked, turning toward Gabriel and waiting patiently for his response.

"You all made it very clear that I was to stay out of Serenity's personal affairs. There is nothing more personal at least in my estimation than what was taking place between her and Graham. You also wanted her to get close to him again, which I believe is exactly what she was attempting to do."

"So you see no issue with what just happened in here?"

"Yes of course I do. Do you really believe I wanted Serenity to be doing that especially knowing what resides deep within the boy?"

Michael turned back to Serenity then and leveled her with his gaze. He was not a happy angel and I knew it was only a matter of time before that unhappiness was directed straight at me..

"Serenity you need to speak now. I cannot speak for you and neither can my brother."

"What exactly am I supposed to say Michael? I mean it's not like what you saw happen didn't happen right? It's pretty cut and dry."

"Nothing is ever cut and dry." Michael shot back, immediately making Serenity scoot closer to the wall on the bed and level her eyes to the floor.

"Tell Ryan what's really going on with you Serenity. The things you said you would eventually tell me, I think you need to tell him." Gabriel spoke up, making his way over to where she was sitting and surrounding her with his light, a move that did nothing for the anger bubbling over inside of me. I didn't want him that close to her. No one needed to be that close to her unless it was me.

196

"You want me to talk then both of you need to leave. I know you won't leave entirely because of what's going on with Graham but please give us privacy at least for a few minutes."

"As you wish." Gabriel said beginning to back away from her immediately turning the light to face that of his brothers. "Let's give them time brother."

When we were both sure they were gone, Serenity stood from Emma's bed and slowly took the steps until she reached her own bed, right where I had placed myself. Sitting down gently beside me, making a point of sitting just far enough away so that we didn't touch, she sighed and I knew she was about to speak.

Putting my hand up to stop her, I realized there were some things I needed to say first.

"I think I need to go first."

"Okay…"

"I've gone the last twenty one years not giving a shit what happens to me. What people say or what they do to me, none of it matters. Walking in the room fully prepared to see you, pull you to me and kiss you like you've never been kissed before and finding you with Graham it's the first time I've ever given a damn and I hate it. I want to go back to not feeling because it hurts too much."

"Ry—"

"No, let me finish please. I want to hate you, hell I want to walk from this room and be done with you and all of this insanity but as much as I want to do it, I can't. I can't walk away from you because I'm the reason this is even happening at all."

"I've learned so much in my time with Michael and I'd try explaining it all to you but none of it would make sense. Just know that I know everything now and I'm so sorry. All of this, what's happening to us now is entirely my fault."

"Ryan…"

"You want to deny it but you can't."

It was risky looking at her but given how close she was to me and the need within me to reach out and touch her, I had to do something so I raised my eyes until they locked on to hers and it was then I saw the tears that were spilling out of them.

197

"This…is…not…your fault." She choked out through the sobs as they made their way through her body. I have never wanted to reach out to her more but I knew that I couldn't, at least not yet. I was still too raw.

"I prayed for you Serenity. I may not have known that it was you exactly but I wanted nothing more than someone else to share this life with. My prayer was answered and here you are except you're more than that. You are also the thing that I had to destroy. If I had never made that prayer we wouldn't be sitting here right now."

"You're wrong."

"No, I'm really not. You were supposed to die in that church and I couldn't let you. So I did whatever I could to make sure I could make right everything I turned wrong. We both made it out though and instead of treasuring it for the gift it is, I pushed you away from me because I was afraid of letting you too close. I caused you to get close to Graham again, whether it was what Heaven wanted of you or not. The way I am caused this. What I am."

"So you're going to blame yourself and then in the same breath push me away again even though you believe pushing me away is what put us here now?"

She's wrong. I wasn't pushing her away; I was just doing the exact same thing Michael had done minutes earlier. I was stating facts, ones that I knew that she wouldn't accept but that I had to tell her none the less.

"I am not pushing you away. Shit, this is not coming out right at all!" I yelled, frustrated that no matter how hard I tried I just couldn't say what I needed to say.

"You need to let me speak now and really hear me because I'm pretty sure you're not going to like any of it."

Could I do that? Knowing that she is going to bring up what happened between her and Graham and what it meant to her, could I really sit here and listen to it all knowing it's going to do nothing but turn me inside out?

"I wanted to kiss Graham. Michael can say whatever the hell he wants but I made the choice to do it. The closer we are the more

198

he turns into the Graham I knew when I lived in Green Haven. The more he becomes my very best friend and the first boy I ever really loved. I know that's going to hurt you, me saying that but you need to hear it. Michael was right; I need to tell you everything."

"I don't think I can hear it."

"I won't ever take your choice away Ryan but you need to hear it."

It was up to me now. I could let her finally tell me everything and we could move on from this or I could push away what she felt she had to say and I could get up and leave, distancing myself from her once and for all. As hard a choice as that should have been for me, I knew what I wanted to do immediately.

"Go ahead."

"You weren't the only one that prayed for someone that would understand. I just did mine later. I had Emma and while she understood she would never truly get it. So I prayed and when Graham came into my life, pushing me to find out more about my abilities I thought for sure he was the answer to my prayers. I latched myself on to him the same way he did with me and well it became something a whole lot more than an answered prayer. It was the opposite of what I have with you. I didn't fall in love with him right away, it was something that built over time but when it happened all I could see was my life with him in it. He was the one thing that kept me going."

"When I met you everything changed. Graham at that point had been separated from me, we hadn't spoken in two years and I seriously started to doubt that he had been the answer to my prayers at all. I never allowed myself to deal with the way things happened between us but then there you were and suddenly I didn't have to anymore. The day you told me that you prayed for me, everything changed. It's like it was all clear."

"What was clear?" I interrupted before she could take a breath and continue. I needed to know what she was getting at. While I hated hearing anything that remotely pertained to her soul mate, hearing that meeting me had changed everything for her just made me want to grab on for dear life and never let go.

"Graham really wasn't the answer to my prayers. You were. I do not love easily. In fact I don't love at all. For a really long time I didn't even think it was possible for me but with you it's like I was hit by a Mac truck. You ran me over. I grabbed so tightly onto the way that I felt when I was with you that when Gabriel told me that Graham was my soul mate I didn't believe him. In my mind and in my heart he couldn't be because that spot was already taken by you."

"You thought I was your soul mate?"

"Yeah of course I did. We were so alike; it's almost like we were each halves of the same whole. It was quick and it was unexpected but what I felt for you was very real. It is very real, at least to me."

She felt everything the exact way I did. I knew that she cared for me, I felt it every single time we were together, the pull between us undeniable but in all the time that had passed since we met I'd never heard her explain to me exactly what she feels. I could feel the anger inside of me beginning to break with her words and the pure honesty that flowed through them.

"Unfortunately I never get anything given to me in life that doesn't come with something attached. That's where Graham comes in. As much as I want to deny it even now, he is my soul mate. He is the one that my heart calls to when we're together and just like Michael said, it's almost impossible to break away from once it's started. So yeah, I kissed him. I let him go further with me than any other guy before because I thought the closer we got the more I could save him."

If this had been any other girl saying the words to me I would have laughed in her face but with Serenity I couldn't. If she said that is what she was doing in kissing him then I believe her. I may not have the most experience with relationships or with girls in general given how closed off I made myself but I knew none of what she is telling me is a line. She wasn't saying any of this to get me to forgive her. She was telling me because I needed to know.

"Do you love him?"

It was a risky question but I had to prepare myself. I needed to know if fighting for what I wanted was the right move.

"Yes I do."

"What about me?"

I was all in now. All the cards were on the table and I had to live with the hand I'm dealt even if it is one I couldn't win. There's no going back now.

"I don't know if there are words for you."

The gravity of her statement wasn't lost on me. She hadn't denied feeling something for me; she'd said that what she felt there are no words for. It should have made me happy but I needed the words, even if they weren't the right ones. It was the only thing that could make any of this right again.

"Try Serenity. Tell me what you feel for me so I know if I can keep fighting."

CHAPTER TWENTY EIGHT

Serenity

There isn't much I know anymore.

Eight months ago my entire life was turned upside down and every single day since has been a struggle to regain the control I had and taken for granted. Where I spent the majority of my life alone aside from Emma and then Graham now it seemed as if I had more people than I could count and I longed for the past again.

There are parts that I wouldn't change, like meeting Ryan. Even though meeting him had only added more turmoil to my already upside down life I wouldn't give it up for anything. Where Emma and Graham had each played a part in getting me to this point Ryan is the person I continued to fight for.

Heaven still believes that I have a much bigger purpose in the world but I still remain convinced I have already experienced it. Saving Ryan was the right thing and the very thing I know I was meant to do. He was meant to realize the light within him and choose his own path. No one should have to live without a choice and I had given Ryan his choice back.

I owe him the words he wants to hear but when I say that there just aren't any it's not a lie. What I feel for him defies the usage of words. It's an all-encompassing feeling that no matter where I am in the world, who I'm with or what I'm doing, he is with me. Even in the moment with Graham while I may have lost myself I hadn't entirely lost sight of him.

"I need to stop fighting it don't I? The bond the two of you share. I mean I'll never be the one you choose in the end."

His belief that he isn't good enough is ripping me apart. He might want to hear words but he didn't seem to get that the words would never be enough.

"What I feel for you has nothing to do with the soul mate bond Ryan."

"It has everything to do with it. Gabriel has a bond with you and he can't even break through what's going on between you and Graham. I can only imagine what he felt seeing the two of you the way you were."

He was right. Gabriel did share a bond with me, one that would not take effect until my time on Earth is done which according to Michael wasn't for a very long time. Though with what was happening that long life may be cut short faster than any of us realized.

I don't understand the bond Gabriel says we share but I don't think I'm meant to at least not yet. What I've been told from the start applies here. Nothing happens until it's the right time and right now it is just not that time, a fact that I believe Gabriel is beginning to understand no matter how much it may hurt him.

"You want me to say a bunch of words in hopes that in saying them it will make everything better Ry but it won't make a damn thing better. It won't erase what you walked in on. It won't make the hurt go away."

"Maybe not, but at least I know if this is worth fighting for."

"You don't already know that?"

The pained expression on his face told me that he didn't realized the magnitude of his words. It was like we were in Heaven all over again and he was giving up on us without a fight.

He was choosing the cowards way out although this time it made a lot more sense. He doubted us because I had given him a reason to.

"I want to fight for us Serenity but I need to know if fighting is what you want me to do. If you're in love with Graham and the bond between you is so strong that you don't think you can go against it, I need to know."

"Graham was my first love and yes we're bonded but I still have the power to choose my own path."

"If what I walked in on is any indication then I'm pretty sure what path it is you're choosing."

I deserved that.

"You want to sit here and assume things about me then fine, I'll do the same. When we were in Heaven, instead of just being

203

with me after what happened with Michael you decided to hide what you were thinking and feeling and push me away. In doing what you did one can only assume you wanted to get as far away from me as you could."

"You'd be wrong."

"Yeah I would be and so are you."

I watched as he turned his eyes away from me finally and began biting on his lip rings almost as if he wanted to say more but was holding his tongue. I knew what Michael warned me about but I didn't care. If he was trying to supress the demon side then he was just hiding a part of himself from me and I wasn't going to accept it.

"Just say whatever you want to say Ryan."

"I want you to say you love me alright? I want you to look me in the eye and tell me I didn't fuck this entire thing up by pushing you away and that this is still something you want to fight for. I want the last words you said to me before tonight to be true."

"What do you think I've been trying to tell you the entire time?"

"Honestly Ser, I have no idea what you're trying to say because you're not saying much of anything."

Did he really believe that? With everything I said to him about the way that I felt could he really believe that I wasn't saying anything at all?

"You want the truth?"

"That's all I ever want."

"I wish everything was different. I wish that I was just a regular girl with regular issues and that none of this other stuff was real. I wish I didn't hear the voices because then maybe my Dad never would have split the way he did. I wish I had never met Gabriel and learned about my destiny. I don't want to have a soul mate. I don't want any of it."

"You don't want...any of it?" he asked, his voice finally lowering and his eyes looking up into mine again, the sadness pouring through as he did.

"You're hearing only what you want to hear Ry. Think about what I just said."

I could tell he was having a hard time figuring out what he needed to hear. That in everything I said I had never once mentioned him and what he brought to my life even though most of it in the very beginning had been dark. I needed him to be able to see it because he needed to realize that while he may blame himself I didn't and that nothing about the way I felt for him had changed. Not one single thing, even after kissing Graham.

"You are what's missing Ryan. I don't regret you. I regret the parts of me that surround you but I could never in a million years regret you."

Realization dawned in his eyes and they immediately began to brighten which calmed my racing heart. I was finally starting to break though. Now I just had to make him understand something I wasn't entirely sure I understood myself.

Graham.

"What happened with Graham wasn't soul mate related at least not entirely. It wasn't even Lucifer related. I didn't want to kiss him in order to get close to him although I do admit that the thought did cross my mind. That's where Michael gets it wrong. I did it because I wanted to forget. I knew what would happen the minute I kissed him, I've experienced the same thing before and I know it well which is exactly why I did it."

"I don't get it."

"I'm not even sure I get it but I know it's true."

"Why did you do it?"

"To forget you."

"I still don't get it."

"Before it happened he asked about you. Where you were, he wanted to know and I wasn't sure which Graham was asking though I thought it was the Graham that I knew and loved. I went to Gabriel with it and he told me I was right. So I told him you were gone."

"Is that what you wanted? Did you want me gone?"

"No. He asked me if you were gone for good or just for now and I wanted to tell him what I really felt but I couldn't because I wasn't sure it was the truth. So I told him that you were gone for good."

I watched as my words sunk in and prepared myself for the hurt he is sure to unleash on me the minute it happened. When no response came I continued.

"If I told him that I believed you weren't gone forever then I would have been lying to him because as much as I wanted to block it out I had no idea what was going to happen with you. So I told him what I believed to be the truth. You were gone for good. I knew what would happen after that and I wanted it to happen. I needed it Ry."

"But why did you need it to happen?"

"Because if he kissed me I knew what my reaction would be and I'd finally be able to forget you which is the only thing I've been trying to do ever since I got back down here. Gabriel has seen it though he hasn't pushed. Emma for all she actually knows has seen it. It's impossible to hide so I just wanted to forget."

"So you kissed Graham in order to get past me?"

"Yes. It's what you wanted me to do isn't it? Or at least what you believed when you told me that we weren't meant to be together."

"I never wanted you to forget me Serenity. Jesus I was a stupid coward that believed in something that wasn't right but I never wanted you to leave."

There it is. What I needed him to tell me that day in Heaven before I left with Michael but the one thing he had been unable to give me. What he really felt instead of what he thought was right.

"Michael was right you know."

"About what?" I asked, unsure of what he's getting at and what Michael has to do with anything that is happening between us now.

"We do always choose to sacrifice ourselves."

"He said that?"

"Yeah and a whole lot of other stuff I can't really remember right now but he was right about that. I sacrificed what I was really feeling in order to get you to do what Heaven needed you to do and because of that you sacrificed what you felt in order to give me what you thought I wanted."

"What do you want Ryan?"

206

"Well I'd really like my memory of the last few hours wiped clean." He answered, his lips rising slightly into a smirk.

"I want that too…" I whispered not letting the fact that he was attempting to be funny win out over the reality of the situation. I did want his memory of what happened with Graham wiped. I didn't want him to see that every time he closed his eyes. It was bad enough that I'd done it to begin with.

"Ser, look at me."

I hadn't even realized that my eyes weren't locked on his but the minute he spoke I raised them up until they were again trained on his, the cloudy blue with the black tinge staring straight through me.

"I just want you. I know I should probably want more than that seeing as I've being given a second chance with my life but all I want is you."

"What if you deserve better than me?"

"There is no one that could be better than you. You are imperfectly perfect."

Imperfectly perfect.

Before I could wrap my mind around his words and how they made me feel he spoke again. "It's your turn pretty girl. What do you want?"

I knew without a shadow of a doubt what I wanted.

"I want to save Graham." I stated speaking again before he could take it the wrong way. "But I don't want to do it alone. Not anymore. I need you."

"You need me to help you save Graham?"

"No Ryan. I don't just need you to help with Graham. I need you period. If you're with me then I know I can do this. I can do anything. I can save him and end Lucifer the way that we need to."

He moved across the bed toward me then and pulled me into his arms, running his fingers down the length of my hair with one hand while locking his fingers in mine with the other.

"I'm right here. You've got me…and Serenity?"

"Yeah?" I asked as I lifted my head and again allowed my eyes to meet his.

"I'm never leaving you again."

207

CHAPTER TWENTY NINE

Gabriel

An angel is seen as flawless, perfectly made in God's image, held in the highest regard as a warrior in the fight against evil. I always felt that depiction suited Michael perfectly. He was everything that Father had hoped for when we had been created. I never knew where I fit in terms of the design but the more time I spend here on Earth I'm beginning to learn I may not be part of the design at all.

I am flawed, the worst kind of angel for Heaven to put their faith in. I feel things that the other angels are unable to feel, I stepped into situations that I wasn't permitted to and I seem to want to put everything else in front of the overall objective in whatever task I am given.

One had to look no further than my handling of the Serenity situation. Where I should have remained steadfast in following the rules and making sure that what needed to take place did, I had not. I had done everything but. I put Serenity in jeopardy by going along with things I knew would only turn out badly and allowing the way I felt about her to blind me to the reality we all faced around us.

Where Graham could have been out from under Lucifer's control by now, he was not. I had failed in following through with my original plan. Figuring out what my brother had in mind was supposed to be my main objective, first only to putting an end to it once it had been realized. Instead I followed Serenity blindly, all in an effort to keep her safe and as close to me as I could manage and now I had nothing to show for it.

We were no closer to finding out his end game then we had been in the beginning. It didn't sit right with me and made me realize even more that I just wasn't cut out for the things Father needed of me.

"Gabriel, you need to heed Father's advice."

"What advice would that be?"

"You cannot let the seed of doubt which has been planted inside of you win."

"Then show me how to do that brother and I will, because right now all I am doing is going over the facts and they all point to exactly what you all want me to deny."

"You believe yourself unworthy of your place in Heaven because of everything that happened with Serenity but you are false."

"It started even before the time with Serenity."

"I am aware of that brother but you must realize one simple thing. You are not Lucifer. You did not choose to go against Father in such a dark and horrible way. You did not continue fighting even when you had been told to stop. You were not cast out. He was."

"It could have easily been me."

"No Gabriel it couldn't have been you. You are different than the rest of us because Father made you that way. He is the one that gave you the heart and allowed you to use it. You care; you feel because that is what he wanted you to do. You could never be Lucifer."

What is he talking about? Father had made all of us at the same time. We were all made in his likeness, in the very same way. There was no difference between us unless we changed it ourselves.

"You are wrong brother. Each one of us is different. I enjoy being the one closest to Father, not because I plan to take his place but because standing beside him gives me everything I need. I want to learn from him. Raphael never leaves Heaven because he believes that spending any real amount of time on Earth will turn him human, the very thing he is most afraid of. Uriel is locked up so tightly with his Beloved that he wouldn't know his ass was on fire until it was already burned off but most of all there is you."

I had never heard Michael speak the way he is and it is taking a little bit of getting used to. Where we all seemed to sound and act very refined he was doing anything but now. Maybe all the time on the planet was finally wearing off on him.

"What about me?"

"You are the one meant for Earth. You are the kind, compassionate, loving and most accepting of all of us. You see Earth and your time here as some sort of punishment for all of your failures but the reality of the situation is, you are right where you are meant to be. No one could handle the humans the way in which you do."

"Lucifer could."

"If that is true do you really think that what is happening to Graham would be happening? All Lucifer knows is how to make things go his way. That is all he has ever been about. He wants nothing more than his own way. It is exactly how it appears. He is much like a human child that isn't getting the toys he wants. You are nothing like him."

"Why are you saying all of this Michael?"

"I am saying this because it is time that you saw your true worth. You have spent the last six human months doing nothing but throwing yourself a gigantic pity party and the time has come for that to end Gabriel. You need to embrace the parts of you that you see as weaknesses because they are your greatest strengths. If you are unwilling to listen to me then you need to speak to Father because he will tell you the truth."

"How can my feelings for Serenity and everything that has happened since be a strength Michael? It has done nothing but cause pain. There is no strength in pain."

"There is nothing but strength in pain Gabriel and you better than anyone know the truth of that statement. When has your charge been at her strongest?"

Of course he would give me the right example so that I am unable to deny it. Serenity was the perfect example of strength in sadness and pain. She had faced my fallen brother in the midst of it.

"It still does not change the facts Michael. Maybe you're correct in what you say but how does that help us now? We are no closer to knowing what his end game is then when we began."

"That is where you are wrong brother. We know more now than ever before. We know he has chosen Graham as his vessel in

210

an effort to bring Serenity to her knees. In doing that he knows she will bring the walls of Heaven down around her. It is only a matter of time before he makes his intentions known."

"When he does make his intentions known how are we going to be able to formulate a plan to save Graham? It is not just defeating Lucifer anymore; it is doing that and still managing to get the vessel out alive."

"I am aware of that and you already know the answer, you are just unwilling to accept it."

I did know the answer. The only way we would be able to save Graham was through Serenity. The bond between them is the only way this could end any other way then tragically. I know she is aware of it as well, which had been her intent in getting close to him from the start but Michael is right, I couldn't accept it.

"He is going to come to her especially now given that the other person he wants to see dead has returned. With Ryan by her side he will come and he will give her a choice. What that choice will be I am unsure but it will be up to her from that point on what happens next. She wants to save Graham so she will do whatever it takes to reach that end result."

I knew that to be true. She would go to her grave in order to save Graham from the fate that she faced only a few short months before. Another thing I could not accept and let happen. She is meant for more than just a casual sacrifice and this time I had to make sure I remembered that.

"You would allow her to sacrifice herself for Graham knowing that his is the lesser of the two lives between them."

"No life involved in this is more important than another. We are all equally important but if her choice is to sacrifice herself in order to save Graham then we cannot stand in her way. We can only support her and hopefully end it before it gets to that point."

"Like we did the last time?"

"You look at what happened that night as a failure but it was a victory brother. We saved both Ryan and Serenity and in the process we took down our brother. We may not have ended his destructive path the way we intended but we did make him take a

large moment of pause in between which is better than not doing anything at all."

I want to believe in him so badly. I want to put aside everything I feel but it is difficult. I am limited in the amount of help I am able to give in battle and that very fact could mean life and death for everyone involved.

"It is time you were given the truth Gabriel."

"What do you mean?"

"Your powers, you never lost them. Father would never have stripped you of them knowing that you were only doing exactly what you had been made to do. As I told you, you were created to be exactly what you are, punishing you for that would serve no one."

There was no way I hadn't been stripped. I had been there when Father did it. He had taken my light; I witnessed it with my own eyes. Michael wasn't making any sense.

"You have spent forever in the arms of our Father and you have not realized that he can manipulate a situation and make it appear any way he wishes? Gabriel you really are too trusting." Michael said laughing, a sound I hadn't heard from him in as long as I could remember. As happy as I was to hear it now I hated that it was at my expense.

"Father hoped that you would realize everything on your own but that hasn't occurred so he's left it up to me to put you on the right path. You are still very much the same angel you have always been. You just need to believe in yourself."

I did need to believe in myself but not because of anything that Michael said. I needed to because in not accepting it, I was causing more damage to every situation I touched then I should be. If I am still the same angel I had been before I met Serenity Richards then I needed to embrace that and put what I believed to be my failures in the past.

Michael is right, that is the only way we are going to make it out of this alive.

Graham

212

I don't understand what is going on with me. It has been well over two hours since I left Serenity's room and I could still remember everything that had taken place between us. He hadn't followed through with any of this threats and he hadn't taken me over.

Something about this didn't feel right. He should have successfully beaten me down and overtaken me by now. Just what was he playing at?

Having the ability to think about everything that happened since I'd gone to her room is doing me in. I could still smell the vanilla scent of her hair as if she's still underneath my body now. I could still feel the way her lips felt pressed against mine. The way her tongue tangled itself in my own so urgently that one taste wasn't enough.

The guttural sounds from her throat the deeper I kissed her were enough to cause my body to react. Thinking of her like this was wrong; she was a woman that is loved by another man. Not just any other man either, a man that she loves just as deeply back. I couldn't allow my body to react to what happened between us.

It's the first time in a long time that I didn't want to be me anymore. I wanted him to take me so that I could forget all of it. As much as I love Serenity what I had done with her had not been the way I wanted our time together to be, soul mate bond or not. I wanted her completely, not just partially the way I had taken her now.

I knew she'd been lying to me when she said that Ryan was gone for good but it wasn't because of the words. It had just been something I felt deep inside. Given everything that I remembered of Ryan before Lucifer tortured me there is no way he would have just gotten up and walked away from her. Even knowing it I still pushed forward and taken what I wanted from her.

I really am no better than the dark angel buried deep inside of me. The light that Gabriel said I had was obviously burnt out because I had known the real truth behind her words and just easily disregarded them. I let myself get carried away with her knowing that in the end I still wouldn't have her the way I wanted.

It was only made worse by the way I acted with Emma. If Serenity had not come home when she did I couldn't guarantee I wouldn't have taken what I wanted from her as well. None of this sat well with me. I am becoming the very thing I hated most in the world and I was powerless to stop it because at any given moment he could come back and I'd be lost again. I could never make up for the things I had done, no matter how badly I wanted too.

I was hopeless.

You played your part perfectly Graham. It went more smoothly then I could have ever imagined.

"What the hell is that supposed to mean?"

Don't you see? Serenity will do anything to save you now. That move in her bedroom was perfection. It couldn't have gone any better if I had done it myself.

What move was he talking about? He wasn't making any sense.

It's time that you knew the truth Graham.

It occurred to me that when he usually came to me everything started becoming hazy as the memories of things I had done began to slip away, which was not happening now. Whatever he hadn't said had something to do with what's happening to me now.

I no longer need to control you through hunger and darkness. You have embraced the darkness all on your own in taking of Serenity the way that you did. There is no greater sin even when the two of you share the bond that you do, than that of coveting another man's wife. As I said to you earlier you did the one thing I needed without even being prompted.

His goal the entire time had been to get me to finally give in to the bond between us?

Yes Graham. The only way I could ever damage Ryan in the way he deserves is through Serenity and the only way I could get to her was through you. A plan that worked out more beautifully then I could have ever imagined. You played your part perfectly my son.

"I am not your son you son of a bitch."

No you are right. You could never be a son of mine as the pesky light within you just doesn't seem to know when to die.

214

Which is where the blood came in handy, that kept you docile and under my control just enough to take the next step.

"Well since you got what you wanted you must be done with me now right?"

That is where you are wrong. You are still needed but no longer in the way that I used you thus far. Your use now is simple. You are a pawn.

He was going to use me against Serenity. He is going to use the bond between us to get her to come to him. I knew it as easily as I knew my own name now that he was no longer controlling my mind. I couldn't let this happen.

You will have no other choice but let it take place Graham. You see after this conversation you will no longer exist. I will take complete control of your body and mind, visit Serenity and inform of her of her choices. She only has one if she wishes to save what is left of your pathetic existence.

"You want to kill her."

One would think that is exactly what I want but my interests have changed in my time on the planet. I no longer wish the girl dead. I want what I did originally. I want to own her and with you as the bait she will give me what I want or she will risk losing you forever.

"You're putting a lot of faith in her choosing to save me instead of herself."

You even saying that tells me that you do not know the same Serenity that I do. She will always choose you over herself. Just the way I want her to.

I couldn't let her do this. I knew I wasn't going to get another chance to warn her and that she would walk into this blind which tore me up inside. She had no real idea what's coming for her and what she was going to have to do in order to make it stop. He might as well kill me because if Serenity ended up choosing to give herself up to save me I might as well be dead anyway.

There would be nothing else left to live for.

215

CHAPTER THIRTY

Ryan

The last time I'd been in this room, I'd been here to tell her everything I knew about her, things I wasn't permitted to speak of but did anyway. Compelled by the feelings I was beginning to feel for her I knew I couldn't waste another moment of her time or mine living in secret.

Now just a little over six months later I'm here again and this time I have the girl in my arms, lying comfortably on her bed, a dire situation on the horizon but not a care in the world because my entire heart, soul and very being were wrapped up in her light. The only place I ever wanted to be.

From the moment I met her there hadn't been a time where it had been just us. Even when we spent time together on the quad having the picnic and just talking under the tree there had always been more going on underneath, at least for me. She believed herself to be faulty, that she is just a broken girl trying to make her way in the world but I knew better. I knew what she was and I'd been there to exploit it.

I seemed to be falling in love with her with each passing moment we spent together but it had been tainted by what I'd been sent there to do. I didn't have that problem now.

I have never been this close with a girl. Sure I had been around girls in my lifetime, a lot of them but I had never taken this step with any of them. Holding a girl had been the furthest thing from my mind. I didn't think I deserved it. Serenity had been my first kiss, she had been my first everything and I liked it that way. I wanted her to be the first and last one I experienced the rest of my life with.

"What are you thinking about?" she asked, meeting my eyes unable to hold back a smile. I could definitely get used to this even though I didn't have the slightest clue what to do next.

I didn't want to admit it but I was worried that my lack of experience would become a problem for her. I know the only experience she ever had before me had been Graham and it wasn't all that much but it still didn't lessen my fear. Most guys even when they didn't know what they were doing still managed to make the moves and have it appear as if they did but I wasn't most guys.

I have no game whatsoever. With the way she is looking up at me now though, her hazel eyes shining I knew she would accept it. She already accepted far more in the short time she'd known me, so my lack of experience would just be another part of me that she would grow to love. It didn't erase the worry though. I really wanted to be the perfect guy for her and not one that fumbled around in the dark.

"You really don't want to know."

She smiled again as she shook her head. "I wouldn't have asked if I didn't want to know Ry."

"I'm just thinking about us."

"What about us?"

Could I really tell her that the thoughts I'm having aren't exactly pure? That with the way she is resting across my body, I'm craving even more. Would she understand it?

"What comes next I guess."

She made a move to sit up and I immediately wrapped my arms even tighter around her. I didn't want to break the contact we shared. I wanted her wrapped around my body this way forever. I couldn't let her sit up and pull away.

"Well we've already done more than most people our age so I'm not exactly sure what you mean by what comes next. I already married you McGregor, I mean what more could you want?" she answered with a laugh as she rested her head back on my chest, bringing a shot of peace directly into my heart. Yes this is definitely where she belongs.

"Please Richards; it's more like I married you. I couldn't handle the begging anymore."

"Oh you're gonna pay for that one." She said as she began running her fingers across my stomach, causing me to squirm to

217

break free. Damn girl had to resort to tickling. The one thing I couldn't handle. Did she really know me that well?

"Oh this is perfect, you're ticklish."

"Yes, yes I am. Now stop it before I flip you over and find out if you are too."

Her hands immediately froze in place on my stomach and I couldn't help but laugh. I got my answer without even having to try, I could definitely get used to this.

She rested her hand across my stomach and even though it was an innocent move the heat wave it caused was anything but. Just when I thought she couldn't affect me in any other ways she had to go and find another one.

"I'm sorry, I won't tickle you anymore."

"Glad to hear it but I'm sorry I can't say the same." Laughing I moved quick flipping her over and before she knew it I had her pinned underneath me.

Taking one of my hands I began running my curled fingers across her stomach and she immediately began to fidget underneath me. What I thought had been a move that would only affect her had the opposite effect. The minute she began to squirm given my close proximity to her body, I felt every bit of it which brought me right back to my inexperience again.

She must have seen my face freeze because she immediately began trying to slide herself up onto the bed.

"You don't have to move Ser..."

"That's not what your face is telling me right now."

Leaning down until our bodies were completely connected again I kissed her nose before making my way down to her lips and kissing her ever so softly.

"My face looks the way it does because of the way being this close makes me feel. Not because you did something wrong. It's about what you're doing right."

Her eyed widened with the realization of what I was trying to tell her and I couldn't help but smile. All the worry I had about my inexperience with girls was erased with the look on her face. I wasn't alone in this.

It wasn't as common as you think finding two twenty year old virgins especially on a campus where sex seemed to be a rite of passage but here we were and neither one of knew what to say or do next. If it had been anyone else that was here with me, I would have just taken myself out of the situation altogether but with Serenity, the last thing I wanted to do is break away from her.

"Oh…okay…so…umm."

"I made you speechless already pretty girl? Man, I was planning on pulling out my best moves but if you're already this far gone, it looks like I don't need to."

Smacking me on the arm but smiling she took me by surprise when she leaned up, her eyes wide open, staring into mine and placed her lips to mine. I wasn't entirely sure what she was trying to tell me but I definitely wanted to know more.

Breaking away, her voice barely audible she whispered words that just shot straight into my heart

"You don't have moves McGregor."

What came next happened so fast that it's almost a blur but the minute the words fell from her lips I knew exactly what I wanted to do. I couldn't fear it anymore; I just had to do it before the chance passed me by.

Placing my hands on her sides I slid her down until she was completely flat on her back and moving to the side I slid down beside her placing my one hand behind her head and the other on her stomach, leaning in as close as I could putting my lips to hers. As she parted her lips to allow me entrance I grabbed her bottom lip between my teeth and I began to suck.

Her body shifted next to mine and before I knew it she wrapped her arm around my back and pulled me until I was completely on top of her. She began kissing me hungrily, our lips crashing like waves into each other, one taste turning into more until I began to lose count. As I felt her tongue enter my mouth I met it with my own and lost myself in the feel of her body below me, her kisses as close to heaven as I had ever experienced.

I ran my hand across her stomach hoping that this time it would spark a different reaction in her, a reaction I got almost instantly as she placed her hand above mine and slid it further up under her shirt.

Both of us were dangerously close to crossing a line, one that we had never crossed before and the realization hit me like a ton of bricks. Breaking my lips away from hers, desperate for air I looked back down at her and saw the same desire I felt evident in her eyes.

"Are...you...sure?" I whispered, drawing each word out.

"I'm sure Ryan, I want this with you."

I didn't need to hear anymore. All of the fears I had earlier about reaching this moment and not being what she needed me to be faded away as I let my eyes travel over every inch of her body. I love this woman more than life itself and there is nothing, on the outside or even in my head that was going to stop me from showing her in every way possible just how much.

Serenity

I'm not sure what you're supposed to feel after having sex for the first time but I'm pretty sure the gravity of what I feel is much more than an average girl.

Sex has never interested me. In high school it was so bad that everywhere you went girls were whispering about it. Who they did it with, how many times, how it felt the first time and just about every other possible thing you could think of in relation to the act itself. It was nauseating really. I really didn't understand the hype, at least I didn't before.

What Ryan and I did was so much more than just sex. Even the word making love doesn't do it justice. Where we had been close before, after what we had just been through we were inseparable. What I experienced with him I would never want with another living being as long as I lived. He had been gentle and loving and I couldn't have asked for more. The concern in his eyes when he pushed himself inside me the first time would be with me forever.

When we finished talking earlier I never expected this to be where we ended up. If all I am ever able to have is his arms around me that would have been enough. I didn't need or want anything more. It's not that I didn't want to do this with him but it isn't something I would die from if I didn't experience.

I am more than a little thankful that Emma remained true to her word and hasn't come back to the room sooner. While we shared everything this is something I want to keep just between me and Ryan. Seeing as I'm having a hard time even finding the words to describe how it makes me feel, the last thing I want to do is break it down for my very over eager best friend.

"Where did you go pretty girl? I can feel you here with me but you're so quiet it's like you're a million miles away."

God I could get used to way he sounded right now. I heard him in what felt like a million different ways during our time together but never like this. He was relaxed to the point where his voice sounded like a slow song and it's definitely one that I would love repeating.

"I'm here with you, there's nowhere else I wanna be."

"Okay then what you thinking about?"

"This, us, what happens next."

He lifted his head and my heart melted at the sight of the smile that covered his face.

"Wasn't that my line from earlier?"

"It might have been." I said giggling. "It doesn't make it any less true though."

"What about us exactly? You're not having second thoughts about what we did are you?"

"You're joking right?"

He lowered his head back to the bed and I knew he wasn't joking. For whatever reason he really did believe I would regret this.

"Are you regretting it?"

"Serenity when it comes to you and me I don't regret a single thing."

I wanted to believe that was a lie given he had to regret walking in on what he did earlier but I wasn't about to call him on it. We were finally in a good place; the last thing I'm going to do is screw it up.

"I actually do regret something but it isn't what we did "

"What do you regret?" he asked the cracking in his voice speaking volumes to what was now running around his mind.

"Not praying for you sooner."

He smiled and I knew that whatever he had been worried about had been pushed away with the words I'd spoken. This was the way I always wanted him to be, smiling and calm. He deserved nothing less than a life full of this. I only hope I will be the one to give it to him.

"Okay smartass you wanna tell me what you were thinking about earlier?"

"Just how much I love you and how perfect this is."

"I did promise you an audience free experience didn't I?" he asked laughing.

"You remembered!"

Where there was nothing funny about the experience we'd been through when it happened, that was the one bright spot through it all. We still somehow managed to keep our sense of humor which made it the only good memory we could take from everything we endured.

"I remember everything Serenity. There's so much I don't want to but that is definitely not part of it."

"Well thank you for delivering on your promise."

"Oh the pleasure was all mine believe me." He said with a grin which only made the smile on my face even bigger.

There is something to be said for the comfortable silences that seem to appear when you surrounded yourself with the people that you love. Where this kind of silence would have normally been awkward for me, I found it to be the complete opposite with Ryan. Just listening to his heart beat steadily in his chest as I laid with him in my bed, the sound of his breathing matching my own was the most comfortable feeling in the world.

I've always felt safe with him but now it was so much more than that. It's almost as if the rest of the world doesn't exist and it's just the two of us. Nothing would ever be able to touch it, or anything that we'd said and done tonight. It was perfect.

"You're doing it again pretty girl."

"I could easily say the same thing about you."

222

"You could but then I would just tell you that I was enjoying the moment."

"Well that's all I was doing too, at least this time." I answered as he reached over and kissed the top of my head, sending another load of butterflies fluttering through my body. I could definitely get used to the way my body responded to this man. It was like every nerve ending in my body is alive.

"I love you Serenity…"

I let the words sink in as he said them and allowed myself to finally melt inside. It took everything in me not to pinch myself to make sure this wasn't a dream. Given everything that we had both been through it just seemed out of this world for us to be here now, wrapped up in each other without a care in the world. Life for us could never just be this easy.

"I love you too Ryan, more then you'll ever truly know."

As he placed another kiss on my head I felt his eyes on me and instantly looked up to meet them. He was right about the pull between us, there was no controlling it. It really did own us.

"I know."

I could have easily argued that he had no clue but there's something about the way he said it that makes me believe that he does. He knew everything I was feeling because he felt it just as strongly. We were more than just husband and wife or the best of friends. We have something that even the soul mate bond with Graham can't touch.

We were living proof that no prayer ever goes unanswered.

CHAPTER THIRTY ONE

Gabriel

While it had only been a couple of weeks since I had seen him, it was still strange to be standing here before him now. Father called both Michael and I home the minute he got wind of Ryan leaving. It appeared that in his haste to do what Ryan wanted Michael hadn't felt the need to inform him.

I didn't want to find it amusing but it was impossible not to. Michael freely admitted to me what his place in Heaven really was and the very thing that he wanted to do is exactly what he had gone against in order to give Ryan what he wanted. No matter what way I looked it, it was obvious that the more time Michael spent in my company the more he seemed to mirror me.

"My sons, we have been able to ascertain what Lucifer's next move is and I believe that in order to move forward the both of you need to be made aware."

I wanted to ask him how he was able to find out but I knew that it would be a pointless endeavor.

"Michael before he chose to go against what he had been told informed me of what he learned from his time with the half demon. It would appear that your fallen brother has been using angelic power for dark purposes."

Now I was confused. If Lucifer is using power that we have full access to here at home than how he has he been able to get ahead of us every step of the way?

"What power exactly?"

"Long before I created you and your brothers to be warriors I was the only one with these powers. I still to this day remain the only one that can contain the power he now uses. How he managed to obtain the power I have not been able to ascertain and I fear I may never be able to but now that we know the power is angelic, only a true angel can destroy it."

"So how do we do that Father?"

224

"You cannot be the one to do it Michael."

Michael looked back and forth between me and our Father, obviously not understanding how an archangel of his caliber is unable to end Lucifer's reign of terror which only made me question what was going on even more. There was power before we were created, that's something I had already known but the magnitude of that power and our inability to be the ones to end its usage is beyond my comprehension. Were we not true angels?

"You are Archangels not true angels. I know that only creates more questions, all of which I will answer when the time is right but for now just know that you cannot be the ones to stop this."

"Then who can?" I asked, finally putting the question out there.

He could take his sweet time and tell us everything when he felt like but he wouldn't hold this back now. Lives depended on it, the very lives that he wanted us to protect so carefully.

"He's talking about our little ball of light. Aren't you Father?"

"I am not."

If it isn't Serenity then just who is the one true angel that could end all of this? It was just another time where I wished Father dealt more in black and white then offering only small bits of information. He may be all knowing but he really didn't know as much as he should.

"Gabriel your belief about my abilities is not now nor will it ever be acceptable. I give you the information I feel is most important when it is meant to be given and not a minute sooner."

Biting my tongue to keep from saying something I knew I would regret I looked to Michael for support. If there was any other angel who understood my frustration with Father it was him and he did not disappoint.

"Father you cannot blame him for questioning you. You say that you know Lucifer is using age old power that we have never even seen the likes of yet you won't tell us who the person is that can stop it."

"It is the very half demon that you released from here just a short time ago, against my orders."

Jesus Christ.

225

"Gabriel, I will not warn you again."

"Nice one brother." Michael answered his face breaking out in a grin.

"Michael if you value your position at my side you will cease all efforts at egging him on. It is not the time for this."

Father was right about that. It is most definitely not the time for it because with the bombshell he just dropped into our lap everything is changing and we were going to need the time to adapt before something more tragic happened.

"Ryan is the only person that can stop him? I thought you said it was a true angel? You do realize he is still part demon right?"

"He is only demon because of the sins of his human mother. This was never the path he was meant to take."

If I heard him right he was telling us that Ryan is another Heaven plant, something that would have been good to know over six months ago when he entered into Serenity's life and ours by association. Had he really kept something this important from us the entire time?

Did I even really know my father at all?

"Are you telling me Heaven screwed up?" Michael asked as he put the pieces of everything together.

"That is exactly what I am telling you. When I informed you earlier of a plan that I was putting into motion, this is it. We need to use Ryan. He is the only hope we have of defeating the power that Lucifer now holds."

He wasn't the only option.

"Then we need to get Serenity out of there now. If Ryan is the one that you believe can end this she needs to be pulled out and brought back here immediately."

"I don't normally agree with him but this time I do believe Gabriel is right Father. She is in an extreme amount of danger that she isn't even aware of."

"We will do nothing of the sort. She is integral to making this work. Ryan lives and breathes for her and her alone. If you take her away then you might as well smite him dead where he stands because he will no longer want to fight."

I can't believe what I am hearing. This is not the father I know and believe in. It is not the man I loved. This was a side of him I had never witnessed and a side I wished I had never come home to find.

What he is suggesting is wrong and as all knowing and seeing as he is he had to see it. He couldn't honestly think that keeping Serenity down there given her increasing powers just so that he could have Ryan reach his full potential was right.

"She will remain down there with him and when the time is right we will remove her and Ryan will end this for us at which point he will come home where he belongs."

"What are we supposed to tell her? She will have no problem staying there as long as she believes that she is going to be the one to save Graham but to learn that it is to be the very man the human part of her loves? She will not handle that well at all. It's not right Father."

"You will not tell her, it is as simple as that. When they need to know they will be informed. Until that time comes she is to remain of the belief that she will be the one to save Graham Hudson. Disobey me in this regard and I will make sure that neither one of you uses your powers again."

"I'm sorry Father but I cannot agree to this." Michael spoke up causing me to look up in surprise. This was a side of Michael I had never seen manifested before today and I wasn't quite sure how to take it.

"Then it is a good thing you do not have a say in this. You do as I say or you will be stripped of your powers immediately. Lucifer's reign on the planet has gone on far longer than it ever should have. I plan on finally putting an end to it and neither one of you will stand in my way."

I couldn't stand to listen to any more of this but there is still one question that hadn't been asked and I knew that in order to move forward, I needed to know the answer.

"I will do as you ask Father but there is one thing that I still need to know in order to move forward."

"What is it Gabriel?"

227

"Does Lucifer know that Ryan is the very being that can put an end to him?"

"No he does not and that is exactly why you are not to say anything until the time is right. In order for this to work and for us to take control of the humans back from his darkness he has to remain blissfully unaware. Do I have your word that you will maintain the illusion until it is time?"

I don't want to say yes to this. There is keeping a lie such as Ryan's return from Serenity but keeping something this huge would do nothing but damage her trust and faith in the very light that she had been born into.

"You have my word Father."

As I turned to find out just what Michaels answer would be I noticed an absence where he had been which only filled me with a sense of dread.

I guess I know what side Michael stands on.

His own.

CHAPTER THIRTY TWO

Lucifer

Some would believe that I am all about the shock value with the situations I find myself in and they wouldn't be entirely wrong. The way in which Graham reacted to my news and what came next had been exactly what I had been hoping for. The goodness that resided him despite all of the work I had done to overcome it could not let him consciously go through with the end of my plan.

It was just too bad he didn't have any say in the matter. I rather liked enjoying myself and leaving him to clean up the mess I left behind. He was always meant to be a means to an end and while he assumed that he would be saved in the end they were both going to be in for quite the rude awakening.

I had no plans on letting Graham live once I was done with him. He had served his purpose and there was no further use for him. Once Serenity agreed to be mine and I was able to brand her again I would shed him like dirty laundry. He may still have levels of strength to fight within him but he wouldn't once everything was said and done.

Where every time before had been easy when I needed to control him, even when the hunger had gotten the best of him, this time was different. Call it will to survive or him wanting to warn Serenity of what came for her but he was just not going as willingly as I wanted him too. He had finally done it but it had taken a longer amount of time then I liked.

It was just another reason the boy had to die. I could not let Heaven get their hands on him. He could turn out to be quite the weapon for them and that I was not going to allow.

The time is now upon us. It is time for me to inform Serenity of what she had to do. She wasn't being given a choice, just as she hadn't been given one the last time we had dealings together but I could make her believe she had one. I just knew that the light in her would determine her next move and she would bend willingly if it meant that she could save someone, especially her soul mate.

It is an added bonus realizing that she is inside the room with the other person I want to see destroyed. Ryan McGregor had shown so much promise but is now nothing more than a useless waste of air. He should have died in the church and it was going against all the laws of Heaven and Hell that he hadn't. I needed to rectify that situation but I am not going to do it now. No, I am going to save that pleasure until Serenity gave herself over to me. Not only would she become mine but she would watch the man she loves perish at the same time.

I could hear what sounded like laughter and it concerned me. After what had taken place before I was sure there would be nothing to laugh about between the two of them. It mattered little because once I told her what had to be done; it would only push them further apart. He would want to save her, be unable to and she would make the sacrifice regardless. It is in her DNA. She is meant to be the sacrificial lamb.

Placing my fist on the door and rapping three times in succession I heard silence from the room and began to wonder if my mind had been playing tricks on me. Is it possible that because of the energy needed to control Graham again my other senses had shifted?

"Emma just come in, the doors unlocked."

I was most definitely not the roommate but I wasn't going to turn the invitation down. If she isn't going to guard herself then it served her right that it be me that walked into the room. The girl obviously had no clue who she is really dealing with, even after having her life force drained.

"What the hell are you doing here?" Ryan spoke up, his voice a mix of loathing and true hate. While he had been healed during his stay in Heaven it is apparent that they had not removed the part of him I cared most for. He is still inherently evil. This was definitely going to be fun.

"It's none of your business. I need to speak with Serenity."

"Over my dead body."

"Careful with your words Ryan, you have no idea how easily that can be arranged."

Ignoring my threat as if it didn't even affect him he glared at me before speaking again.

"Did you not do enough to her earlier? You come back for more?"

"I did the right amount of damage earlier. The reaction on your face was well worth what I experienced with your wife. How does it feel knowing your wife desired me Ryan? That she still does?"

"Graham, stop it." Serenity called out immediately putting her body between us, sensing the escalation.

"You see Ryan, she isn't denying it."

"You want a denial?" She shot back at me, her voice seething. "What happened between us was a mistake. It never should have happened."

"I do not believe you. I felt the way your body responded to mine." I said as I bridged the distance between us. Getting as close as I could without touching her I smirked.

"You're delusional man. If that was true wouldn't you be in the room with her instead of me?"

Ryan had a point but one that I could easily talk away. My time on the planet had proved itself a success just in my ability to pick up on the way human's interacted with one another. Debating is now something I could do and win.

"She needed a moment with you of course. With how deeply I care, I want to give her whatever she needs. I've given her enough time now. I'm back and I would very much like to talk to her."

"Then you can say whatever you want with Ryan here."

"I'm afraid I cannot do that."

"Why not?" she shot back, her eyes doing as they have always done and searching me for some kind of sign as to what this was all about. It would appear she is gaining her powers much more quickly now that she has embraced what she truly is. It was a sight to behold.

I could see Ryan out of the corner of my eye and the look of shock leveled on his face was quite distracting. His eyes remained

231

wide and his mouth was now hanging open where moments before it had been tightly closed. He knew what was happening here, there was no doubt in my mind. He knows who I am.

"It's not Graham..." he spit out and I laughed.

Yes he was indeed figuring everything out and it is priceless. He knew that he couldn't do anything to stop whatever came next. He was not in full form anymore. The damage I had done to him in the church had left its mark just the way I intended.

"You would be wise to listen to him Serenity and then give me the moment of time that I need with you." I stated with finality.

This is going to go one of two ways and if the both of them were smart they would do it the easy way. I am not in the mood to end the both of them. Not quite yet anyway.

"No, I don't care what you do to me but he's not leaving the room."

"Serenity, I know you don't want to me leave but I think it would be best if I did. I won't go far; I'll be right outside the door but let's not make this any worse than it already is."

The way the half demon bended to my will is remarkable. Did I still have a hold on him even after all this time? It is definitely something I am intrigued by and would focus more on at another time. For now though I needed time with Serenity. I had a time table to keep and nothing, not even the demon was going to stand in my way.

Watching as he made his way to her and placed a kiss on the top of her head I felt my stomach turn in revulsion. It appeared that even though Graham was no longer with us he is still affected by what is taking place right in front of my eyes.

"No Ry...I don't want you to leave."

"He won't hurt me if I go but I can't say the same if I go against him. Pretty girl trust me."

She nodded her head and he placed his lips to hers at which point I had to turn away. The bond between the vessel and Serenity was being driven crazy with what was taking place and the only way to stop it now was to not witness it.

When I was sure Ryan had taken himself completely from the room I turned to face her again, this time complete with a grin. I finally had what I wanted and I was more than a little eager to move forward.

"So he's gone. What the hell do you want?"

"I thought that was glaringly obvious Serenity. I want you of course."

Ryan

I knew it the minute he spoke. At first he sounded like Graham given what happened between them but it became glaringly obvious quickly that while it was definitely Graham's body he is walking around in, the guy isn't in control of anything anymore.

The last time I had seen Lucifer he had been in a different vessel so my mind didn't want to accept the form he was in now. That guy was gone and now I'm left with facing down the very guy I caught my wife locking lips with.

Not beating the sh:t out of him the moment I realized everything had been hard. He was due a good beating the way I saw it. After what he put me through I wanted nothing more than to be the one to end him. Not only had he taken my very life from me but he had almost done the same to Serenity and while my life might not mean much in the long run, hers did. I would fight for it every chance I got.

I had no idea what he wanted with her and I really didn't want to leave her alone. I promised her I would never leave her again and I was fully prepared to die doing that but I knew that in the end it wouldn't be what she wanted. I had to give in to his demand.

We both knew that what happened between us before he arrived wouldn't last forever. That eventually we would have to come up for air and focus on what was happening around us. Lucifer may have allowed us the moment, same as the angels but he wasn't going to sit dormant forever. Our moment is over and now real life is setting in.

"*Ryan...* "

I knew that voice.

"Gabe, no one is around, why don't you just appear?"

"I will not appear as I do not have the time. I need to find Michael."

"How did you manage to lose your brother? I mean big angel, all bright and shit, it's hard to miss."

"This is not the time for jokes Ryan. Has Michael come to you?"

"No but your other brother has."

"Lucifer has appeared before you?"

It's obvious that Gabriel hadn't been expecting to hear that but whether he wanted to hear it or not he was going to.

"Yeah he's in there with Serenity right now."

"This is not good...not good at all but not entirely unexpected. I knew it was only a matter of time before he put his plan into motion."

"What plan? What do you know that we don't?"

"In regards to him I am afraid I do not know as much as I would like and what I do know is useless. I was hoping to find Michael here so that we could both speak with you and Serenity."

"About what?"

"Something that impacts the both of you greatly. I am not permitted to tell you myself. It would have to come from Michael given that he did not give his acceptance."

Angels and their riddles, it never changed no matter where it happened. I just wanted him to spell it out already.

"Well as you can see Michael isn't here but since your other far more dangerous brother is, do you think you can put whatever it is you can't tell me in the background and help me figure out a way to end him?"

"You are the one that must end him."

"Excuse me?"

"I have said too much. If he has allowed you to wait out here then it means that he is not here to hurt Serenity now. I am going to find Michael but when you learn what his business is please call for me again. I will return right away."

I wanted to respond but I knew it would fall on deaf ears. He was gone and all he left me with was a whole lot of confusion and more riddles I would need to solve before I could figure out what was really going on.

What did he mean by me being the one that ended him? I know how badly I want to be the one to do it but is it possible that I am the only one that could because of my history with him?

For now I needed to do as Gabriel said and focus on Serenity because in order to get answers from Michael I was going to have to give some of my own and the biggest thing I could think of that they would want was exactly what his next move is.

I plan on giving it to them.

CHAPTER THIRTY THREE

Serenity

"The last time you wanted me you tried to kill me. What makes this time any different? Why not just kill me now?"

He laughed and it made my skin crawl. I can't believe I had been stupid enough to actually feel sympathy for him when I thought he died. Whatever they did to heal me in Heaven must have gone to my head because he is definitely still the same lunatic he has always been.

"You misunderstand me Serenity. I will be the first to admit that the plan changed the first time around and that you were more use to me dead but I was wrong."

"You were...wrong?"

"Yes. It is not often I admit that but in your case I was very wrong. I am not here to kill you. That wouldn't have been a fitting end to what is the brightest light in Heaven. I intend to do things differently this time around."

Of course he is going to do things differently. He failed in his attempt to end me so now he was going to try a different tactic and use my soul mate to do it. Well I wasn't about to let that happen.

"Alright, you got my attention. What do you want with me this time?"

"I want you to be mine."

Oh this is too much. "Didn't you want that very thing before? What's so different now?"

"I believe that with what I am proposing that you will be more inclined to say yes to me now."

If I had to say yes to him it meant that he wants me as a vessel, something he is only getting over my dead body because I wasn't about to ever say yes to him, no matter how much he tortured me.

"You misunderstand me again Serenity. I do not want you to be a vessel. I want you to be my equal as was the original plan. I

236

want you to rule Hell beside me and I think when I lay all of my proverbial cards on the table, you will be unable to say no."

"Well then let me spell it out for you now. No."

"Not even if it means saving the life of the very one you are bonded too?"

There it is. The one thing other than Ryan he knew I would be unable to say no to. I knew that when he had taken Graham in the end it was going to come back around to me but I never imagined that he was going to use him as a bargaining chip. I actually figured he would have Graham kill me.

"You know you've got my attention so just spit it out."

"I wish you to join with me as I have said and rule Hell together. Your power alongside of mine would be unstoppable. I do not understand why I deviated away from the original plan to begin with as it was brilliant. You give me what I want and I will release Graham as my vessel."

"So I agree to go to Hell and you give Graham back alive and well? You'll excuse me if I don't believe you'd do anything remotely humane without conditions."

"You believe me to be without compassion Serenity but you would be wrong. I felt you mourn for me and the true way you believe me to be and you would not be wrong. You believe me to be soulless now and that is where you are false. I will give your soul mate over to my brothers just the way he was when I took him provided you agree to my terms."

This is my chance to save Graham. I know what Ryan said about us always sacrificing ourselves but if in the end it meant that Graham could go back to normal and live a productive and happy life then maybe this is the right time for a little sacrifice.

"You already want to say yes to me, I can tell."

"I do and you know why but I can't say yes to this yet. I think you also know the reason why."

"The demon."

"Ryan."

"Fine, you cannot say yes to me because you need to speak to Ry--an." He sneered dragging out the sound of his name and I immediately wanted to reach out and smack him. I didn't care if he

237

was in Graham's body or not, he didn't have to be a douchebag and I had no trouble making him pay for it.

"The anger within you is delicious. It will come in handy during your reign as my princess in Hell."

Okay now that was just gross. I didn't want to be the princess of anything, especially not Hell and his use of the word delicious sent shivers up my spine. It was creepy.

"I will concede to your wishes this once given that I already know what your decision will be in the end but you must make it quick. You have twenty four hours Serenity. Inform the demon and then meet me at the place where it all began."

Green Haven. He wanted me to make my choice and go back to the very place where he had almost taken everything from me before. What is it about that place that kept him coming back for more?

"You do not remember it but you resided in Green Haven on more than one occasion Serenity. It is also where you spent your second lifetime. It is of great significance not only to you but to me as well so it must be where this happens. It will be where everything happens."

"Why is it so special to you?"

"That is a story for another time my princess."

"No actually, it's a story for now if you want me to give you my answer and meet you there tomorrow."

I could tell by the smile on his face that he enjoyed the way I spoke to him but I couldn't understand why. Maybe he liked demanding women, something I didn't even want to focus on just for the sheer gross factor of it.

""When Father cast me out and I fell to the Earth it was in that exact location that I fell. At the time it was not known as Green Haven, that came later but it is of great importance to me which is why it must happen there."

"If it means so much to you, why did you level Graham's house? Isn't that destroying something that you love? If you are as compassionate as you say and you have a soul doesn't what you did go against everything you claim to be?"

"It caused me great agony doing what I did to that location but it had to be done in order to secure the very vessel I walk around in now. Everything I do leads to a much bigger picture."

I wanted to blow him off but he made it impossible when he was being completely honest. I could feel it in him. He's telling me the absolute truth about the way he felt and everything that had occurred there, both for him and for me. I'm beginning to really hate this new ability. Knowing Lucifer as anything other than a cold bastard was not working for me.

"You've stated your case and I've heard everything you've said so you need to leave now. I will see you in twenty four hours with my answer."

I had no idea how I was doing it, keeping my voice level when inside I was freaking out. I saw the end and what I would have to agree to in order to reach it and also what that is going to mean for every single person, angel or otherwise that's involved. I knew that Ryan would not agree to letting me do this but all I could see is the end result.

Graham would finally be free and the world could go back to normal again. Without the threat of an angry fallen angel looming over its head. I could finally do what I had been told I was supposed to do all along.

I could actually save the world.

CHAPTER THIRTY FOUR

Ryan

There is no way in hell she's doing this. No damn way. I would lie down and let him kill me again before I let her give herself over to him.

I am sick of being haunted by Michael's words because they are true. I need to change both of our destinies and stop the constant back and forth sacrifice. I could not let her do this again even though I knew she wouldn't listen to me.

We had to save Graham Hudson some other way that didn't involve Serenity walking straight into the lion's den.

I've been there before. Hell. It's not a walk in the park and Lucifer wanting to take her there and subject her to all that is contained in it, the least of which was the torturing of innocent souls just went to show just how far off the reservation he had gone even in the short time we had been apart.

He may have fallen but he was still an angel and a very powerful one. He had to know that what he was asking of her was not the right thing. That she's meant for better things but his anger had gotten the better of him. Where my demonic side had been born of that very anger, his was pure and it is stronger than any other emotion he might actually be able to feel.

Serenity was strong but even the strongest entities could not survive Hell which is why so many of us wanted to stay topside. It is easier going about our business on Earth then it could ever be doing it from Hell. There were too many ways to get distracted and not in the good way. She is not going to do this, it's settled. We would find another way.

"I know how you feel about this Ryan but what other choice do I have? I need to get Graham seeing as I'm the reason he's going through it at all."

That's another thing that pissed me off. It drove me nuts the way she took the blame for everything when really none of it was her fault. Until eight months ago she believed she was just another human girl and could have easily gone on believing that for the rest of her life if Heaven hadn't seen fit to unleash itself on her.

I played a part in it given that I'm the one that told her about what she really is but I'd only done that because of my feelings and because I knew the angels already made themselves known. While I had no problem laying the blame on myself I still didn't do nearly as much as they had and where were they now?

Conveniently absent. They were off looking for one another because they couldn't even manage their own problems, leaving the final choice to again be in Serenity's hands and by default mine.

"You did not bring this on Graham. Gabriel did when he went to him that first time. I know you care about him Ser but you have to see that he took the steps first. Not you."

"It doesn't change the fact that this is the only option we have."

"There has to be another way. I know what he wants to do with you and I can't let him do it. Bringing you to hell, pretty girl you won't survive it no matter how strong the light is inside of you."

I know the way it looks. Like I don't believe that she can handle it but I don't care. I do believe she can handle anything thrown her way but not Hell. There are times I'm amazed that even Lucifer could handle the pure darkness he created there. It is not a place for someone like her, it wasn't even a place for me and I had done more than enough in my lifetime to be damned for.

"If it saves Graham I don't care what happens to me."

"Well you might not care but I do. Serenity…after everything we've been through and I do mean everything; do you really think I can just accept this? It means you will be taken away from me forever. There is no coming back from there unless he drags you back up here later and you know how time moves between realms. It could be centuries before that happens."

Her eyes hit the floor and I knew I was getting through to her. That while she wanted to do the right thing and save Graham she also knew that she would be giving up the only other thing that she wanted in her life if she did. I only hoped that right now, my need for her to be selfish would win out over the true goodness in her heart. I wasn't ready for her to be taken from me.

I don't think I ever would be.

"I don't want that..." she whispered so quietly I had almost not heard her.

"Then don't do it. Call Gabriel, tell him everything and let him find another way. We still have another day to decide right? Well make them do what they're supposed to do."

I need her to do this for me. I need her to stop wanting to save the world and every single person in it on her own and let someone else take control. I want her to realize that she can't do this on her own and work with me to find a better way.

Most of all I just want more time with her. I want her in my arms where I could keep her safe and never have to think about any of this again. I want to be selfish with her because I love her so damn much.

"What do you think I've been trying to do since he left?"

I wasn't expecting to hear that. If their connection was as great as he made it seem, where the hell was he?

"He must still be looking for Michael."

"Wait...what?" she asked her eyes rising to meet mine finally.

"He came to me earlier. He was being vague as usual but he asked me if I had seen Michael and that if something happened with Lucifer to call him. I mean there was more to it but none of it made any sense so I didn't focus on it."

"Focus on it now, maybe we can figure out what he was trying to tell us."

"You really think there is some hidden message in that mess he was spouting off at me?"

She shrugged. "I have no idea but since he's not exactly answering us right now maybe it wouldn't hurt to take a look at everything he did say. Maybe we can figure out what's going on and get another way out of this."

There is no way she could understand exactly what hearing her say those words did to me. I wanted her out of the one track mindset she found herself in and I was finally being given it as she is willing to find another way. It meant that we were in this together.

"He said that there is a way to deal with Lucifer and that Michael had to be the one to tell me because he made some sort of agreement not to. Then he mumbled something about me being the one to end Lucifer and well he was gone after that."

"You're the one that has to stop him? Then what is all this drag me to hell business?"

Now it was my turn to shrug. I had no idea. Gabriel's words still made no sense and added to what Lucifer wanted with Serenity it didn't seem as if it ever would.

"If I'm the one that is supposed to end Lucifer then he doesn't seem to be aware of it otherwise I wouldn't have made it out of the room earlier but that means that Heaven knows something that the rest of us don't and I don't like that."

She nodded her head in agreement. We both knew what would happen if Heaven was following their own agenda and not filling us in. It would be a direct repeat of the situation we had been in before. Serenity would be going in blind and the angels would be almost too late to save her, if they even showed up at all. This was not good.

"We need Gabriel."

"Yeah pretty girl we do."

"Ryan..."

She moved toward me then and I opened my arms instantly, sensing what she needed and more than willing to give it to her. As she wrapped her body around mine, I let myself enjoy the moment for as long as it was allowed to last.

This is all I wanted with her. No talk of angels and demons and fighting to the death with Lucifer. I just wanted her and me alone and connected the way we were now. The rest of the world could cease to exist for all I cared as long as this exact feeling never went away.

"If there is no other way out of this, I need you to accept my choice."

I was fully prepared to give this woman the world if she asked for it but that is something I could never accept. I loved her for the person she is, for the light that resided inside of her but my heart could not come to terms with giving her up. I was going to let her down because I couldn't concede on this.

"I can't give you that baby. I can't lose you."

"What if there is no other choice? I know you Ryan, the real you. You don't want Graham to suffer even though you know what he means to me. You want to hate him and you can't and that overrides your natural instincts. You want him to be saved because you know it will give me peace and happiness."

"You're right; I don't want him to die."

"Then please accept what I'm going to do if there is no other option. I don't want to leave you but if it means saving Graham and you then I'm going to do whatever I have to."

Son of a bitch she was getting to me. She's hitting the selfish part of me with a healthy of dose of reality and there is no way I could argue with her. I wanted to hate Graham, she was right about that but I couldn't because I knew he was an innocent. I want him saved as much as she does because I do know what it would mean for her. Not being able to argue with her was pissing me off though.

"I'll accept it if I have to Ser but not until there is no other alternative. I refuse to do it until then."

Nodding her head into my chest and sighing I knew that she was accepting my answer. It was the only one I could give her so I hoped that she wouldn't continue to push it.

"Call Michael…"

"Don't you think that might be better coming from you?"

"No. If what Gabe said is true and you are the only one that can end all of this once and for all and Michael is the only one that can tell you then it has to be you that does it. It's time we got some real answers."

I couldn't argue with that. So holding her as tightly as I could, focusing on the one good thing I knew would get me the result we needed I did the only thing I could do and I prayed.

I just hope that in using the love I have for Serenity, Michael would hear me and come, otherwise I am going to have to prepare for the one thing I'm not willing to do.

Give Serenity up.

CHAPTER THIRTY FIVE

Gabriel

I had been positive that when Michael vanished from Heaven that he would head straight for Ryan given everything we learned. While I agreed with my brother in that Ryan and Serenity needed to know everything as it pertained to them, I knew that in agreeing to Father's demands I cut myself off from being able to do it.

There was no way I could have chosen any other response. I needed to keep my power for what is to come and so did Michael. I am sure Father had not stripped him of his power yet otherwise he would have been much easier to find. It was a small comfort.

I had come dangerously close to telling Ryan everything when I popped in on him. With as strongly as I felt that he did deserve to know it was increasingly difficult to not share my knowledge. So I had done the only thing I could and told him that he needed to get his answers from Michael. In a way I was hoping I could kill two birds with one stone.

He was nowhere in Heaven and from what I could tell he was also nowhere on Earth. Even Raphael who has always been good in tracking us down was having a hard time placing him which annoyed him to no end. Michael had really fallen off the face of the earth and it filled with me with dread. Given how close we were to our fallen brother I feared that Graham's fate would befall Michael.

"Oh ye of little faith little brother. I assure you that Lucifer has not gotten his claws into me quite yet."

The relief that flooded through me at the sound of his voice could never be explained. I had allowed myself to delve into some dark places in my search for him and I was eager to bring myself out of them. As long as he is okay and was speaking to me everything would be fine.

"Where are you?"

"I cannot tell you that. I am sorry Gabriel, as much as I love you I cannot be around you and the agreement you have made with Father right now."

"I did the only thing that I could given what we are facing as I thought you would as well."

"Agree to let Serenity and Ryan go into a fight blind? That seems like the best possible choice to make Gabriel? Since when have you become this blinded by Father?"

It was a valid question. I have always been the one that questioned every step taken whether from our father or another being of Heaven. I never accepted things for what they were, at least not until this moment. He had every right to ask the question and also every right not to trust me or my responses to it.

"I agreed only to keep the power."

"Power means nothing when we are turning into the very thing we are supposed to fight against. I would rather be powerless."

"Just tell me where you are Michael. Let's face this together."

"You will soon find out where I am and where I have been brother. That is all I can tell you now but know this. The humans are calling to me, they want answers and they deserve to have them. I plan on telling them everything. What they choose to do from that moment is on them and also you and father."

He had no idea that he is about to do exactly what I want him to. That I wanted him to do this so I would be able to follow suit and go to Serenity and Ryan and finally face this head on with no secrets between us.

"Tell them everything brother, it is the only way we can handle this. I do not agree with Father's plan and while I know that you do not believe in me in the way I wish that you did please believe in that. I want a better result then what Father is planning."

"I will never agree with his plan. He can take my power away, he can lock me in Heaven the way he wanted to do with you for the duration but I will never agree with this. He wants to use Ryan as nothing more than a weapon in order to do away with his son. I know you heard what he said as I did. He wants to use him and

then bring him back to Heaven where he belongs. He wants to take him from Serenity."

I heard our father say those words and I knew what they meant not only for Ryan but Serenity as well which only made their need to know that much more important. They were both going to be alone in this at least where Heaven is concerned. Our father had turned his back on the right thing and was settling for ending Lucifer instead.

Ryan is much more than a weapon just as Serenity is more than a heavenly light and it is time we did the right thing, even if it meant going against everything we had ever known or been taught.

"Then do what you must. I want you to tell me where you have been but I also respect the fact that you can't. You must see this through because right now we are all they've got."

"They are calling to me now Gabriel. If you mean what you say then you will arrive there with me and we will tell them together. Be sure of your choice before you make it though, because once taken you will not be able to turn back."

"I have no desire to turn back Michael."

"Then I will see you in a few minutes...and Gabriel?"

"Yes?"

"It's good to have you back."

Serenity

I don't want to lose faith in the angels. Given everything that Gabriel has been accused of just since I've known him I wanted more for him. I wanted to believe in him where before I gave up. He has done everything as he's been told or to look out for me and I spent a lot of time holding that against him even though to my own credit, I hadn't known everything the way I do now.

Unfortunately the faith I wanted to have in him and even in Michael was dwindling the longer they kept us both waiting. I was beginning to believe that we were truly alone in this. I believed the angels had figured it all out long before we did and were finally jumping ship. If that's actually what is happening that it meant there really is only one way out of this.

248

I am going to have to do whatever Lucifer want in order to save Graham.

In order for things to be the way they are meant to be then you had to let go of the selfishness and accept your fate. My fate was tied up in Lucifer and the sooner I realized that the sooner I could save Graham and set the world right again.

I didn't care that I was always the one on the chopping block. That I was the one facing certain death because if it meant everything could be the way it should be then I would choose the same end every single time.

"You're giving up on them aren't you?" Ryan asked quietly, reading my mind easily.

"I'm starting to think we're in this alone Ry. I don't want to think that way but what other option could there be for them not showing up when we call?"

"I have no idea but I don't like it."

"Part of me thinks that if Gabriel had never bailed on me before that I might have more faith in him now but I know that this has nothing to do with that. Neither of them answering now is either because something is wrong or because they really have given up on us. I don't like either option."

"Me either."

There was so much being left unsaid in his words. I know he is trying not to focus on what the angels not answering meant but with the more time that passed I knew that he was going to have to. I was going to have to make this choice because we both know I have to save Graham.

"I never thought I'd ever say this but I actually miss the way things used to be." He spoke with a deflated sigh.

"What do you miss?"

"At least with Lucifer when you called him he always answered you. He's a sick bastard but he never leaves you hanging."

As much as I want to hate the way he spoke about the very person who had put us all in this mess I couldn't stop myself from agreeing. It's been proven that even when you think he isn't around he's there. He never leaves. He was actually the complete opposite of his brothers but even admitting that much was upsetting.

"I know you don't want to face it but—

I was cut off as the room became bathed in light, taking me off guard and causing me to fall back onto the floor, Ryan's attempt to catch me coming just a little too late.

"Better late than never I guess." Ryan whispered under his breath as he held out a hand to help me up from my place on the floor.

"What I wanna know is how you can be so unaffected by that."

"I don't know, maybe it's because of all the time I spent with Lucifer I've become immune. I do enjoy the way you fall all over yourself though. I hope that never changes." He answered with a grin which only made me want to focus on his mouth instead of the two very large angels that just appeared in the room.

"Laugh it up buddy." I say slapping his hand away once I was steady on my feet.

"I plan to" he shot back sticking his tongue out.

"So you're what…five now?"

"If the shoe fits."

"As entertaining as the two of you are we have urgent matters which we must discuss."

Leave it to Michael to get right to business. I guess I should have been happy he even answered the call at all but I wasn't. I was annoyed.

"You bet your ass we do." Ryan said before taking a seat on the bed. The way he moved reminded me of Graham and how he always wanted to be comfortable when hearing bad news. I didn't want to compare them but they did seem similar in the way they handled situations.

"Have you garnered more information from your time with Lucifer?"

This was my cue. I needed to tell them exactly what Lucifer planned and hopefully find a way out of it before meeting him the next day.

"He used Graham purely to get to me."

250

"We assumed as much. Is there more or is that all you have to tell us?" Michael asked sharply which only made me want to cross the room and hit him. He had no right treating us this way considering we were all on the same team.

"Yeah he did. He used Graham to get to me because he wants what he did originally. He wants me to be his partner."

"He does not mean to end you?" Gabriel asked, obviously as shocked by the turn of events as I was when I'd heard them. It did seem unbelievable.

"He will release the hold he has on Graham if I agree to join him and go to hell."

I could tell by the expressions on their faces that they didn't know what to make of what I just dropped on them. For beings that were supposed to know everything they sure didn't act like it.

"Well that is not going to make what we have to tell you any easier."

What they had to tell us?

"Does this have something to do with all that vague crap you said earlier?" Ryan spoke up, calling my attention away from the angels and back on the man now sitting beside me on the bed.

"Yes it has everything to do with what Gabriel was trying to tell you earlier Ryan. It all has to do with you."

"What about me?"

"You are the only person who can end this."

"As much as I love getting answers from you guys do you think just this once you can spit it out?"

"What Michael is trying to tell you is not going to be easy to hear Ryan and just as it was with Serenity when I came to her I am unsure if you will even believe it."

I remembered that time well. Ryan had told me about everything and even though Gabriel had expanded on it, I could never really believe what he told me. It hadn't sat well with him and I now understood why.

"Well then just tell me but beating around the bush and trying to make it easier is not going to help you right now. It's too late for that. If I can end Lucifer then just tell me how and I'll do it."

251

We must start from the beginning in order to explain that. You are not as you appear to be Ryan. In fact you are much more."

I had no idea what he meant but I was willing to agree without any other information. I always knew Ryan was different which is why he had the light around him. It's about damn time they were finally admitting the same thing. I hated being the only one that seemed to get it.

"You are the purest form of angel there is."

Ryan began laughing and I felt my stomach twist in knots. He didn't believe it but I did. It made sense.

"You're joking right?"

Placing my hand over his and locking my eyes with his the minute he looked up I shook my head. "I believe it."

"I assure you there is nothing about this that is even remotely amusing. You are a pure angel. There was an issue in Heaven that sent you down at the wrong time and has brought about everything that has happened to you since."

I couldn't even begin to understand how there could have been an accident that would cause something like this but I knew what Michael was saying is the absolute truth. Even without my abilities I would believe it. Ryan had the light around him because he was an angel and not the demon that everyone made him out to be. He had just gotten a shit deal.

"Father did not learn of the mistake until recently which explains why nothing was done about it until now but there is far more that you need to know."

"Like what?"

"As a pure angel you are the only one that can stop Lucifer but in doing so you must forsake the life you have built here. Once you have done as Father needs you will be sent back home where you belong."

I didn't realize I'd been holding my breath until Michael spoke again and it all came rushing out of me. Ryan was nothing more than a weapon and would be taken from me the minute he was done completing what he had been created for.

"He's just going to what…die and be sent home?"

"He will not die. He will go willingly back home with Father when the time is right."

It wasn't lost on me that neither of them had put their own names in. That meant that they didn't agree with what they were saying which explained why Michael had to be the one to tell us because they had been sworn not to.

I couldn't help agreeing with Ryan's earlier assessment. Things almost seemed easier with Lucifer. At least with him you knew what you were getting. He didn't hide how evil he was. Heaven was far more complex and headache inducing.

"No!" I screamed causing all eyes in the room to land on me. "This is not happening."

"Serenity we knew that is how you would react and we want it to happen no more than you do which is why we have both gone against father. You cannot fight that which you do not know."

"I'm gonna figure that Lucifer has no idea what I am." Ryan cut in again.

"You would be correct. He knows nothing of your true form and what you mean in terms of whatever he is planning. He is under the influence of most powerful magic and has become almost drunk on the power it contains which is where you come in. Father wants to use you while he remains unsuspecting."

"Then I say we let him have his way."

What? Did I just hear him right?

"Excuse me?" I asked turning to him. I couldn't believe I was hearing this. He was going to do what God wanted yet hated when I wanted to do the very same thing only minutes before.

"You heard me. If I can end this then I damn well want to end it."

"No!" I cried out again. There is no way I am going to let him do this.

"It would appear as though you two are at a standstill but unfortunately I have no time to dwell on that because I need answers."

"What do you want to know Michael?" Ryan asked, answering for me since I couldn't seem to find my voice after what Ryan had just decided so easily.

"When is Serenity due to give him her answer?"

"Tomorrow." I managed to choke out before going back to the silent treatment again.

"Then we must prepare quickly. We do not have much time."

This is a joke right? They couldn't possibly be here to help make their fathers plan a reality. Didn't they just agree that they didn't like what their father planned? So why were they hell bent on pursuing anything right now? Didn't we need to figure out a different way out of this?

My mind was overflowing with questions that I couldn't trust my voice to ask.

"There is nothing to plan guys. I hate to say it but if I'm the only thing that can end Lucifer then I am going to have to go there tomorrow with Serenity and end this once and for all. I don't need heavenly intervention to end the son of a bitch."

"That is where you are wrong Ryan. You will not walk into this blind nor will you do as our father wants. We are here to fight with you and we will find another way. Neither one of you is going to be sacrificing yourselves anymore."

"If it's the only way to end this then that is EXACTLY what I'm doing." Ryan snapped, jumping from the bed and making his way over to where both angels stood. I feared what his next move would be and only prayed that whatever happened, Gabriel and Michael would realize that it wasn't him talking and leave him unharmed.

I understood wanting to do the right thing better than anyone and right now this seemed to be the only real way to end everything and keep Graham safe in the process but I wasn't going to just blindly accept it. We would find another way, just as the angels said and that's all there was to it. I am not losing Ryan. Not today and not ever.

"Be mindful of your next move demon. You may be an angel to our father but to us you are still very much the dark entity you have always been."

Ryan stopped immediately and shook himself. If I hadn't seen it with my own eyes I wouldn't have believed it. Whatever Michael said had gotten through to whatever part of Ryan that was reacting and he was immediately backing up from his earlier stance.

"I'm sorry. I don't know what got into me."

"It was your anger, something that should have been fixed during your stay with us." Gabriel answered immediately.

I couldn't take any more of this. Ryan resigning himself to what he believed needed to be done was just too much to take in. If I didn't get out of here right now I was going to break and I knew that once I did there is no way I was going to be able to help them.

I needed to be alone. I needed to come to terms with everything I heard and decide what the right thing to do is and I wasn't going to be able to do that in this room. I couldn't handle being anywhere near Ryan if all he's going to do is plan what would be the end of him and the end of us.

Standing from the bed, I made my way for the door hearing my name being called with each step I took but not wanting to look back and acknowledge any of them. If they wanted to find another way around this then they could do it but right now they'd have to do it without me. I had about all I could take tonight.

I was done.

CHAPTER THIRTY SIX

Gabriel

"Go after her brother. You may be the only one that can get through to her."

Watching Serenity walk from the room without so much as a word or glance in our direction had been extremely difficult for me. I could only imagine the thoughts running through her mind and as much as I wanted to access them I knew I couldn't.

She had every right to be upset given the way Ryan had easily accepted Father's plan for him. I wasn't sure if it was a knee jerk reaction on his part or if he really did want to see this through but whatever it is it's beyond upsetting to not only her but me as well. He needed to give this a lot more thought before throwing away everything he had fought so hard to come back to.

"Tell her I'm sorry."

I didn't even want to acknowledge Ryan's plea. If he was actually feeling sorry for the way he acted then he should be the one to go to her and make it right, not leave it for me to handle. It was actually something about him that I greatly admired as I came to understand him. He always accepted his mistakes and moved forward in efforts to fix them.

"Tell her yourself." I said as I made my way from the room to do as my brother asked of me.

"You must make sure she doesn't make any rash decisions in her current state of mind Gabriel. That could mean certain death for all of us."

Michael is right. Serenity had a track record of making choices when her emotions were running high and I couldn't allow that to happen now. Not because it might mean the end of all of us but because of what it would mean for her and her alone.

I felt her immediately the minute I made my way out of her dorm and after what felt like only a few steps she came into view.

256

She was a vision in her own right as she sat beneath the oak tree that stood just outside of the college.

A tree reminiscent of the one in Green Haven that she sat beneath on more than one occasion during her time there. It had been a source of comfort to her then and I could only hope that it is serving as one now. Given all of the information she just had to take in, she needed that now.

Instead of speaking to her right away I made my way over and stood to her right. I didn't want to push myself, wanting more for her to come to me herself. I hadn't done that with her before but seeing how distraught she was I knew it is something I had to learn to start doing now.

"How can he just be okay with this?"

"I do not know Serenity. I can only assume he accepts it so easily because the other alternative is something he cannot bring himself to accept."

"It's always going to be like this for us isn't it Gabe? Always trying to one up each other in an effort to protect?"

"It does appear to be that way but I do not believe that to be the case, at least in terms of forever."

She looked up at me then and the minute her eyes leveled their gaze upon me I was lost. There is so much sadness behind them that I ached to take it all away for her and bring her back to a simpler time where none of this would have been a concern. She may have had to live a life of solitude but at least she wouldn't be forced to put her life on the line.

"Tell me there is another way out of this."

That is the one thing that I could not give her. There was no other way out of this. It was either going to have to be Ryan doing as Father wanted him to or her giving herself over in order to save Graham.

"I wish that I could tell you what you want to hear Serenity but then I would be lying to you and that is something I promised myself I would never do again."

"So then I just have to let him do this?"

257

"No, you can do it before he gets the chance to but given his resolve and Michael's strength I do not promise you will make it very far before you are stopped."

She sighed and I felt my resolve cracking. The reality of the situation is hitting her now and there is no way she can deny it any longer. She was either going to have to accept Ryan taking this next step or she was going to have to do it for him, neither of which any of us wanted but were unable to stop.

"I love him Gabriel, more than I think I've ever loved anything in my entire life. I mean how crazy is that? He was sent here to kill me and yet here I am head over heels in love with him."

I understood her completely because it is the way I felt about her even knowing that her human heart beat for another and would always. We were both cut of the same cloth in this regard and there is nothing either of us can do to stop how we feel even though we'd probably like to.

"He wants to sacrifice himself to save me and the world, ending this once and for all and I'm angry with him. He wants to do the most selfless act there can be possibly be and I just want to scream and hit him until I can't feel it anymore."

"Michael made me aware of your new abilities. The anger you're feeling is most likely not your own Serenity. You are feeding off what remains of Ryan's."

"Of course it is because it's impossible for me to feel something of my own anymore. I'm either feeding off Ryan or I'm bonding with Graham. When does it end and what I feel is my own again?"

Another question I did not have the answer to though it didn't stop my need to give her something to ease her mind anyway.

"It is okay to be upset about this Serenity. You care for him and he is choosing to do the right thing instead of what you want him to do."

"Yeah I know, I'm a selfish bitch."

"No that is not what you are. You're exactly what you should be."

"Oh? What's that?"

"You are an imperfect human."

She went silent then and I found myself enjoying the silence that surrounded us. We both knew what was looming on the horizon but in this moment we wanted to forget about it and just be, no words required. It is the most peaceful I've felt in as long as I could remember.

When she spoke again the tremor in her voice was gone and she seemed to have gained control of her emotions again.

"I'm ready to go back now."

"Are you sure? You can take as much time as you need. Michael would inform me if we were needed."

"I don't need any more time. I'm good."

I'm not sure where it came from or why but when she told me she was good a chill began to rise in me. Serenity may be a lot of things but I knew beyond a shadow of a doubt that the one thing she wasn't is good.

I saw beyond the weak smile she wore on her face and knew that while she may appear stronger and in control again, she was anything but.

I just wish I knew what it meant.

CHAPTER THIRTY SEVEN

Serenity

I knew what had to be done and I am determined to see it through.

The time for discussions was over as all the arguments we could make had been exhausted. There could be no turning back now. We all knew what happened from this moment on and even though none of us wanted to acknowledge it we knew that no matter what way it all played out it had been the right decision to make.

The only one we could make.

It hadn't been an easy road getting there but then nothing truly worth fighting for ever is. The four of us were all living individual destinies, paths that we may not have chosen but ones that we were going to take regardless. Michael and Gabriel realized that sometimes you can't just follow blindly on a path set forth by a parent. That sometimes you have to go it alone even though it hurt to do it. They were the epitome of free will.

I learned that as important as I am to the world I didn't have to sacrifice myself every time in order to live up to it. I could be me, with all of my faults and failings and still manage to do the right thing. I may have to save the world one person at a time but I could save them all. It was just going to take longer than anyone wanted.

What Ryan learned is different from me even though we both share the same problem with ultimate sacrifice. His realization is harder than ours because he needs to learn his true worth. I hadn't seen it at the time but spending the time listening last night as he told me how he really felt and what he believes he needs to do, I finally get it. He had been redeemed the last time we had been in this place but even going through that and what happened next he never accepted that he is worthy of anything other than the darkness he knew so well.

So we plotted and planned and finally agreed on what needed to take place.

Ryan would be going up against Lucifer and he would do what needed to be done even though he knew it meant he would be taken immediately once it was over. He was willing to do it because it was his way of learning his lesson. This is how he would finally accept that he is more than just the demon he believed himself to be.

When I told Gabriel I was okay the night before I meant it. I could no longer deny what was in front of me and whether I liked it or not, I had to think of the bigger picture and not just the one that included me. It's about more than me, or even Graham. It is about the human race and making sure that it thrived instead of slowly dying off.

I knew no one believed me. They all just assumed I was numb to everything I'd been told and was going through the motions but that wasn't the case at all. I just finally accepted what I had always known yet refused to believe. He was always meant for this. I had seen it the very first time I noticed the light surrounding him and as much as I wanted to shield my eyes from it because I didn't want to experience the hurt, I couldn't because I wouldn't be letting him shine the way he so desperately needed to.

As we all stood taking in the church in front of us, mentally preparing for what was to come I am reminded of the way everything had turned around the night before. That if this was the last experience I ever had on the planet I was glad that I'd gotten the night I did before it all ended.

*****

Ryan is crying.

That was all I could see the minute I walked back into the room. He was on his knees on the floor in front of my bed and he was wiping away tears angrily with his hands. It didn't matter why he was doing it because all that mattered was the reason why. He was crying because of me.

"How long has he been like this?" I asked Michael as I made my way over to where he rested and knelt down beside him,

261

immediately wrapping my arms around him even though I worried it might be the last thing he wanted.

"Pretty much since the moment you walked out and Gabriel followed."

He was trying to speak through it but the sound was muffled and I couldn't make out anything that made any sense. This was not working for me at all. If anyone should be in tears given everything it should be me and there wasn't a tear in my eye to be found. I had cried all of my tears before Gabriel had made his way out to me. It was time Ryan did the same. We needed to face this.

"Ry, it's alright. I'm here now." I whispered to him as I ran my hand up and down his back trying to soothe him.

He had always been the strong one, the stoic one who never betrayed his feelings in any given situation. It was like the roles had been reversed and I had no idea how to fix it.

"I...didn't...think."

"Didn't think about what baby?"

"About..." he said, catching his breath before continuing. "You. I didn't think about you."

"What are you talking about? You're always thinking about me."

I wasn't saying it to soothe him anymore. I meant every word. He was always thinking about me and every step he'd ever taken in the short time I'd know him proved that.

Raising himself up from his knees, his arms instantly came around mine as he pulled me towards the bed. Positioning both of us on the end he turned to me and grabbing my face with his hands leaned in as close as he could.

"When Michael told me what I am, what I really am and what they needed me to do something in me snapped. I couldn't see anything but ending Lucifer's path of destruction once and for all. I stopped thinking about you."

I understood what he meant now but didn't fault him for it because when Lucifer told me that the only way to end this for Graham was for me to sacrifice myself I had done the exact same thing. If I wasn't allowed to blame myself then I most definitely could not blame him.

"It's okay Ryan. I get it."

"It's not okay Ser, not by a long shot. The only reason I am even here at all is because of you. They could have easily left me for dead in that church and I would have understood it because I did right by you. You are the only thing I've ever wanted to fight for and in ignoring how my choice would make you feel, I made you run from me."

I couldn't argue with the last part of what he said because it was true. In hearing him accept the responsibility so easily it scared me.

"I was wrong Ryan. I never should have run from the room or from you. I should have heard you out."

I knew he could see the truth in my eyes and I was thankful for whatever connection we had between us because he really needed to see it.

"I need to do this Serenity. I don't expect you to get it or hell even accept it but I need to do this."

"I know you do." I whisper weakly. "I just wanna hear you tell me why."

I could see it was a struggle for him, saying this to me knowing that for once he wanted to do something that had nothing to do with me and everything to do with the light inside of him.

"I'm twenty one years old and I've never done anything good in my life other then what I did that day in the church. I've stolen the best parts of people, I've used them for my own gain and I've hated myself every single day since. I don't believe that a person that does the things I did can ever really be redeemed even though I'm living proof that it can. I need to do this because for the first time in my life I need to do the right thing without reservations."

The love I have for this man knows no bounds. He is finally beginning to see what I have seen all along. He's finally realizing his true value.

"There is this part of me that no matter how hard I try to push it down it continues to fight its way back up until I can no longer control it. It comes through in my anger and it comes through even more when I become determined and tonight I have never been more determined."

263

"You don't need to explain it to me Ryan, I get it."

I understand the demon side of him better than he thinks and while I may not fully understand how I tap into it so easily he doesn't need to hide it from me or try to protect me from it. I might not like it but it is a part of what makes him who he is, whether it was a mistake on Heaven's part or not and I loved every part of him.

"No, please let me. I need to say this because after tonight I might never get the chance again. It was a risk tonight accepting everything the way I did knowing what could happen. Knowing what did happen. You fed into it and it broke you. I never want to break you Serenity you have got to believe that."

"I know." I whispered leaning my head into his until our foreheads were locked together his hands still tenderly placed on my cheeks. "Sometimes though, when you love someone the way that we do, things get broken."

"What are you saying?"

"The fun is in the fixin'." I answer, not knowing where it came from but knowing it is exactly what I'm trying to get across. He might believe that he broke me but it wasn't something that couldn't be fixed.

"Where did that come from?" he asked trying not to laugh and failing.

"I wasn't sure when I said it but I think it's something my dad used to say to me."

"It's perfect." He said, finally releasing the laugh he'd been bottling since the silly quote popped out of my mouth.

"I know you need to do this Ryan. I also know why you need to do it so I'm not going to fight you on it anymore. I was being selfish when I ran from you but I'm not going to do that anymore. It's time I stopped doing that and did what I need to do."

"What do you need to do?"

"Fight."

"You will not be fighting alone either because Michael and I will be right there with you."

*****

Gabriel kept true to his word because standing to my left was none other than my guardian angel and he wasn't alone. Michael is there beside him, as large and imposing as ever both of them ready to fight their fallen brother in an effort to make everything right again.

"Does everyone remember what they need to do?" Gabriel asks as his gaze shifts over each of us.

"Yes Gabe, for the hundredth time since we got here, we're more than ready to get this over with. We're just waiting for you to stop asking."

I smiled and looked at Ryan, noticing the way his eyes lit up and his lips rise in the grin he was trying his hardest to hide.

Yeah there was no doubt about it. We were ready and this time we weren't gonna leave until it was finished and we'd taken everything Lucifer had stolen from us back.

Ryan

Watching Serenity walk across the lawn and into the church was probably the hardest thing I've ever had to do. I knew it was all part of the plan we put together the night before but knowing she was about come face to face with the man who wanted to take her from me was tearing me up inside.

This is the one area I still needed work in. I still couldn't come to terms with letting her go. She is going inside to do what we had planned and the way it felt inside my chest watching her walk away from me was like it's going to be the last time I saw her even though my head knew better. I would be joining her soon enough but my urge to keep her near me was so overpowering that I wanted to break the plan just so she wouldn't have to go through this alone.

It had been the same way the night before after Michael and Gabriel had left to inform their father of what was going to happen. We'd made love again only this time we went slower, wanting to savor every single moment knowing that we would not be able to have another one. We'd been unable to talk about what was going to happen today, neither one of ready to say goodbye to the other

265

so we'd chosen instead to just enjoy every last second we had wrapped completely in each other.

There had been hardly any conversation, the both of us just content to be with each other in silence. I planned on carrying every moment I ever spent with her with me when I finally said goodbye to my life and this memory would be the one right at the top of the pile.

I wanted to remember the way she looked as she slept in my arms, complete with her ever present strawberry vanilla scent and the way her lips always curved up into a smile when she was dreaming. Yes I would most definitely be spending the rest of eternity with that image of her locked tightly around my heart.

"She's in. Michael go around the back the way we discussed and get yourself into position. Ryan and I will be right behind you."

I was brought back again to the reality of the situation I was in. Michael filled me in on Lucifer's powers and exactly what that meant for us and I only hoped that he wouldn't realize we were out here before we were ready for it. I couldn't imagine what he would do to Serenity if he knew he was being ambushed.

"Are you sure he won't know we're here?"

"We are angels Ryan. We do have powers to block that sort of thing." Michael shot back as he made his way around the back of the building, his form moving so quickly I could barely keep track of it.

"He's actually starting to grow on me."

"That won't last long believe me." Gabriel said, his focus never leaving the front doors of the church.

The last time we'd been here there had been demons guarding the doors and even ones located in the windows on the upper floors but this time there was nothing. Lucifer must really believe he is going to get his way if he had no precautions whatsoever.

"Does this not bother you?" I asked finally bothered enough to voice it.

"I am unsure what you mean."

"I would have thought given the way he is that he would have guarded himself better but there is literally nothing here."

"He knows Serenity just as you do Ryan. He knows that if it's a choice between her own life and that of Graham's she will choose him every time. He does not need to be guarded if she is willingly going to give herself over to him."

Getting confirmation was great but it didn't make me feel better. Shouldn't Michael have said something by now? Was Serenity alright? Did we need to get in there now?

"Ryan you must relax your body and your mind. If you push yourself you know what will happen and right now that is something we cannot afford."

I knew this. I was just having a hard time keeping my focus on it. The last thing we needed was for the demon to make an appearance, especially when confronting the very creator of it. Serenity wouldn't be the only one at his mercy and that was something that would seriously blow our entire plan to hell.

"I'm in position."

"Michael is where he needs to be and he is fine. You have nothing to worry about. Serenity will handle herself flawlessly. Now brace yourself Ryan because we're about to begin."

Swallowing one final lump in my throat I felt him grab a hold of me and prepared myself for what was to come next.

I only hope that I wasn't going to be too late.

Lucifer

She is such a stunning creature.

It would not be obvious to the casual eye but to me I could easily see how she is made of Heaven. The light within her added a glow to her body that no other woman on Earth could ever replicate. Even the unease running through her body as she made her way up the aisle toward me was enticing.

Yes I had most definitely made the right decision in choosing her. She would make the perfect companion for the lifetime we would share together in hell. Where Lilith had failed me in every imaginable way much the same way that Ryan had, Serenity would make up for in spades.

267

"Do not be afraid. I will not hurt you but I cannot promise to keep my hands to myself."

The twitch in her body told me that my words affected her deeply though not in the way that I wanted them to. I could have easily become disheartened with her reaction but I knew once we made it back home everything would change. She would adapt nicely into the new routine that would be her life and she would respond to me in a more favorable light.

Just the mere thought of it filled me with an excitement I had never known.

"That's what I'm afraid of."

"Oh Serenity, your attitude is so refreshing."

Completely disregarding me she spoke again but instead of bothering me the way most humans did I became even more intrigued by her and what was to come.

"So I'm here, just the way you wanted me. You win, so it's your turn to deliver."

"All in due time Serenity. We still have much to discuss."

"Of course we do." She answered with an eye roll.

Moving closer to her but making sure to keep my distance in an effort not to ignite the bond she shared with my vessel I smiled. "You must tell me. How did Ryan react to your decision?"

"He hated every part of it just the way you predicted. He didn't want to let me go. It's too bad for him that he isn't the one making the final decision."

Oh yes, I am definitely going to enjoy my first taste of her. The body in which I resided in could barely contain the heat building within it at the words spoken. It ached just as I did to have this wonderful gem beneath me.

"Splendid. I want him to feel the loss of you for generations."

"I have no doubt that he will."

It would take no effort at all to bend her to my will. She was already showing how willing she is to accept what is laid out before her and it pleased me ever so much knowing that the hard work was finally over.

Unable to control myself, I reached out to her and ran my hands across her cheek enjoying the way her body shivered from

268

my touch. Soul mate bond be damned, I needed to taste her. Moving so quickly she was unable to prepare herself I grabbed her up into my arms and brought my face mere inches from hers, so close I could feel her labored breathing across my face and allowing the fire building in me to ignite.

"Just one taste Serenity and I will give you what I have promised you."

Indecision flooded her features, the connection she had with Ryan obviously running paramount in her mind as she broke eye contact with me and looked down toward the floor. I wanted it to be her choice as it would be the only choice she would ever make but the desire within me both from the bond and from the urges of my own making were making it hard to wait.

"You want to kiss me?"

Lifting her face up with my fingers so that she could look nowhere but directly into my eyes I nodded. "Just one small taste. That is all I ask of you and then you can have your precious Graham back in your arms one final time before we leave."

"Okay…"

"You are so beautiful Serenity." I whispered as I leaned in until my lips were only a mere breath from hers. "I have waited forever for this." Bringing my lips to hers, waiting for the explosion of desire that I knew would come I was stunned into silence as she lifted her hands and placed them on each side of my head squeezing as she did.

"That's the one and only taste you'll ever have of me you sick bastard!" she screamed as she backed her face away from mine, her hands never leaving my head. Watching as her eyes closed, her body going completely still I realized with stunning clarity what she was trying to do and I immediately began to fight back.

"You foolish little girl. He's gone, he's been gone since before I came to you."

"Then let him go!" she yelled back just as loudly not giving an inch.

As I fell to my knees on the floor powerless against the level of strength she controlled I looked up into her eyes and all I saw was the black that resided within them. Whatever power she was accessing it was not her own. It was of my making. She is taking me down with my own power and there is nothing I could do to stop her since she had her hands tightly held on my only defense.

Yes she's definitely the right choice.

"Graham if you can hear me fight! Fight with everything you've got."

"It is pointless Serenity." I choked out. "He is already dead."

"I don't believe you. I will never believe that." She screamed at me, her voice no more than a muffled screech as her hands began slipping down over my ears.

I could hear her begin to chant and the blood running through my veins ran cold. She really did believe that I am lying to her and is now going to do everything in her power to prove it. Falling even further to the ground under her power, I heard the familiar words begin and knew that time was running out.

"Vi esorcizzare, ogni spirito impuro. Ogni potere satanico, ogni incursion Dell'avversario infernale, ogni legione, Fand la congregazione e la setta diabolica. Così, maledetto demone, e ogni legione diabolica, noi scongiuriamo voi. Cessate ingannare le umane creature e dando loro il veleno della perdizione eterna."

Gabriel

I was unsure of what I would find when I made my way into the church but standing in the doorway and watching as Serenity performed the rite of exorcism on my brother, I realized with sudden clarity that it was most definitely not that.

"What is she doing?" Ryan asked finally coming to a stop beside me and watching the scene unfold before us.

"She is attempting to free Graham from the hold that my brother has on him." I stated simply. There was no other explanation I could give him but I now understood everything much more clearly the more I stood watching her.

"Is that something you both planned on when you were outside last night?"

No it most definitely was not. At least it wasn't something that we planned together. Remembering the way she sounded when she told me she was good I immediately knew what she had been doing. The entire time under the tree when she had been breaking apart she'd been looking for a way out of this and she found it.

It still wouldn't change what Ryan had to do next but she would definitely succeed in her goal of taking care of Graham, which is what meant more to her anyway. She could worry about Ryan fully once she had done what needed to be and saved the only other person in her human life that held a piece of her heart.

"Do we just let her keep doing this?" Ryan whispered as we stood transfixed watching her continue with the incantation.

"We have no other choice but Ryan you should know I did not plan this with her. This was all of her own design."

"She lied to us?"

"It would appear that way yes. In order to save Graham from what she believes to be the fate she damned him to, she lied to all of us."

I watched as Graham's now lifeless body fell to the floor with a resounding thud and immediately began moving forward. If Lucifer was long gone from his body then time really was of the essence. I needed to get him out of here before anything more took place.

It is then I saw Michael making his way from the right and rushed toward her.

"Gabriel, you need to take Graham and you need to get out of here now!" Michael yelled through my mind.

Doing as he instructed, I pulled his lifeless form into my arms and I disappeared immediately knowing I was leaving Ryan to fend for himself but trusting that he would be in good hands with Heaven's strongest angel fighting alongside of him.

If anyone could get the rest of them out of there it was Michael.

Ryan

Something is very wrong.

Serenity's eyes changed as she had been chanting in Italian over Graham's body and it was a change I recognized immediately. It was the same change that occurred inside of me every time that I allowed the demon inside of me to take over.

How it was happening to her I had no idea but I knew I had to do whatever I could to make it stop. She isn't meant for the darkness. Lucifer had done this to her, that's the only way any of it could make sense. He had done something before we'd gotten there and now she was paying the price even though she was saving Graham's life in the process.

"Serenity stop!" I yelled as I raced toward her, immediately wrapping my arms around her and bringing her as close as I could into my body shielding her. Before I could say anymore Michael appeared beside us, his face ashen. Something was definitely not right. Even though Graham had been taken from the church it was still not over. His color began dimming right before my eyes and it solidified my fears.

"You need to release Serenity."

"I need to do what?

"You need to trust me and you need to release her now."

Before I could ask why, I felt the blast to my stomach and immediately felt myself flying. Opening my eyes as wide as I could I saw what Michael had been trying to tell me. Serenity, my sweet, gentle Serenity was no longer herself. Her eyes were now the color of blood and the grin on her face didn't belong to her.

Lucifer.

He began to speak and though all I could see is Serenity's lips moving I knew that it was never going to be her again. In her attempt to save Graham she had done the unthinkable. She had given him exactly what he wanted. He now had control over her his ultimate goal from the start.

"I have to hand it to the girl. She did take me by surprise with her knowledge of the Rite but she didn't prepare herself for every possible alternative."

"Lucifer let her go!" I heard Michael cry from across the room.

Don't hurt her Michael. Even if it's him inside of her she's still there. I can feel her. Don't hurt her.

272

"I'm sorry Michael but you know I cannot do that. I wasn't prepared to let the boy live. I wanted her to believe in me so that when I took her home she would be more accepting of what was to happen to her but I had no intention of letting him live. As it appears, I don't have to concern myself with that because I still have her."

"I can fight him Ryan but that will only damage her in the process. I am afraid the only way to save any of now is to stick to the original plan. You must kill him."

No I could definitely not do that. I could not go up against the woman I love and kill her. It wasn't her anymore I knew that but there is no way I could look into those eyes even knowing that and do what Michael, Gabriel and even God himself wanted me to do. I could not end her life.

"I can't do that Michael, you know that."

"You have no other option Ryan. If you do not do it then we shall all perish."

"You do it."

"It cannot be me. You are the only one who can do this. Focus on the love you have for her Ryan, it will carry you through. She would want this. End him. Once you do that the two of you can be together on the other side."

I didn't want to do it but I knew that Michael was speaking the truth. I had to be strong and do this. Serenity wouldn't want to be stuck this way forever and she would definitely never be able to live with herself if she knew that we all died trying to save her.

Pulling on whatever strength I had left I slowly got back up to my feet and locking my eyes on the body before me now, the woman I would spend the rest of my life loving, I began taking the steps to where she stood waiting for me.

"Take the blade Ryan and do it. Do not think about it. Just do it. It is your destiny."

Before I had a chance to ask him what blade he wanted me to take I saw it begin to shine in my hand. Continuing on with the blade lighting the way I reached my destination and stopped short as she spoke the words my heart desperately wanted to hear.

"Ryan I love you…"

Closing my eyes as tightly as I could and remembering Michael's earlier words I lunged forward, knowing I hit my mark the minute I heard the ripping sound of her shirt as the blade went in. Opening my eyes I watched in horror as her eyes went wide and the room immediately began to spin around me.

"I love you too…"

Unable to control it anymore I fell to the floor, immediately curling my body up into a ball as the realization of what I had done washed over me. As Michael reached down to help me up I turned to him and saw the emptiness I was feeling staring back at me.

Standing to our feet we both turned to face what I had done. Her body began to shake and in the time it took for me to blink my eyes, unsure of what I was seeing, whether it was her final moments or something more, she disappeared.

It was real. It really happened despite my heart not wanting to believe it.

Serenity was gone.

EPILOGUE

Ryan

There was this one time just after I turned six when I decided I was tired of hanging around in my room and wanted to take my new bike for a spin. I just jumped on top of it and took off not giving much thought to my own safety, instead leaving the helmet, knee pads and elbow pads at home in the closet where they'd been since my birthday. I thought I was invincible, that nothing could touch me. At least I was until I hit a rock in the middle of the road, it getting jammed in the spokes and flipping head first onto the pavement. I realized pretty quickly that I wasn't Superman and I started taking better care whenever I took the bike out again.

I made it home that day even though I can't really remember how and as I walked into the kitchen and my mother caught sight of the blood matted to the top of my head, tear stains streaked down my face she looked almost concerned for me. I was so happy. I wanted nothing more than for her to finally show me some form of affection. I craved it the way a thirsty dog does water.

It was only when her body tensed and her forehead creased I knew I was wrong. She didn't care at all; in fact the sight of me actually bothered her. Then she opened her mouth, the words fell out and the world came crashing down around me.

"What's with the tears? You're a fucking boy for Christ's sakes. Start acting like it."

I never felt another thing again. At least I don't have any recollection of feeling. I went through every day after that making sure that I did as she said and acted like the boy I was and now the man that I had become. I'd done pretty well to given that I'd never shed another tear since that day.

Until her.

Serenity came into my life like a hurricane; pulling me up in her whirlwind and making me feel things for the first time in

275

fifteen years. It was more than just feeling something again though. It was feeling it and knowing that it was okay and accepted. She did that for me. If I'm honest she taught me so much more than that but the way I loved her and the way that she accepted it so easily despite knowing the darkest parts of me is definitely the most important part of everything she brought to my life.

It's been ten days, six hours and 15 minutes since she disappeared in front of me and despite trying my hardest I am unable to feel anything. I can't cry. It's like I shed all the tears I had in the church the night she vanished. I'm just numb now and until I find out what really happened to her, I don't think I will ever feel anything but numb again.

I miss her so badly sometimes that I find it hard to breathe. I want to know what happened to her when she left me and if she's somewhere else and okay or if what I had done had really been her end. When Lucifer possessed her I could still feel her life force strong and wild, just the way she was in life but now I don't feel anything at all.

It's like when she disappeared she did it into thin air. Michael and Gabriel have been trying everything in their power to find her but it seems that even their power isn't strong enough to reach her.

I want to believe she's still alive and that somewhere out there she is thinking of me the way that I am about her. That she misses me just as much, if not more, than I miss her and that she's fighting tooth and nail to come back to me. I can't seem to allow myself to look at it any other way. I can't believe she's really gone and that the only things I have left are the memories and pictures of our times together in my mind. It's unacceptable to me. She's got to be out there somewhere and I won't rest until I bring her home with me again.

Because I didn't succeed in achieving my destiny there has been no reason for me to go back to Heaven. I understand what I am now and what my path in life will be from this point on but I just can't go there, even though God wants me to and that's because the last time I was there, I fought with her and I don't want to remember anything that wasn't completely beautiful between us.

So I'm Ryan McGregor, half demon, pure angel and average human college student and I hate every damn minute of it because when I look beside me in Psych class every day, instead of seeing the hazel eyed pretty girl I cherish more than life, I just see a random empty chair. It's ironic really seeing as that how my heart feels.

Empty.

Graham is back to school now and when we finally came face to face I'd been ready for a fight. There will always be a part of me that will hate him for what he meant to Serenity and for being the reason she's not here anymore but I can't focus on it. It's not what she would want. I can't fight him because he's the only one aside from the angels that truly understands the loss I feel deep and rough inside of my chest.

I won't ever love the guy but at least now we can pass each other around campus and not give each other death stares. I only hope that wherever she is, she sees all of the changes I've been making and the new way I'm going about living my life. I may still live in solitude the way I did before I met her but at least this time it's happening only because no one else can bring to my life what she did so there's no real sense in pretending.

I've started writing a lot lately, songs mostly but it's a way to get the feelings that are constantly building up inside of me to break free without hurting anyone. It's another way I'm coping with the way that I am. I haven't caused harm to a single person since I've come back and I don't ever intend to. That part of my life is behind me and if I have to write a million songs to make sure it stays that way, it's exactly what I'm going to do.

I told her on more than one occasion that the reason I'm here is her, that I was living for her and since she's been gone I've realized just how true that really is because from the first breath of air that I take in the morning until the very last one that I take at night I am doing exactly that.

I'm living for her until she can live for herself again.

Another day is about to pass and I'm about to close my eyes to the world around me, counting the minutes until sleep takes me but

just like every night since she disappeared, I stop myself right before the darkness sets in and I make my solemn promise.
I will find you Serenity and I will bring you home.

Where is Serenity? Can the Angels and Ryan find her or is she lost to them forever? Find out in the next book in the Love United Series: Wanted.
Coming Spring 2014

ACKNOWLEDGEMENTS

To my real life Ryan McGregor. Knowing you has brought a joy to my life I was unaware I could ever experience. You have touched my life in so many ways. You continue to inspire me with your words, your smile and everything in between. My heart beats for you love, and it always will. You will forever be my pure angel.

My ladies in the HMC, without your constant love and support and delivering of eye candy this book probably wouldn't have seen the light of day. Each and every one of you means the world to me and your never ending support in my endeavors will be forever treasured. Jennifer Ankles, Jennifer Hicks, Jenn Lierman, Linda Rabinowitz, Faith Walsh, Jill Fritz, Lisa Morris and Savanna Decker.

To my four little angels that put up with Mommy spending way too much time attached to her laptop. I love you more than life itself and I swear once the writing has been put to bed we will have our famous Winchester dance party.

My best friend Joey for never giving up on me and this novel in the times when I wanted nothing more than to walk away. You are more than just a friend you are also family. Welcome to the Winchester clan! I adore you and everything you stand for. You can now proceed with the pat on the back you're dying to give yourself.

To the Hummel to my Berry, the Blaine in Klaine; this one's for you princess. Situations may separate us, time may divide us but in the end you have always been my biggest fan and I yours. I wouldn't be here without you and I can't go another minute without acknowledging it. To us!

To every writer that continues to write, published or not, the world over. Your dedication to the written word and the worlds you create has and will remain a constant inspiration for me and without the stories you've written I wouldn't be doing the same now.

To each and every person that takes the time to read my stories. I appreciate you all more than you know. Thank you for choosing to spend your hard earned time and money on me and my dream. You are the true angels here. Much love to you all.

ABOUT THE AUTHOR

Melyssa is a mother of four from Toronto, Ontario, Canada. Previously spending her daylight hours freelance editing for friends and family, she happily traded in her gig for a rewarding career writing young adult supernatural novels. The best part being that in working from home, she gets to spend more time with her own set of real life angels, and maybe a demon or two as well.

When she's not writing, you can find her buried under the covers with her portable DVD player, watching marathons of Supernatural and Veronica Mars. When those aren't available, you can find her curled up in a corner with her e-reader and a plethora of books, falling in love with characters written so well she deems them her book boyfriends and girlfriends. If you want to find her, check Facebook or Twitter as she may just have an addiction to both. If those don't work you can always keep up with her progress on her personal site where she more than loves blogging about her various endeavors.